I0627731

PULSE

Hell's Handlers MC Florida Chapter
Book 7

Lilly Atlas

Copyright © 2025 Lilly Atlas

All rights reserved.

ISBN-13: 978-1-946068-57-6

Thank you so much for joining me in the worlds I've created. <3

Ty
Pulse

Mayhem Makers Series
Solo Rider

Blue Collar Bensons
First Comes Loathe
Shock and Aww

M/M Standalone
The Duality of Swams

Audiobooks
Audio

Join Lilly's mailing list for a **FREE** No Prisoners short
story.
www.lillyatlas.com
Facebook
Instagram
TikTok

Table of Contents

Prologue

They were early.

Not by much—only fifteen minutes before he expected them, but it was enough to devastate everything.

Everything.

"Yo, you in here, man?" Enrique pounded on the door with his heavy fist.

How did Max know the power that fist wielded? Well, he'd been on the receiving end of that fist a time cr two. It hurt like a bitch when it made contact and left massive bruises as a parting gift.

"I'm here," Max called out. "It's open. Come on in."

"You fucking decent?" Enrique asked as he always did. "I walk in on your scrawny ass doing unspeakable shit to my sister, and I'll fucking die on the spot."

Chuckling, Max strode to the door. He opened it and gestured into the empty room with a flourish. "How long have I known you? Have you ever once caught me and Camila getting busy?"

Enrique shuddered. He wasn't the biggest man at only five-eight, but he made up for that height with his bulky width and massive personality. "Nah, but you can never be too careful." He strolled into the room, hiking up his sagging jeans. He wore his jet-black hair slicked back, showing off his

1

tanned face with the strong jaw women went nuts over. His dark eyes and thick eyelashes didn't hurt. Enrique raked in women like no one Max had ever met. They flocked to him. Two, sometimes three a night. The man couldn't get enough of them either.

"Lucky for you, I respect her too much to risk anyone catching a glimpse of her. She is for my eyes only."

Enrique grunted. "Lucky for you, you mean." He plopped into Max's desk chair and pushed aside a pile of paper, leaving a smooth, blank expanse of wood in front of him. "The only reason the old man and I let you near her was cuz you're a respectful motherfucker." He drew a vial from his pocket and began tapping a few lines onto the table. Cocaine was Enrique's drug of choice, probably in his top three favorite things. "If you were any other man, we'da cut your nuts off for how hard you went after her. Ya know?"

Oh yeah, he knew—two years of carefully earning Enrique and his father's trust while making his interest in Camila obvious. More than once, he'd feared for his life after a night spent heavily flirting with the very pampered and protected cartel princess.

But he'd had nothing but success. Max had not only worked his way deep into the cartel's circle of trust but also into the heart and bed of the revered Camila, daughter of the most powerful cartel leader in recent history.

They'd been together ever since Enrique's father gave his blessing—nearly a year and a half.

While he didn't love her and never would, they'd built a bond he would mourn the loss of once this assignment ended, not to mention the weighted guilt that would live on his shoulders for the rest of his life for ruining her family and her life.

"Want some?" Enrique asked, staring up at Max, who stood by the open door.

"Nah." He shut the door and strode to the empty chair on the opposite side of his desk. Enrique often spent time in Max's office eating, snorting coke, fucking, and doing whatever the fuck he wanted. What was Max's was Enrique's —well, the cartel's.

"Don't know why I bother offering to share." His dark head bent over the desk as he inhaled his first line. "Damn, that's good shit." He wiped his nose and went for a second line. "You're so fucking straitlaced," he said with a laugh as he came up, blinking and brushing the excess powder from beneath his nose.

"You know that's not true." Max had participated more times than he liked to admit. He'd had to. Sampling the merchandise was part of the game, and he knew how to play it well. But he hated coke. He spent ninety percent of his life an anxious mess of hypervigilance, worried the cartel would find out he was an undercover DEA agent. Living in that heightened state was hard on the body and mind, but he'd accepted that fate when he accepted the job. Coke made it worse. He didn't need anything to increase his heart rate or make him sweat more. It was only a matter of time before he dropped dead of a heart attack—coke would only speed up his demise.

Unless the cartel discovered who he was and put a bullet in his brain. Nothing he'd done the last few years would matter in that case.

Enrique's grin turned mischievous. "True. You can be a wild motherfucker when you want to be. So, you set for tonight?"

Ah, tonight. Max had been both dreading and anticipating this moment since he went undercover almost four years ago. He'd finally be able to rejoin the world and shed the crooked persona he'd played every day for years. Leaving this assignment behind was a monumental relief but also terrifying.

He'd done things as the third in command for the Del Rios Cartel. Hell, he'd been promised to slide into the number two position when Enrique eventually took over, a powerful station he'd receive over Enrique's brother, Tomás. Tomás was young and soft, a kid who would struggle to make it in his family's world but would have been given the title of number three when he came of age if Max hadn't arrived. However, Enrique's father viewed Max as invaluable to their operation and much better suited for the position than the book-loving Tomás. Becoming vital to the cartel didn't happen by accident. And it didn't happen without great personal sacrifice and a long leash from the US Department of Justice.

Late at night, while the woman who loved him slept by his side, Max wondered what would happen to him when this job ended. It was easy to compartmentalize the vile things he'd seen and done in the thick of it. But once he returned to his shoebox apartment in New Mexico, would his conscience flare to life and destroy him?

He'd find out soon.

"Of course I'm ready," he said with the exaggerated confidence Enrique had come to expect from him. "Could do this shit in my sleep."

Laughing, Enrique bent over his final line. "Always such a cocky fucker," he said before snorting the last of his coke. "Any last details to be sorted? This one's bigger than most."

That was the understatement of the year. Tonight, their most significant shipment to date would arrive from Colombia on multiple small boats. Max would oversee the crew meeting the boats, supervise the unloading, and then see it safely delivered to one of the cartel's many secret warehouses around the city.

It never ceased to amaze him how much of the cartel's

operation happened right under the noses of unsuspecting citizens and oblivious law enforcement.

"It's all good," he said, folding his arms over his chest. He'd bulked up to his largest size since taking his job— working out like a fiend provided one of his only outlets for the stress. It was either that or becoming a raging alcoholic, and he couldn't afford the risk to his safety by being drunk all the time. "Your father and I have been through every detail of this thing a million times. You coming to the dock?"

"Nah, but Dad and I'll be at the drop location to help you unload when you get back."

"Perfect."

And it was. The more people the DEA could round up in one sting, the better.

Enrique stood, so Max followed suit. "You call me if you need anything tonight, okay?" Enrique said as he grabbed the back of Max's neck and drew their foreheads together. The Del Rios were affectionate with those they considered family, and Max had been so since the moment they agreed to let him date Camila. "I mean it, man. If one fucking thing feels off, you call me. I'm here for you. You're my brother in all but blood. As soon as you grow some balls and ask Cami to marry you, you'll be my brother by law too. I got your back. You hear me? If just *one* fucking thing feels wrong."

A sick feeling settled in his gut. He'd become accustomed to it over the past few years, but it still sucked. "I hear you." The worst part of this assignment was trying to find a way to reconcile the way he both loved and hated Enrique and his family in equal measure. "Thank you."

Enrique wasn't a good man. Some called him a sociopath, but he knew damn well right from wrong and could empathize with those he loved. He enjoyed choosing wrong. Max had witnessed Enrique do things that would haunt him for the rest of his days. He'd watched the man kill in cold blood without being able to do a damn thing to stop it. One time, Max witnessed Enrique torture a man for hitting on Camila at a nightclub. Last month, Enrique carved his initials into a man's tongue for mouthing off during a meeting.

As a law enforcement officer, allowing these atrocities to happen went against everything he stood for. As an undercover agent, it was just another day at the office.

But the flip side of Enrique's violence was the man Max had spent every holiday with for the past few years. The man who called him brother. The man who had saved his life two years ago when a rival cartel member planted a bomb in his car. The dichotomy fucked with Max's head. The shrink his superiors sent to deal with him after all this would have a field day rooting around his fucked-up emotions and unhealthy attachments from this assignment.

Three hours later, Max drove his pickup into the lot behind the cartel's sneaker warehouse, a few minutes behind the semi-truck full of product. The legitimate side of the business did so well that he'd never understood why Domingo Del Rio bothered to run drugs. Then he'd met the man and realized money wasn't why he ran the world's most dangerous and profitable drug cartel. The man craved power like most craved water. He thrived on it, reveled in it, couldn't survive without it, and he had it in spades.

Max parked his pickup next to the big rig backed into the loading dock. Hundreds of sneakers with drug-filled false bottoms were being unloaded into the warehouse. The shipment had arrived without a hitch. The hard part was over. Or so they all thought.

Little did they know that in exactly eighteen minutes, the DEA would flood the warehouse with agents armed for war and prepared to go to battle. They'd arrest everyone on site, Max included, to keep up appearances, then dismantle the cartel, ending the most prolonged and complicated operation the DEA had ever run against a drug cartel.

All thanks to him.

They'd give him a medal and maybe a promotion.

They'd debrief him until his hair turned gray, and he'd answer the questions correctly to keep them from putting him in a padded room. But at night, when he laid his head down, he'd be alone with his fucked-up thoughts and traumatizing memories.

Sixteen minutes.

He blew out a breath and exited his truck. If he lingered too long, someone would become suspicious.

"Yo, the man of the hour," Enrique announced with a victorious grin as Max entered the warehouse. Men scurried all around, unloading the truck while at least thirty women sitting at multiple tables began breaking down the shoes and removing the product. He slung an arm around Max's shoulders. "This man never disappoints. There's no one I fucking trust more," he bellowed as he slapped Max's chest.

Max forced a smile. "Thank—"

Boom.

A ground-shaking blast rumbled through the building.

Enrique's arm fell from his shoulders. "What the fuck?" he shouted, eyes wide and wild.

Men in tactical gear rushed in from all angles with weapons drawn and shields in place.

"DEA, get on the fucking ground!"

Max froze.

They're early.

Why are they so early?

Even five minutes off schedule could fuck up the entire plan.

"*Feds!*" Enrique screamed. Fury transformed his face into a terrifying mask of death and violence. He lunged forward while reaching for the gun forever tucked into the small of his back.

"Don't." Max barked. He snagged Enrique's arm before the man could grab his weapon and force the DEA to fire on them. "Just get the fuck down and don't do anything stupid. They'll mow us down like animals." And they would. He had no doubt the strike team would end any immediate threat with deadly force. It's what they trained for.

"Max…" Fear bled into Enrique's voice for the first time since Max met the man. This entire warehouse was a prosecutor's dream come to life. All it would take was five minutes of searching for the DA to have enough evidence to lock up Enrique and his father for life, and he knew it.

This moment was what Max had spent the last four years of his life working for, sacrificing for, and lying for. It was necessary and deserved. Enrique and his father did things even the most depraved nightmares couldn't rival.

They belonged behind bars and away from the public for the rest of their lives so they couldn't hurt another innocent soul.

So why was his heart racing and his stomach sour with guilt and dread?

Ah, the murky waters undercover cops swam in—the fine line between doing his job well enough to fool his mark and actually becoming what he pretended to be.

"I know," he said, letting his dread bleed into his voice. "Just do it. We're fucking dead if they start shooting. Think about Marisol." Enrique's wife. "Think about Camila." His sister.

A hard shove knocked Max a few feet forward. "I said get down!"

He allowed the momentum to drop him to his knees, then pitched onto his stomach, immediately interlacing his hands behind his head as ordered.

"Get your fucking hands off me." Enrique struggled, but

the trained agents had him prone and cuffed in seconds. He shouted and cursed the entire time, but they ignored him, all business in their actions.

Max was restrained next. He didn't belong there, lying on the ground like one of the bad guys. A heavy boot pressed down in the center of his back, immobilizing him on the filthy warehouse floor as an agent slid cuffs around his wrists. The click of the metal jolted through him like a gunshot.

Get these off me.

Get these off me.

His chest tightened, and the boot restricted his lung movement.

I can't breathe.

For four years, he'd tried to prepare for this moment.

Nothing could have prepared him for the panic that seized his lungs and stole his air.

This isn't real. It'll be over, and you'll be set free soon. Pull it the fuck together.

The pressure eased off his back, and he sucked in large gulps of air. The oxygen eased some of the panic but not the hatred of being restrained. He was dying to glance over his shoulder to see if he recognized the agent who'd cuffed him, but he resisted. The risk of blowing his cover was higher than ever. The only way to get out of this without an enormous blinking target on his back was to play along. He'd done it for four years, so he could pull it off for a few more hours.

"Fucking pigs," he shouted, jerking his arms against the cuffs. "You have no idea who the fuck you're dealing with."

"Big talk for a man in cuffs," the agent behind him said with a laugh.

He recognized that laugh. Mosley, a veteran agent Max considered a friend, or he had before New Mexico's dark underbelly swallowed him up.

Now Mosley was the arresting agent Max needed to make

everyone believe he'd kill if he had the chance.

"Fuck you," he shouted as best he could with his chest on the ground and his hands behind his back.

A dark chuckle rang out as Mosley yanked him to his knees with a vicious tug on the cuffs. Agony tore through his shoulders, making his pained cry legitimate.

"You fucks," Enrique shouted from the same kneeling position as Max. His jet-black hair stuck out in all directions, much the same as it did the many times Max caught him strolling into his father's compound after a night spent cheating on his wife. "I'm going to fucking kill every last one of you. You're fucking families too."

"Shut the fuck up, E," Max said, as would be expected of him in this situation if he were looking out for Enrique.

"Someone ratted, brother," Enrique whispered when the agents left them to assist in arresting others.

Max's blood ran cold, but somehow, he managed a scoff. "No fucking way," he muttered back. "No one is that stupid, E. You'd fucking kill them. Everyone here knows that. No one is stupid enough to betray your family."

Wild-eyed, Enrique shook his head. "No. Death would be too easy for them. I'd make them beg for death every minute of every day. But I wouldn't grant it. Not until I peeled every inch of skin from their bodies. I'd snatch their babies from their cribs and make them watch while I snuffed the life out of the little bodies. I'd carve up their wife and make them watch as I coat myself with her blood."

Ice ran down Max's spine. He did not doubt the truth of Enrique's lethal promise for one second. Max didn't have a family. Well, maybe there was someone out there somewhere, but his grandmother raised him, and she'd passed during his senior year of high school. That lack of connection was part of why he'd accepted the DEA's offer after getting out of the Army.

He'd be the only one to endure unspeakable suffering should the Del Rios discover his true identity. That fact comforted him, though he'd prefer his skin to remain on his body if given the choice. But seeing as how that choice might be taken from him, at the very least, he knew no one he loved would suffer for his actions.

Because he didn't love anyone.

And no one loved him.

Well, one person loved him. Someone he had no doubt would turn as brutal as Enrique should she find out he destroyed her family. If the DEA did its job, she never would. She'd mourn his arrest and whatever story they'd concoct about why he didn't get a trial. Most likely, they'd fake his death, but she'd never discover the truth.

Max Dominguez, her beloved cartel boyfriend, was Maximus Gabriel Varga, an orphan from Texas turned undercover DEA agent.

"What the fuck do we do?" Enrique whispered.

He turned to the panicked man beside him. "We're chained on the floor. What can we do?"

"I don't fucking know, but I gotta do something. I won't let —"

"Drop the weapon!"

The harsh shout had both Max's and Enrique's heads whipping in the direction of the command.

"Cami, no." The cry left Max's lips before his consciousness registered her standing there with a semi-automatic rifle jammed against her shoulder. Fire blazed in her dark eyes, not unlike the heated gazes she gave Max when she wanted him, but this was full of fury and hatred instead of lust.

His heart hammered against this ribcage.

Why was she there? She wasn't supposed to be there. He'd booked her an entire day at her favorite spa to keep her far away from this disaster.

"Kill every one of these fuckers," Enrique shouted at his trembling sister.

"Put the gun on the ground and get on your knees!" one of the agents shouted. "We will shoot you if you discharge the weapon."

Fuck.

Max hopped to his feet in a move that would make ninjas proud. "Everyone shut the fuck up." Most guns remained trained on Camila, but a few turned his way.

"Cami," he said, trying for a soothing tone even though his stomach was tangled in a million knots. "Cami, honey, please put the gun down."

She shook her head, her long, dark hair swishing around her tear-stained face. "I-I can't let them take you from me."

Guilt was a ruthless motherfucker. It twisted Max's insides until he nearly screamed out his anguish. Camila wasn't innocent, but she didn't deserve a life behind bars as her family did. She was aware of who her father and brother were, but she was also a woman born into a militant, male-dominated drug cartel. She held no power and never would.

Max might not love her, but he cared for her deeply. She was the one person he wanted to spare in all this—the one person who didn't deserve the backlash of his betrayal.

And the one who'd suffer most for it because he'd done a damn good job of convincing her she was the love of his life.

All part of the job.

His fucked-up job.

"It's okay," he said as though speaking to a frightened animal. "Just put the gun down, and we'll sort it all out."

"Fuck that." Enrique climbed to his feet and shot Max a disgusted glare. "You know what you need to do, Camila Del Rios. This is family. Blood. The most important thing in the world."

Her face crumbled. "Enrique," she whispered, heartbreak bleeding through the words as she stared at him. "I love you, but…"

"It's okay, baby. Just put the gun down."

Camila's gaze bounced between him and her brother. Silent tears rolled down her beautiful face, dragging her mascara with them.

"Max…" Her arm lowered a few inches.

He nodded as relief flooded him. "That's good, baby, keep —"

Her spine snapped straight, and she whirled left, lifting the rifle back up.

"Camila!" he screamed as his gaze locked on her tensed trigger finger.

It sounded as though every gun in the room fired at once.

Bullets entered Camila's body from all angles, jerking her in an unnatural but unmistakable way.

"No!" Enrique screamed so loud Max's ears rang. He lurched forward with a feral cry only to be slammed back on the ground by the one agent not shooting.

Max stood frozen, staring at the body of the woman he'd pretended to love crumpled to the ground. Inside, he wailed as long and loud as Enrique, but he couldn't move a muscle. He should scream. He should cry and try to attack the agents. It would help his cover, and it was what he wanted to do.

But he stood paralyzed.

Camila didn't move. She lay in a lifeless heap with a crimson pool expanding all around her.

She wasn't supposed to be there.

Why was she there?

He'd tried so damn hard to keep her from the fallout of her family's business.

But he'd failed.

And now she was dead.

Was it worth it? Were the lives saved by ending the Del Rios Cartel worth more than the ones lost in the process?

The day he'd accepted this position, he'd believed that. Now, he wasn't so sure. Four years deep undercover fucked with his head, heart, and soul in a way he might never recover from.

For one heart-stopping second, the warehouse fell deathly silent.

Then all hell broke loose.

For his part, Max stood staring at Camila's body until someone finally dragged him to a waiting DEA vehicle.

He rested his head against the rear window, his gaze still fixated on the slain body.

I'm sorry, Camila.

He barely noticed the agents who slipped into the front seat and drove toward the government detention center.

"Heard you've been in four years," the driver said after a few minutes of riding in silence.

Max merely stared at the shrinking warehouse as they drove away.

His partner gasped. "Four years? Shit, you must be glad this shit is over, huh?"

It was over all right—permanently for Camila.

And for Max too.

Chapter One

"*Pulse,* I think I'm getting sick. Can you look at my throat?"

The only thing louder than Jinx's laugh was his whine, and his laugh broke the sound barrier, which made listening to him whine unbearable.

"What the fuck is me looking at your throat going to do for you?" Pulse looked up from his burrito into the pitiful face of his club brother. To be fair, Jinx's eyes were puffy, his skin paler than its usual deep tan, and his nose was raw from frequent tissue use. Even a layperson could recognize that he felt like garbage.

Jinx's hulking body dropped onto a barstool next to Pulse. He frowned. "What do you mean?"

Shrugging, Pulse pressed his lips together to keep from laughing at the huge guy who never failed to act like an oversized child when he was sick. Men everywhere balked at the term *man flu*, but then Jinx went and proved all their irritated significant others right. "I mean, I won't be able to tell you shit by looking at your throat. If you think you're sick, go see a doctor."

Horror transformed Jinx's expression from sullen to indignant in a second. "A doctor? Fuck no. I'd rather die of tonsilitis or whatever the fuck I have."

Pulse snorted. "You're not going to die. You're just being a baby."

"Puulse…" The whine was back and as pathetic as ever.

"He might die," Spec called from across the room. "If he doesn't stop pissing and moaning, I'll have no choice but to kill him." He disappeared into the kitchen with a case of beer on his shoulder.

"Come on, man, you're a medical professional. Help me out. Think of the mess if Spec kills me. You know that fucker doesn't ever do it neat and tidy."

Pulse stared at him. "I'm a trauma and ER nurse."

Jinx sniffed, and it sounded like he was working his hardest to keep a gallon of snot from pouring out of his nose. "And?"

A huff came from across the room. "Oh my God, Jinx. Are you harassing Pulse after I told you to leave the poor guy alone?" Harper sidled up to her ol' man, folded her arms over her chest, and glared. "Sorry, Pulse. I tried to spare you from his serious case of the grumpies."

Chuckling, he stood and greeted Harper with a kiss on her smooth cheek. "Don't worry about it, sweetheart. Comes with the territory." That was true. As the club's solo medical professional, his brothers asked him for advice on everything from hangnails to bullet wounds. He preferred the latter and tolerated the former.

Sometimes.

"Why you so nice to her and so mean to me?" Jinx grumbled as he snaked an arm around Harper's waist and pulled her onto his lap.

"Because she's so much better-looking than you are."

"Can't argue with you there," Jinx said, leaning in for a kiss.

"Oh, no." Harper arched away from his searching lips. "Do not bring that germy mouth anywhere near me until you are feeling better. The shelter opens tomorrow, and I cannot be sick."

Jinx pouted. "Baby…"

"Look, brother, if you're feeling like shit, go home, take some cold medicine, and sleep it off. That's all anyone would tell you to do right now. That and drink lots of fluids."

Jinx lifted his near-empty tumbler of whisky. "Working on that one."

"Not what I meant."

"Tried that," Harper muttered while Jinx said, "I can't leave. We're having a party," as though missing so much as five minutes of fun was unfathomable.

Spec stuck his head out from the kitchen. "Fire's roaring, and drinks are flowing. Come on out, you three."

Instead of taking the sound advice of resting and drinking something besides alcohol, Jinx gathered Harper in his arms and hopped to his feet. "Let's go, baby," he shouted before sneezing so loud the damn clubhouse shook.

"Oh my God," Harper shrieked. "You sneezed on me, you big ogre. Put me down!"

Pulse shook his head. This place was a madhouse on a good day. Throw in a celebration, and the chaos ramped tenfold.

But they were the only family he had.

A family he sometimes felt like an outsider around but still valued above anything else in his life. The occasional discomfort was his fault. He had secrets he could never divulge and thick scars that prevented him from letting people get too close—even his brothers, who he'd kill and die for. The same went for their ol' ladies.

Now that every damn man in the club had coupled up, he was even more of the black sheep. But it was all right. He was safe there and had the brotherhood he'd craved since the day he left his life as an undercover Del Rios Cartel member.

How fucked up was that?

Returning to the real world had been more complicated than acclimating to a life of crime in a drug cartel. The DEA's psychologists would have had a field day with that information had he let them poke at his brain. But he hadn't.

After two weeks of leave, gallons of liquor, and countless hours of self-recrimination, he'd turned in his notice and vanished before his mandatory counseling and reintegration sessions.

From there, he'd struggled for a few years, bouncing around shit jobs and wallowing in self-pity. It was a lonely time that nearly crushed him. As fucked up and evil as cartel life had been, it'd given him something he hadn't realized he'd craved—something that filled a gaping hole in his life.

A brotherhood.

Family.

People who gave a shit about him.

Eventually, he'd pulled his head out of his ass and gone to nursing school, a career on the opposite end of the job spectrum from being a federal agent—saving lives rather than destroying them.

At one point, he'd met Ty when the man suffered a nasty case of road rash in a bike accident. They'd bonded over a love of motorcycles and became friends. Eventually, Ty told him about his cousin, Curly, the wrongfully imprisoned MC president looking for solid guys to start a new club.

From federal agent to one percenter.

Fuck, if the club ever found out he'd been a fed, Spec would make the torture he'd witnessed in the cartel look like child's play.

"Dude, you okay?" The man in question stood near the kitchen, staring at Pulse with a frown.

"What? Yeah, sorry. Zoned out for a second."

"Shitty day at work?"

No. He loved every second of his job. Maybe he'd one day

help save enough lives to make up for the one he hadn't been able to save.

"Uh, yeah. Stressful shift." He strode toward Spec and gestured for the man to precede him into the kitchen.

Spec slapped him on the back. "Let that shit go, brother. It's family time."

Nodding, he followed his brother through the kitchen and out behind the clubhouse, where chairs had been set around a roaring bonfire. A few hours and too many drinks later, the conversation turned to the reason for their celebration. The women's shelter the ol' ladies had been working their asses off to perfect would open its doors and accept its first client tomorrow.

Pulse was so damn proud to be part of this group.

"Hey," Jinx shouted, seeming to have found a cure at the bottom of the whisky bottle. "Speech! Brookie, give us a speech."

"Speech, speech." Pulse participated in the chorus of chants. Thankfully, the alcohol loosened him up and helped chase away his reflective mood.

"All right, all right." Brooke climbed off Curly's lap. She swayed, almost losing her champagne flute, then giggled at herself.

"I think it goes without saying, I… we…" She waved her hand, indicating the other ladies. "Couldn't have done any of this without the help of every single person here. So much blood, sweat, and tears have gone into creating a safe space for women. Tomorrow will be an amazing day, and I want to thank you all for supporting Liv and me in our lofty idea. This project is special for so many reasons, but the main one is how it has allowed me to grow closer to all of you wonderful ladies." She sniffled and chuckled. "Damn allergies," she said, swiping at her watery eyes. "You're my sisters in every way that counts, and I can't wait to take this journey with all of you."

Spec raised his glass with a shout. "To the ol' ladies."

"Hell yeah," Pulse yelled.

"I'll drink to that."

It was time to stop drinking when the whisky no longer burned. He had to work a partial shift from seven to eleven tomorrow morning, covering for a coworker, and couldn't do his job with a raging hangover, so he set down his empty glass and refused Jinx's offer of another.

They all stayed for a bit longer. Ty and a very drunk Kelsie were the first to announce their departure.

As they said their goodbyes and goodnights, the telltale crunch of leaves crushing under a boot had everyone's heads swiveling toward the intrusion.

Two people in rumpled suits strode toward them with severe expressions and a pompous air of authority. Pulse could have tagged them as cops from a mile away.

"What the hell?" Jo's spine snapped to attention. As a former police officer, she'd probably worked with them at one point and looked about as happy to see them as Pulse felt. Hell, there wasn't a single man or woman sitting around that fire who was comfortable in the presence of cops.

Forget no more drinking. He leaned forward and snagged a beer from an ice bucket on the ground.

"What are you doing here?" Jo barked without an ounce of warmth.

"We're looking for Max Vargas. I believe he is known to you as Pulse."

He froze, beer hovering near his lips as all eyes swiveled his way.

Max. Fuck, he hadn't gone by that name since the day he tossed his resignation on his boss' desk five years ago. No one, not one single person in his current life, knew him as Max Vargas. He'd legally and officially changed his name when he'd moved.

These assholes knew precisely who he was, and that sucked. He set the beer down and cleared his throat. "I'm Max. Who are you?"

"Mr. Childs, please stand."

Fuck that. He didn't so much as twitch. "I'm not doing shit until you tell me who you are."

"The fuck?" Jinx muttered. "Isn't his name Gabe?"

"Pulse," Jo whispered. "They're cops."

Yeah, that much he got.

The female cop had a pixie haircut and an annoyed expression. Her face was slender with sharp, makeup-free cheekbones and a pointy nose. She stared him down as he'd done to his fair share of criminals in the past while reaching into her blazer lapel. "I'm Detective Wallace, and this is my partner, Detective McGee."

Twin badges gleamed in the light.

"Please stand."

Ty stepped toward him, as did Curly, but McGee held out a hand, halting them in their tracks. The detective wasn't tall—he might hit five-foot-nine on a good day. Bulky muscles made up in width what he lacked in height. Not someone he'd want to receive a punch from. The detective's stature reminded him of Enrique. Just what he needed—to be dragged back in his mind to those days. Calling him Max had done it, reminded of time undercover with the Del Rios Cartel.

The worst thing that could happen tonight would be for the detectives to inform his club exactly who Max Vargas was. Thankfully, as an undercover agent, his former DEA status wasn't publicly searchable for his safety, so if his brothers got curious and googled him, they'd come up empty.

Mostly.

That didn't mean these detectives wouldn't blurt it out if

they got annoyed with his lack of cooperation.

He set the beer down as he stood. "Something wrong, Detectives?"

Wallace whipped out a pair of handcuffs. "Max Vargas, you're under arrest for the assault of Alicia Minor. Turn around and put your hands behind your back."

"What the fuck?" What a load of horse shit. "Who's Alicia Minor?"

Instead of answering, the cop rattled off the Miranda warning.

Jo jumped to her feet. "Wallace, what the fuck is this?"

"This is an arrest, Jo. You know how this works." Her thin nose turned up. "Or you used to."

"Oh my God, Ty, we have to do something." Kelsie's fear made his heart clench. That girl had been through so much shit recently she didn't need anything else to stress about.

"You didn't answer my question. Who the fuck is Alicia Minor?"

Wallace turned him around with a rough hand on his shoulder. "She's a prostitute who works a corner in Tampa."

Cool metal clasped around his wrists with a deafening click. Memories tried to assault him—Camila appearing where she shouldn't have been, Enrique encouraging her to fire on the agents, Camila's body riddled with bullets. Sweat broke out across his forehead as he shoved those horrors back into their box.

"Miss Minor was found beaten and bloody earlier tonight," Wallace said. "She was able to give us a name and description that both match you perfectly."

"What the fuck?" What was this? He'd worked in Tampa earlier but came straight from his shift to the clubhouse long before dark when the streets woke up. He whirled around and stared at Wallace, trying to find any indication of what she was playing at.

"Pulse, don't say another word." Jo had her phone in hand, no doubt calling the club's attorney.

Wallace's eyes held a twinkle as though she was enjoying this fucked-up game a little too much. Whatever this was, these detectives did not think he'd roughed up some prostitute. Something deeper was going on. And that was more terrifying than if he'd been arrested for an actual assault.

He narrowed his eyes and said what anyone would in his situation. "But I didn't—"

Jo pointed at him. "Not another goddamn word until the club's attorney gets there. Got me?"

He only had the chance to nod before the detectives were leading him away in cuffs as he'd done to so many criminals in his former life.

Chapter Two

Was there anything better at the end of a long, taxing day than being engulfed in warm, fragrant water with candles flickering in the background and a generous glass of wine waiting to be consumed?

If so, Talia had yet to experience it.

Okay, fine, some might argue that coming home to a hunky man who would cook her dinner and give her orgasms all night would be better, especially if they shared the steamy bath first. But she wasn't convinced those scenarios existed outside fiction and fantasy, so she'd stick with her original claim.

Nothing beat a relaxing bath and a glass of wine at the end of a long day.

Air drifted from her lungs in a satisfied sigh as her muscles unwound. She closed her eyes and settled against the warm porcelain tub, letting the day in court float away. She'd done her best for her client, a nineteen-year-old young woman on trial for stabbing a man, resulting in the loss of his spleen.

Her goal had been to make sure the jury knew the fucker deserved what he got and more. She hadn't phrased it quite so bluntly, but they learned her client had acted in self-defense by the time she'd been done. She'd saved herself and stopped the asshole from sexually assaulting her. As far as

Talia was concerned, her client deserved a medal, not a criminal record.

But, again, she'd schooled her emotions and argued the objective legalities of the case on her client's behalf.

And she'd won. After only two hours of deliberation, all twelve jury members found her client acted in self-defense and would not spend another day in prison.

Talia became a criminal defense attorney for two reasons. The first was to represent people like her client today, those thrust into impossible situations who faced horrifying choices and did their best to survive. The second was to defend those she truly believed innocent from the horror of wrongful imprisonment.

And she was doing it.

One client at a time.

Suds clung to her arm as she reached for the wine glass perched upon her tub's ledge. She didn't bother to open her eyes as she brought the glass to her lips. The chilled, crisp white wine contrasted with the warmth from the bathwater.

Heaven.

"God, I needed this," she whispered against the lip of the glass.

That was the entire reason her phone rang with her boss' ringtone. She'd inadvertently breathed her contentment into the universe and now must pay.

She couldn't ignore that ring.

Water dripped onto the screen as she swiped the call and hit the speaker button. Her phone sat on the side of the tub, next to the wine glass.

Her boss didn't bother to wait for a greeting before she dove in.

"Sorry to call you this late, but you asked for this, Tal."

The amused voice on the other end of the line had Talia sitting up straight. Water sloshed down her back, leaving a soapy film from the bubbles.

"The MC?" she asked as her heart thumped with purpose.

"The MC."

Yes.

"Last chance to back out. Are you sure you want this account? Those boys bring a fair amount of business, and, like tonight, the hours aren't usually predictable. It can be a lot to handle. Plus, the women's shelter opens tomorrow, and the club covers all legal fees for the women they serve. All that business will become yours as well. Your workload is about to go through the roof."

A grin stretched across her face. Hard work didn't scare her. She relished in it. Some might call her lack of life outside her job unhealthy, but she liked it that way.

She needed it that way. Focusing on work from the moment her eyes opened until she passed out at night kept her mind off other things. Painful things. Even relaxing in her enormous garden tub, she'd been about to run through cases in her mind.

"I want it. I can handle it, Margo."

What was it someone had told her once? Idle hands do the devil's work. In her case, an idle mind was far more dangerous than idle hands.

Her boss chuckled. "I have no doubt, Tal. I'm more concerned with your work-life balance. Sometimes, you get so wrapped up in your work that you forget there's an entire world outside the courtroom."

Was there?

She snorted.

"I appreciate the concern, Margo, but my life is balanced just how I like it."

"Mm-hmm." The agreement was heavy with doubt. "That's exactly what I'm worried about."

Talia stood as she rolled her eyes. Water cascaded off her

body and into the tub. "I gotta hang up so I can get to the station. But you don't need to worry about me, Margo. I'm fine."

"Says every person who's a hot mess."

"Goodbye, Margo. See you tomorrow."

"Bye, Tal. Oh! Before I forget, drinks tomorrow after work at Blu."

"You're on." Margo might be her boss, but she was also her friend. They'd known each other since Talia's first day of law school when frazzled, she'd appeared in the wrong class. In her final year, Margo had pointed her in the right direction. They'd been close friends ever since. When Margo called her two years ago to let her know she was opening a law firm in sunny Florida with all female partners, she hadn't needed much seducing to leave her male-dominated firm in Rhode Island. Unfortunately, she'd signed a contract binding her to her old firm until six months ago. Now settled in Florida and working with Margo's firm, she was happier than she could remember being.

Smiling, Talia hung up, then set the phone back on the ledge. She shivered as she climbed out of the tub and dripped water across the bathroom on the way to the shower. After a quick rinse to remove the suds, she was ready to choose her battle outfit.

It had to be something that commanded respect but let her feel good in her skin. It amazed her that even in this day and age, women in professional roles were judged harshly for their clothing choices. Talia was youngish. She had a good rack and an ass she'd hated when younger but learned to appreciate in her adult years. She enjoyed looking good and refused to hide beneath boxy pants and suits. That said, she wasn't planning to walk into the station in a crop top and booty shorts either.

After a few minutes of hemming and hawing, she chose a

leather pencil skirt and her favorite white sleeveless blouse. The ensemble was classic and professional but still feminine. Three-inch red heels capped off the outfit. Once dressed, she slicked her long hair back into a low ponytail and applied the barest makeup. Then, she grabbed her bag and left her house with quick, sure steps.

She used the twenty-minute drive to the police station to get back into work mode. Not that she ever left it far behind, but interactions at this particular police station always left her frustrated and a bit ragey, so she needed the time to prepare herself. A handful of dinosaurs worked there—the kind who pretended to talk under their breath when they made their sexist comments and went out of their way to make her job harder.

She loved facing those men in court. Nothing beat the looks on their faces when they realized the 'girl working a man's job' had wiped the floor with them.

Her heart sped up as she whipped her Mercedes into a free spot between two official department vehicles. After killing the engine, she checked her lipstick in the rearview mirror. "Give 'em hell, girl," she whispered to herself.

They were the exact words her grandfather had told her every time she saw him. God, she missed that man. The only man she'd ever fully trusted.

With a swift exhale, Talia hooked her bag over her shoulder and exited the car. Bright lights gleamed from the police station, which was still bustling with activity at eleven p.m. As she approached, a baby-faced officer in uniform who had probably graduated from the police academy last week held the door for her.

"Thank you," she said as she breezed into the building.

"You're welcome, ma'am."

Ah, the politeness of the South, combined with the politeness of low-ranking officers, never failed to make her grin.

"Good evening," she said to the man behind the reception desk. He, too, wore a uniform but was much closer to retirement than the police academy. A pin on the left side of his uniform announced his last name as Blasetto.

He glanced away from his computer and the game of solitaire he had completed. When his eyes landed on her, he smiled. "What can I do for you, pretty lady?"

Inside, she cringed but somehow managed to keep it from her face. "I'm Max Vargas' attorney."

Instantly, the temperature of the conversation plummeted. The officer's grin flipped to a frown, and his eyes hardened. "You?"

"That's right," she said with an overly sugared tone. "Me. I believe he's in a holding cell. Can I please be taken to him? Now."

Officer Blasetto shifted his attention back to his computer. He opened a program and clicked a few keys before reading what popped up on the screen. Was he planning to answer her or ignore her like a child?

With each passing second, Talia tapped her foot with greater force. "Officer Blasetto, I'm going to give you the benefit of the doubt and assume you didn't hear me. I need to be taken to my client. You know, Miranda rights and all that."

Not a question, and no 'please' this time.

He answered her with a low whistle. "You sure you want this?"

Talia gave him the same indulgent smile she'd give her niece or nephew if she had one. "Yes, I am sure. You see, that's how the justice system works. Clients ask for a lawyer, and I show up."

"Well, this one's accused of beating the shit out of a hooker. Figure you ultra-feminist types might have a problem with that."

Talia opened her mouth to blast the Neanderthal for, one, announcing Max Vargas' legal business to the lobby and, two, daring to make judgments about her. Before any words could leave her mouth, a man in a crinkled suit stuck his head around a corner. "You Vargas' lawyer?"

"I am."

"Follow me."

She smiled and flipped Blasetto off, earning a host of snickers from others in the lobby. Then, as requested, she followed the man.

There wasn't any point in making friends in this police station. She had fantastic working relationships with some departments. They respected each other, and while the end goals of their jobs occasionally collided, they could have a civil and even friendly rapport. Since the men in this particular county office couldn't see past the fact she had a vagina, she'd never be given a chance to prove her worth and ability to play nice, so she didn't bother. How the few women who worked here tolerated the day-to-day misogyny was something she'd never understand.

"It's Detective McGee, isn't it?" she asked as she hurried to catch up with the fast-walking man.

He slowed until they were walking side by side down a long hallway. "It is, yes. I apologize, but I can't remember your name."

"No worries." At least he seemed to have a modicum of respect. "Talia Davenport. May I ask what the charges are against Max Vargas?"

He hesitated just long enough to have her spine tingling.

"A prostitute was found beaten in downtown Tampa. It was nasty. He messed her up, but she was conscious at the scene. She called him out by name and perfectly described Max Vargas." The detective shrugged but didn't meet her eyes as he spoke, causing Talia to narrow hers. "Open and shut."

"Hmm." She pursed her lips. Something about this entire situation tickled her suspicious side. "We'll see."

They stopped outside a closed door. "He's in here. My partner, Detective Wallace, is with him."

"Not questioning him without his attorney present, of course?" she asked, raising an eyebrow.

"Of course not."

Detective McGee opened the door, and Talia strode into the room only to come up short at seeing a devastating man cuffed and on his feet, scowling at a slender woman in a suit.

McGee swore and jumped into action so fast Talia's head spun. He grabbed his weapon and trained it on Vargas in under a second. "Sit the fuck down!" he shouted at a man she assumed was Max Vargas.

Rapid footsteps pounded behind her, and then a third officer shoved past her into the room, weapon drawn. "You heard the detective," the new arrival, a woman with a short helmet of hair, yelled. "Sit your ass back down."

Wild, furious, and yet gorgeous crystal blue eyes met Talia's. They weren't often seen in combination with his dark hair and olive skin, as though he had Hispanic blood. Talia nodded to him once. Hopefully, he understood she was on his side, but threatening whoever he was trying to murder with his eyes wouldn't do him any favors.

After a second, he lowered himself to the metal chair bolted to the floor.

The woman he'd been snarling at stood. She had to be at least six feet tall and thin as a bean pole, with her light hair pulled back in a severe bun, making her slim face appear almost gaunt. "I'll take that as my cue to leave."

Talia frowned. Who the hell was she? And what was she doing harassing Vargas when he'd requested an attorney?

Time to get some answers.

"Well," she said with a grin. "Seems I'm late to the party. Detectives, put away your weapons. I want a few moments alone with my client." She didn't bother saying please. They weren't about to start this game with the detectives thinking she was soft or sweet.

Max's distrustful eyes stared at her beneath a full head of dark hair that could have used a trim a few weeks ago. Dark stubble covered his strong jaw as though he hadn't bothered to shave in a few days. He had sculpted arms littered with tattoos and wore a faded Led Zeppelin concert T-shirt. Had she met him anywhere else, she might have swooned, but his looks had nothing to do with why she was there.

Though they did holster their weapons, neither detective left the room, probably to goad her or get a sense of her technique. To see how she'd react if they pushed a bit. That was fine. She had no problem asserting herself or being a bitch if the situation called for it.

Talia cleared her throat as she set her bag on the metal table that separated her and Vargas from the detectives.

She stared straight at Detective Wallace. "I wasn't asking. Clear out. I need five minutes."

Wallace's eyebrow arched, but she stood, and Talia swore she saw a glimmer of respect in the female detective's gaze.

"Keep your ass in that seat, Vargas," Wallace said as she motioned for her partner to leave Talia alone with her client.

"Turn the cameras off," Talia called before they shut the door.

As soon as they exited the room, she glanced at the camera in the upper right corner. Once the recording light disappeared, she turned her gaze to Vargas.

"What the fuck is going on?"

Chapter Three

"You know if there is any deal to be made, it has to happen now. With every minute that passes, our generosity fades."

As he'd been doing for the past thirty minutes, Pulse stared Detective Wallace down. He'd uttered exactly four words since being cuffed and shoved in the back of a patrol car.

I want my attorney.

That's it.

When they first showed up at the clubhouse tossing his name around, he'd assumed they knew his history as a DEA agent. He'd been wrong. These idiots thought he was nothing more than a lowlife who'd beat a hooker on the street. They weren't aware, but he knew every tactic in the book to get a perp to talk. Getting his lips to part would take much more than basic psychological tricks.

Another five minutes passed in a silent visual standoff. McGee hovered in the corner, arms folded across his broad chest. They'd yet to establish who'd play good cop and who'd get the role of bad, but it didn't matter. They could threaten or sweet-talk him until he hit old age, and he wouldn't utter a damn word without an attorney present.

A sharp rap against the interrogation room door had McGee frowning. He opened it and muttered back and forth for a few seconds before looking over his shoulder with a frown. "Wallace, step out with me for a minute."

Her brow wrinkled, annoyance clear in her tense posture, but she listened, and a few seconds later, Pulse was alone.

He exhaled pressure from his lungs and rolled his shoulder as he stared into the two-way mirror.

Who watched on the other side of that glass? The district attorney? Police chief? Other cops? The police have had it out for the club since its inception, though Curly did a fantastic job of keeping the MC's less-than-legal activities on the down-low.

The door opened, and his eyes narrowed as a tall, slender woman with slicked-back hair strode into the room. Her basic black pumps clicked on the linoleum. Everything about her screamed government employee, from the cheap black pantsuit to the minimal makeup to the I-don't-get-paid-nearly-enough-for-this bland facial expression.

What the fuck was going on?

"Hi, Max," she said as she slid into the seat Wallace vacated. "Long time no see."

He quickly scanned his memory before recognition hit him like a ton of bricks. "Jesus," he whispered as the woman smiled a predatory grin.

"Nah, just Agent Dixon. Jesus was busy tonight."

He could talk all he wanted now. Dixon wouldn't give a shit about his request for an attorney. She'd have a fancy way of justifying whatever she was about to do or say, and the law wouldn't matter.

He knew it because he'd done it.

"You were a rookie when I left."

"I was. Now I'm a veteran agent, and you're a criminal. Crazy." Her light brown eyes sparkled as she spoke. She loved every second of this, thinking she was so superior to him. She knew nothing. Understood nothing.

"How'd you find me?"

Her sharp burst of laughter made him jump. She'd been annoying as hell as a rookie. Dixon was a classic suck-up who did anything to get the approval of her superiors. Rumor had it she'd sucked more than a few dicks to make up for failing the entrance exam. At the time, he'd dismissed it as typical sexist bullshit, but then she'd offered to drop to her knees for him when she wanted a more critical role in the cartel takedown.

He shut that shit down fast.

"Oh, Max, we've known exactly where you've been every second of every day since you betrayed your country."

He snorted. "I didn't betray my country. I quit my low-paying government job after a traumatic undercover role. I won't be the last to do that, and I certainly wasn't the first." He tilted his head and smirked. "Did it hurt your feelings? When I left, that is. I know you had a little thing for me."

Annoyance flashed in her gaze, and Pulse bit his lip to keep from cheering. He might have left law enforcement behind him, but he still knew how to ask a question that would get under someone's skin. After the shitty past hour, it felt good to have a few seconds of power in this fucked-up situation.

"You're kidding yourself if you think I—"

"What the hell does the DEA want with a beat-up hooker?"

As though he'd hit her with a happiness wand, her annoyance transformed into glee. "Absolutely nothing," she said, her grin so wide he could practically see her molars. Had she been a child, she'd have bounced in the seat and squealed in delight.

Fuck.

"But we are very interested in outlaw motorcycle clubs, Max. So interested, we now have a task force dedicated to taking all you criminals down. You'll meet the agent in charge soon enough, but I wanted to be the one to deliver the news."

He rolled his eyes. "Well, you've wasted a shitload of your time dragging your ass here. We don't traffic drugs. If you'd done five seconds of research, you'd have learned that. Guess you better crawl on back to DC and disappoint the agent in charge."

Good riddance.

"Not so fast, Max. This is a joint task force across alphabet agencies. I'm just the lucky one who got to pick the team."

Fuck. Fuck. Fuck.

"I'd like to make you an offer."

"No."

She plowed on as though he hadn't spoken. "Funnel us information on your club, the mother charter in Tennessee, and other clubs yours works with, and we'll—"

"Fuck off."

Her eyes narrowed, the first crack in her arrogant armor. "Okay, fine. It's not an offer. You give us what we need, or you spend the next chunk of your life in prison for beating Alicia Minor near to death. Poor thing. She's just trying to make a living in any way she can. Did you know she's a mother?" Dixon tsked. "Juries do not look kindly on men who violently assault young mothers."

What a fucking monster.

He'd been away from federal law enforcement long enough to have forgotten how dirty they were willing to play. But not long enough to ever be willing to participate in this charade.

He stood, pressing his cuffed hands to the table. "Fuck. Off."

Dixon grinned. "I'll give you a little time to think. Imagine how your club will feel when they discover you were a DEA agent for a decade. If a big dude named Bubba doesn't take you out in prison, I imagine your club's president will. He sure seems to have a dislike of law enforcement."

If they were anywhere else, he'd reach across the table and wrap his hands around her scrawny throat, squeezing until her face turned purple and her eyes bugged. But the camera winking at him from the corner kept him from losing his shit.

"I'll say it one more time," he announced in as threatening a voice as he could muster. "Fuck. Off."

Dixon opened her mouth to speak again, but the door opened.

"Sit the fuck down!" McGee shouted as he rushed in, making Pulse shift his focus from Dixon.

The detective stood in the open doorway with his weapon drawn. A woman stood next to him, frowning.

For fuck's sake.

Wallace appeared, shoving past her partner. "You heard the detective," she added in a sharp tone. "Sit your ass back down."

Pulse shifted his gaze to the woman he didn't know. His gut tightened when their gazes met. Goddamn, she was a stunner. Call him a cliché, but a pretty woman all buttoned up in a professional outfit was sexy as hell. He'd love to mess her the fuck up, starting with that long, slick ponytail.

Whoever she was, she nodded to him once, and for some reason, he trusted her, so he sat his ass back down on the hard-as-hell metal chair. God forbid someone be remotely comfortable while being grilled by the cops.

Dixon stood. "I'll take that as my cue to leave," she said with a wink that let him know this wasn't over.

"Well…" The newcomer grinned as Dixon slipped out of the room. She strode around the table and came to stand next to him. "Seems I'm late to the party. Detectives, put away your weapons. I want a few moments alone with my client."

Pulse's lips twitched. So, she was the club's new attorney. She sure had spunk. He liked a woman who knew how to command a room. The club had recently changed law firms, and anyone who worked with them would need a spine of steel.

She cleared her throat, her eyes on Detective Wallace. "I wasn't asking. Clear out. I need five minutes."

Damn, that was hot as hell. This time, Pulse didn't try to stop his grin.

"Keep your ass in that seat, Vargas," Wallace said before gesturing for McGee to leave with her.

"Turn the cameras off," his lawyer announced. She didn't miss a trick.

They both stared at the camera in the corner of the room until the light changed, indicating they were no longer being recorded. Then she turned a pair of intelligent green eyes on him.

"What the fuck is going on?"

Pulse snorted.

She sighed. "Sorry, I haven't even introduced myself. I just hate it when they pull shady shit, and I have a feeling whatever was going on before I walked in was shady as fuck." She held out a hand. "Talia Davenport. I'm an attorney with Miller and Carmichael. I specialize in criminal defense and will be the main attorney for the Hell's Handlers moving forward. I will also counsel the women staying at the shelter who might need a legal representative."

"Pulse," he said as he slid his hand against hers. Her palm was smooth as damn silk, but there wasn't anything limp or weak about the way she clasped his hand. She gripped him confidently and shook, staring him straight in his eye.

Sexy.

"Have a seat," he said, nudging the chair next to him with his foot. "Sorry you got called out in the middle of the night."

She waved away his concern as she pulled the extra chair out and sat sideways, facing him. "Part of the job." Smiling, she crossed her legs, a movement he had no choice but to zero in on.

He nearly swallowed his tongue.

Her legs were gorgeous.

Smooth, tanned, shapely. They'd feel amazing against his tongue as he dragged it up her thigh. Would she get wet? Would she cream herself, then let him bury his nose against her pussy and inhale the scent as it soaked her panties?

Fuck, this was not the time, and she was not the woman.

Of course, she pulled a pair of black framed glasses from her bag. Was she trying to fuck with him? He bit off a groan as she slid the frames on her face before picking up the file the cops left for her.

"Okay, from what I gather, a woman working as a prostitute in Tampa was severely physically assaulted, and the detectives claim she mentioned your name and description before losing consciousness."

Her words squashed his inappropriate lust. He shook his head. "Such fucking bullshit."

She raised an eyebrow. "So you deny the charges?"

His spine snapped straight. "Excuse me? Of course, I fucking deny it. Do you know a damn thing about our club? I don't give a shit how much evidence the cops say they have, it's bullshit. I'd be kicked out on my ass if I beat a woman."

Her smirk had his eyes narrowing. "Oh, I know," she said. "I did do my research on your club, and I wouldn't be working with you if I thought you were the types of lowlifes who'd beat on women. So that leaves us with a few questions."

"Who hurt the woman?"

"No, well yes, that is a question but one for the cops. My concern is for you and why the hell she named you if she really did."

After speaking with Dixon, he wondered if there was an

injured woman or if the entire situation was a ruse to get him to rat on his club.

God, he'd rather fucking die.

"No idea," he said with a shrug. It felt as though he'd swallowed a pint of sawdust. Had the DEA orchestrated this whole thing to reel him in, or did they piggyback on some poor victim's trauma? He wasn't sure which was worse, but they'd done something to get him in their interrogation room.

And now he had to lie to his attorney to keep her from finding out he'd been a DEA agent. They might have attorney/client privilege, but the club paid the bills, so her loyalty would lie there. If she found out he'd been a fed and they wanted him back, she'd tell Curly.

As she should.

The club came first.

"Who was in here talking to you before I arrived?"

He shrugged. "Just another cop trying to get me to talk. You know how they are." He needed the one thing he didn't have—time. Time to think about the best response. Time to plan and process.

Talia set her papers down and narrowed her eyes at him. "Hmm."

Could she tell he was lying? Could she see right through him? Curly wouldn't hire a law firm without significant vetting and research. This woman had to be at the top of her field, which meant she'd be skilled at sniffing out bullshit. He'd worked alongside plenty of lawyers in his day, and the best could spot a lie from a mile away while blindfolded.

"Okay, guess we'll come back to that."

Pulse released the breath he'd been holding.

Picking up the file again, Talia gnawed on her lower lip. The silence allowed him to study her as she read the case notes.

Those fucking glasses.

"Victim's name is Alicia Minor. She's eighteen... *Christ*, and goes by Kitty on the streets. The poor baby," she muttered. With a huff, she lifted her gaze and stared straight into his eyes through those pornographic glasses. "What's your connection to the victim?"

It was Pulse's turn to huff, but it came off as more of a grunt. "Never heard of her."

"No?" She pulled an eight-by-ten photograph from the file and turned it his way.

He shook his head as his stomach soured. "Jesus, she looks like a child."

"Eighteen. She basically is."

He racked his brain. Had she been a patient at the hospital? Did she have an affiliation with one of his club's enemies? Or the most likely question to have a big fat yes as an answer— did the DEA pressure her into implicating him by offering her an out on prostitution charges?

"I've never seen her before."

She studied his face for at least thirty painful seconds before speaking. "Okay, then."

"I work in Tampa but got off shift before three. After that, I drove straight to the clubhouse. I've been there all night, and everyone there can vouch for me. The whole damn club was there. And if they don't want to take the word of a bunch of bikers they fucking hate, there are photos and videos from throughout the night. Phones timestamp that shit."

"They do." Talia frowned. "And they're saying this assault occurred around eight. I know you said this already, but to clarify, you were at the clubhouse surrounded by others at eight o'clock, correct?"

He nodded. "I arrived around four and did not leave until the detectives shoved me in their car at ten something."

"Well, I guess there's nothing left to do but invite the detectives back in and see what garbage evidence they have on you, and why this young woman named you when you couldn't have been there." She tilted her head and pursed her lips before asking, "Are you the type of client who's going to drive me batshit crazy, or are you going to listen and only open your mouth when I tell you to?"

He snorted. "I'll be a good boy." He'd do anything she wanted if she wore those glasses a little longer.

Talia winked. "Just how I like 'em."

Five minutes later, Detectives Wallace and McGee sat across from him once again. Did they know? Were they aware the DEA had their grubby hands all over this, or did they think this was a typical investigation?

"Let's get this show on the road," Talia said. "My client would like to get home, and I'd like to be able to grab a few hours of sleep tonight."

Pulse's lips twitched as the detectives frowned. Talia had a way about her, that was for sure. He liked her no-nonsense style and almost aggressive approach. No way in hell would anyone be walking all over her.

"I wouldn't hold your breath there, Ms. Davenport. Our victim has both named and described Mr. Vargas in detail as well as exactly how he beat the absolute shit out of her. So how about you start by telling us where you were this evening between seven and ten p.m.?"

They'd be sorely disappointed if they were looking for a 'gotcha' moment. Pulse glanced toward Talia. Gone was the playful grin and wink. She was all business now as she gave him a single nod.

"I was at the clubhouse."

With a background in law enforcement, he didn't need an attorney present to tell him what to say or not, but he'd play the game to avoid arousing suspicion.

"Care to elaborate?" McGee asked with a huff of impatience.

"No." The most straightforward answer was always the best when being interrogated.

Talia shifted beside him, and he swore she pressed her lips together to keep from grinning. "He answered the question, detectives. If you want more, you'll have to be more specific."

McGee's glare would have incinerated Talia on the spot if she'd been anyone else. "What time did you arrive at the clubhouse?" he asked through clenched teeth.

"Four."

"On the dot?"

"Give or take ten minutes."

"And you know the exact time because?"

He glanced at Talia, who nodded again. "Because I went there straight from work. Also, I got a text from Brooke as soon as I parked. You can check my phone. She said she saw me pull in and asked if I could grab a case of beer from the back of her SUV on the way in."

"Convenient," McGee said, shaking his head.

Asshole.

Pulse opened his mouth, but Talia placed a hand on his forearm. Maybe he needed an attorney to keep him in check, after all.

"Convenient timing, maybe…" she said, "… but that doesn't make it untrue."

"Did you leave the clubhouse at all?" Wallace asked.

"No."

She raised an eyebrow. "And I suppose your club members can vouch for you."

"Yes."

"Mm-hmm."

"There are also multiple photos and videos on more than one phone taken throughout the evening. Feel free to verify," Talia cut in. "I'm not sure what's going on here, detectives, but it sounds like much more investigative work needed to be done before an arrest was made. We can wait while you corroborate Mr. Child's story and check the evidence, but I don't recommend keeping him too long. I don't take kindly to my clients being falsely arrested."

He'd have whistled if it wouldn't worsen the situation. As it was, he couldn't keep a broad grin from stretching across his face.

The temperature in the room rose as the detectives' white-hot fury heated the air. Wallace stood stiff and frowning. "We'll be back after we make some calls."

"You do that," Talia called after the retreating detectives.

All Pulse could think was how grateful he was that this firecracker was on his side.

Chapter Four

Three hours of sleep wasn't conducive to a productive and enjoyable day, but the previous night's events hadn't given Talia much choice. When the detectives finally verified Pulse's alibi and released him, she'd only had a handful of hours until the sun rose and not much more until the next workday began.

She'd slathered on more makeup than usual to hide the under-eye circles and trick people into thinking she felt refreshed and ready to tackle the day.

Extra makeup and a vat of coffee, too.

After chugging half a pot, she arrived at the courthouse on time and then hit the office for a quick meeting with her paralegals. Ten minutes into the meeting, her assistant disappeared for a few moments, only to reappear with an extra-large coffee from the shop in their lobby. So much for fooling everyone.

It was only noon, but Talia felt as fatigued as if she'd worked a full day. And now she had to attend a grand opening luncheon for the Hell's Handlers' women's shelter. Yesterday, she'd been excited for this event. Today, she wished to grab a nap first.

She admired the landscaping as she strode up the light stone walkway toward the main entrance. Beautiful flowers native to Florida adorned the path in a variety of colors. They provided a welcoming, safe, and comfortable atmosphere that was so important when creating a space for women who'd been traumatized. The building itself was modern and gorgeous, with fresh tan siding. A tall, sandy-colored door beckoned to her. It opened before she reached the stoop, and a beautiful blue-eyed blonde wearing a sundress that Talia swore she had seen on an episode of *Real Housewives Miami* met her.

"Hello, welcome," the woman said with an open and inviting smile. "I'm Liv."

"Talia Davenport," she said as she extended her hand. "I'm the club's new attorney."

That news transformed Liv's face from curious to ecstatic. "Forget the handshake. You're getting a hug." She leaned in and gave Talia a quick squeeze. "Thanks for helping Pulse last night. These guys will keep you busy, especially my man, unfortunately."

Laughing, Talia returned the hug with one arm. "Why does that sound like a mild threat?"

"Come on in, let me give you a tour," Liv said as she chuckled. "And I promise it's not a threat. I'm with Spec, the club's enforcer, so occasionally, he needs some... legal advice."

"Ah, got it." The enforcer. "The club's bad boy." The one most likely to land himself in trouble. She and Spec would probably get to know each other well.

"Something like that," Liv said, but her blissful smile let Talia know he wasn't all bad. A woman didn't beam like that unless her man was taking good care of her in all ways.

Talia stepped into the foyer and sucked in a breath. An immediate sense of calm and comfort stole over her. "Oh, wow, Liv, this is impressive." She took her time moving around, her hand pressed to her chest as she absorbed the grays and pale blue decor. Ahead, a large common room with a plush light gray couch and a soft blue ombre rug begged her to kick up her feet and relax. The room also had a large-screen television and a modern fireplace built into the wall.

"Thank you, although I can't take an ounce of credit for the design choices. That's all Brenna. I'm sure you'll meet her soon."

"I've done quite a bit of pro-bono work with women's shelters in the past, and this place gives the feeling of home and safety more than any I've seen, and I've barely stepped inside."

Liz blinked quickly as though trying to control her emotions. "Thank you. That... that means the world to me. This project means the world to me. C'mon, let me show you the rest."

They spent the next twenty minutes touring the immaculate building. Each bedroom had been lovingly crafted with the goal of security and serenity. They each had a double bed with a simple light wooden bedframe and matching dresser and nightstand. The walls had a few art prints and photos, but Liv explained they wanted to leave wall space for their clients to have the ability to decorate some during their stay. The kitchen was as stylish and beautiful as the rest of the house with stainless appliances and white cabinets that reached the tall ceilings. The place was a masterpiece that would be the perfect landing spot for women needing a haven.

"Liv, thank you so much for showing me around," she said after they had toured each room. "I've really enjoyed this. You've done something wonderful here."

"Thank you," Liv said, nearly giddy with happiness. "Can I have your number? I know we all want to set up a meeting with you to discuss how everything will work with you providing legal counsel for our women."

"Yes, absolutely." She grabbed a business card from her purse and handed it over. "You're welcome to call my cell at any time, but if you want to schedule something, you'll have better luck going through my assistant. She pretty much runs my life."

"Hmm, maybe I need one of those."

"I highly recommend it," Talia said, laughing. They hugged, and then Liv directed her to the backyard, where lunch was being served and the reception would take place.

She wandered outside, immediately heating after being inside the cool of the shelter. The backyard was as lovely as the rest of the space, with flowers, a large deck, and a round firepit. An eight-foot fence surrounded the property with multiple security cameras, but she didn't feel closed-in. Instead, it felt cozy and secure like a secret garden inside a bubble of safety. Every detail seemed to have been thought of. It was apparent the Handlers' women took great pride in what they'd created.

A table by the door held flutes of champagne, so Talia grabbed one and then went to explore and mingle.

When she'd first heard the shelter would be on the same grounds as the MC's clubhouse, she'd been concerned. Many of the women they'd be serving had experienced violence and fear at the hands of men. Erecting a shelter so close to such big, gruff men sounded risky. But seeing the care they took to ensure a private entrance and plenty of distance from the clubhouse, she changed her mind. Plus, the few club members she'd met seemed as devoted to protecting the shelter as the women who'd created it. Maybe this was the best place for a woman to regain strength, courage, and confidence.

"Talia, glad you could make it." Curly's voice had her turning to find the MC president standing beside a pretty woman in a simple floral maxi dress.

"Wouldn't have missed it," Talia said, shifting her champagne from her right to left hand so she could shake Curly's hand.

"Wanted to introduce you to Brooke, the brains and beauty behind this entire operation."

The woman in question elbowed her ol' man as she extended her other hand to Talia. "He makes it sound like a one-woman operation when I've had more help than you can imagine. This has been an all-hands-on-deck venture. A complete group effort." A handsome German Shepard trotted over as she spoke and plopped down at her heels, panting beneath the warm Florida sun.

"Who is this?" Talia asked.

"That's the love of my life, Ray."

Curly rolled his eyes as both women chuckled.

"Sorry, babe." Brooke patted Curly's arm.

"Don't worry, I've always known I'm second in your heart."

They laughed, including Talia. She always enjoyed being around couples who were confident and secure enough to tease each other.

"He's a beautiful dog. May I pet him?"

"Only if you want him slobbering after you the whole time you're here."

"That's what I'm hoping for." Grinning, Talia crouched down, careful to keep from flashing the entire party. She held her hand out, and Ray immediately nudged his large head against it. "Oh, you're a sweet boy, aren't you? I've always wanted one, but I worry I work too much to provide the care and attention a dog would need."

Heat prickled the back of her neck, and it had nothing to do with the hot sun blazing down on her. She lifted her gaze, still crouched beside the friendly dog, and met the troubled eyes of the man who'd occupied her mind since the previous night.

She nodded once in greeting as she rose back to her full height. Pulse stood about twenty-five feet away, nursing a beer under a large canopy tent. He sported the same dark circles she'd seen in her mirror that morning, only without the added benefit of concealer. Expression pinched, he saluted her with his beer bottle.

"Talia, it was so nice to meet you finally," Brooke said as she placed a hand on Talia's upper arm and pulled her attention away from Pulse. "The caterers are summoning me, so I gotta run, but we'll make sure to invite you to our next girls' night. Oh, and I love your dress."

"Oh, that's... thank you." Talia glanced down at her simple black bodycon dress. It was her favorite, hugging her in all the right ways, but it wasn't anything glamorous. She'd left her blazer in her car when she'd arrived. It was way too hot to stand outside in a black blazer, and she didn't want to come across as stiff and stuffy. "Nice to meet you too."

Curly's eyes smoldered as he accepted a kiss from his ol' lady. He whispered something in her ear that had Brooke's gaze heating and her cheeks flushing.

And then she was off to deal with whatever the caterers needed from her.

"There's no escaping 'em once the ol' ladies get their hooks in you. Girls' night is just the beginning. They tend to adopt people, so expect them to be blowing up your phone from now on."

She highly doubted it. People tended to say things like that without actually meaning them. Smiling, Talia turned her attention to Curly, watching his ol' lady with a possessive stare. "She seems fantastic."

Curly kept his gaze on Brooke as she walked away, then turned his sharp attention back to Talia. "This might not be the best time, but I don't know when I'll catch you again, and

I don't want to miss the chance to thank you for being so available and quick to jump in last night. I want to say that won't happen again, but..." He shrugged.

"Nature of the beast. No worries. I'm very used to the unpredictable nature of my job. It's part of what keeps it exciting." She took a second to study the man she'd met in person a few times but spent a formidable portion of her youth reading about in the papers and watching splashed across the news. Curly's former club made headlines frequently for their criminal antics. He'd been part of a different club back then, one that Talia wouldn't have agreed to represent. Drugs, women, weapons, his club had run it all and with very little respect or care for anyone but themselves.

Yet none of that justified the way Curly had been taken down. The thirteen years he'd spent in prison for a crime he didn't commit due to a corrupt system and a few supremely evil players.

Guilt compressed her chest from all sides like a steel vise. Over the years, she'd grown accustomed to the heavy sensation, but since meeting Curly in person, the shame felt fresh and intense again.

"Is the shit with Pulse put to bed, or will there be more from the cops?" Curly asked.

Her gaze drifted to Pulse again, now deep in conversation with the man claimed by Liv. The enforcer patch on his cut clued her into his identity. He was a formidable man, large and with a cunning gaze she felt could turn lethal in a flash.

Though Pulse had his back to her now, his stiff stance gave off the impression of discomfort. Were he and Spec also discussing last night's arrest?

Talia shook her head as a heavy sigh slipped out. Unfortunately, she couldn't give Curly the answer he wanted. "I'm not sure to be honest. Something was off about the whole ordeal."

Curly tensed. "How so?"

She gave him her full attention, tuning out the rest of the club and their guests drinking, laughing, and having fun. It wasn't her scene anyway. No one would accuse the workaholic attorney of being a party animal. "I'm not in any way trying to victim blame here. There are legitimate hospital records, and she was severely beaten, which is horrifying, and someone needs to have their ass sent to jail for a very long time over it."

"But it couldn't have been my guy. I know that without seeing any evidence. Pulse isn't that man."

"No." She shook her head. "It couldn't have been Pulse, and verifying his alibi was easy. But the detectives didn't do an ounce of detecting. They went straight for the arrest. Why? The report claims the victim was drifting in and out of consciousness when she named him. Why wasn't he questioned as a suspect instead of cuffed and dragged to the station? Why didn't they wait to talk to her again when she was more lucid?"

Curly rubbed a thumb over his bearded chin. "Do you think the cops are starting a campaign against my club? Was this the first of many bullshit arrests we can expect?"

Talia frowned. Her brain whirled as she scanned everything that had happened since she stepped foot in the police station last night. After the interrogation, she'd wanted more time to speak with Pulse alone, but he'd been in a shitty headspace and stormed out without so much as a wave goodbye.

Understandable but frustrating.

"I don't know. Could be, but it felt personal."

Folding his arms across his broad chest, Curly frowned. "Against Pulse, you mean? As opposed to the entire club?"

"Yes, though it's hard to pinpoint exactly why. Do—" She winced and shook her head. "Never mind."

"No. Go ahead. I know you're on our side, so ask what you need to help my men. I'm not stupid enough to keep secrets from you. You'll have access to whatever information you need."

The sincerity in his tone had her smiling. "Well, thank you. It's not often clients are so easy to work with."

"Well..." He shrugged and gazed at Brooke once again. "I have a lot more to lose now than I did before. Don't think I'd survive being ripped away from her. My guys are a family more than a club. So I'm not fucking around when it comes to our legal protection and counsel."

Shit.

He might as well have slipped a knife between her ribs.

"Yes," she whispered, unable to strengthen her voice. "Obviously, I'm aware of what happened to you in the past. And I promise you here and now that I will do everything in my power to keep you and your family safe."

"I know you will. You have an incredible track record of going to the ends of the earth for your clients. It's why I chose you. It's why I trust you with my life and my family's lives."

His solemn gaze bore into hers, twisting the knife beneath her ribs.

She swallowed a painful lump as she nodded. "I won't let you down."

If he had even an inkling of who her father was and how he'd destroyed thirteen years of Curly's life, he'd not only take those words back and kick her ass off his property, but he'd also probably end her life.

And make sure no one ever found her body.

Chapter Five

"You working tonight?" Spec asked as he sidled over.

Pulse had been nursing the same beer for the past twenty minutes. As typically happened in Florida, the air heated his beer within minutes, and he now had a piss-warm drink to finish. Not that it mattered. Cold or warm, every sip settled in his stomach like battery acid.

"Nope."

Talia stood across the yard chatting with Curly. They seemed to be lost in a serious discussion, and it didn't take a genius to know he was the main topic of conversation.

Fuck.

He'd tried so hard to fly under the radar for so long, to not only be the center of attention but to bring the drama to his club. It had his head exploding.

"We gonna stand here like a bunch of assholes, or you gonna talk to me? I've been super patient waiting for details, but I'm anxious now."

Pulse snorted. Patience was the last word anyone would use in association with the club's enforcer.

"I'm serious." Spec elbowed him. He'd buzzed his hair that morning, giving him an even more fresh-out-of-the-army look than usual. "You have no idea the things Liv had to do to my body this morning to keep me in bed so I wouldn't call you at six."

Another snort. "I highly doubt you took much convincing. Your woman breathes, and you're hard."

Spec's shameless grin and wagging eyebrows had Pulse chuckling.

"Finally, a laugh. Fuck, brother, you've been off today."

"Sorry." He sipped the beer, wincing as the warm foam coated his tongue.

"I'll take those details now."

Pulse shrugged. "Not much to tell. Got arrested. The charges were bullshit. Lawyer got them dropped. You know how it goes."

"Hmm."

He could only imagine how much Spec wanted to shake a better explanation out of him.

"Hot, that one, huh?"

"What?" Pulse turned toward Spec, who jerked his chin in Talia's direction.

"You've been staring at the sexy lawyer lady since before I came over."

What? No, he wasn't. "I'm not staring. Just thinking about shit."

"Shit, like her tits in that tight dress? Maybe her ass. She's got a good one. Squeezable."

His eyebrow arched. "Liv know you're checking out other women's asses?"

Spec threw his head back and laughed. "If it helped get you a woman, she'd be fine with me stuffing one in my trunk and kidnapping her."

He blinked. "What? What the hell are you talking about?"

"Brother, you have no idea how badly those ol' ladies want you wifed up."

"Fuck off. They do not give a shit about that."

"Oh, I'm serious, man, they do. They are plotting and

planning, so watch your back. Maybe I should say watch your ring finger."

"You're crazy."

His gaze drifted back to Talia, and he felt the same stirring in his groin he'd felt the night before. He wasn't blind. The woman was sexy as hell. She had curves, an ass built for squeezing like Spec said, and a rack he could get lost in for hours. But the confidence she radiated drew his and probably every man's eye. Talia was a gorgeous, intelligent woman, and she carried herself like she damn well knew it.

Sexy.

If his life hadn't blown the fuck up last night, he'd be all over that, but he had more important things to think about than his dick. Talia got him out of a sticky situation yesterday, but the DEA wouldn't give up. They wanted an inside player in the MC, and they wanted it to be him. Despite his former life as an undercover agent, Pulse wasn't a rat. He'd never willingly hand over his brothers. If the DEA thought he would, they were in for a rude awakening. The only question was how badly they'd fuck up his life as punishment for not playing along.

He'd cut all ties with his former life when he walked away years ago. After four years undercover, he'd had few friends and family connections left outside the agency, but now he had none—no ties to his past. It gave the government little to use as leverage, so they'd threatened to out him to his current MC. If it came to that, he'd leave before they got the chance.

The only way they could possibly manipulate Pulse would be if they went directly after one of his club brothers or their ol' ladies, but he doubted they'd be stupid enough. They wanted to destroy the club from the inside, not start a war.

"Hey," Spec said as he nudged Pulse with his beer bottle. "You good?"

"I'm all right. Hardly got any sleep." He shrugged. "Just

feeling off."

"Look, Pulse, it's no secret you're quieter than most of us fuckers and keep to yourself more, but you know we got your back, right?"

"Yeah, of course."

"No, brother. I mean, we really got you. No matter what the fuck it is. We can handle whatever hell comes our way."

He cocked his head." Even if I beat the shit outta some poor working girl?" He'd meant it as a dark way to break the tension, but his stomach twisted with disgust even as he said the words.

Instead of recoiling, Spec nodded once. "Even then." Then he smirked. "But I know you, Pulse. Even though you're a private bastard who doesn't like to share shit, I know you'd never lay a hand on a woman. You'd have never made it far with this club if you were that kind of dickbag."

"Yeah."

"I'm just tryna say that you don't need to keep your distance, Pulse. Whatever you got, we can handle."

He met Spec's gaze once again. "How do you know I got something?"

Spec grunted. "Cuz we all do, brother. It's how we all found each other. We're a bunch of misfits with truckloads of past trauma." He slapped Pulse on the shoulder and then ambled off, probably in search of his woman. It had been at least ten minutes since he'd had his mouth on her. He was probably getting the shakes.

He needed to shake off this funk. There were things to be done to protect himself and his club, and he couldn't get his ass in gear if his head were lodged up it.

"You look about as exhausted as I feel."

Talia's voice sliced through his mental fog. A fresh, sweet coconut scent wafted his way. Jesus, she smelled like a damn cocktail. Pulse loved tropical flavors. Everything from pineapple on his pizza to coconut cream pie and even coconut creamer in his coffee, though no one knew that particular tidbit. The last thing he needed was the sexy, too-sharp attorney all up in his space while smelling delicious.

"Did you get any sleep?" Her tight dress hugged her generous tits in the best way. There wasn't anything revealing about the dress, but he still wondered if her cleavage would hold the same coconut scent if he buried his face there. And if he licked? Would she taste as good as she smelled?

"Pulse?"

He blinked, then scrubbed a hand down his face. "Sorry. What did you ask? Sleep?"

She nodded with a soft smile.

"Uh..." He shrugged. "I caught a few hours but feel like roadkill today."

"Roadkill," she said with a chuckle. "That's a good description."

He grunted. God, that scent was making it impossible to think. How rude would it be to take a giant step away from her to preserve his sanity? At least she wasn't wearing those fucking glasses. He couldn't have stood there if she had them on.

"Are you doing okay?" she asked, setting her empty champagne flute on a nearby table.

"You a therapist as well as a lawyer?"

Her eyes narrowed for a fraction of a second, but then she smirked. "Let's say I'm full-service. Seriously, though, I'd love to sit down and chat with you at some point. There are some things we should go over. I'm filing a complaint on your behalf with the police department and want to make sure all my I's are dotted and my T's crossed before I submit it."

His eye twitched. "Thanks, but don't bother. I'd rather forget all about it. I'm not interested in making a big thing of it."

She frowned. "They arrested you for felony assault without doing a proper investigation, Pulse. That's bullshit."

"Maybe, but you got me out of there, so it's all good."

Her frown deepened. Instead of detracting from the attractiveness, the pout of her lip made his tingle. Pulse was a picky bastard when it came to women. He didn't fuck them just because they had a willing pussy. He preferred someone with intelligence and liked to have a real conversation before and often after a good fuck.

That meant he was often alone with his hand as he'd been for too many months now.

"Uh, well..." Talia grimaced. "Curly is the one who asked me to file the complaint, so..."

Right. Of course, he did. Because he was a stellar-fucking-president who always looked out for his club. It also meant he'd have to sell Curly on dropping the complaint, which would never happen. Given his history, the prez sought every opportunity to set the cops straight when they fucked up.

"Look, Pulse..." She placed her hand near his elbow. He had to fight the urge to shiver as a ripple of electricity traveled up his arm from beneath her soft fingers. "I know I just met you last night, and it will take some time to build trust, but I can promise you I'm on your side. I am completely devoted to your club. You are safe with me, as is any information you share, no matter what."

She spoke with passion and conviction, pressing her free hand to her chest as her thumb stroked the inside of his elbow in an unconscious, soothing motion.

It didn't soothe.

It only made him clench his teeth against the blood pooling in his groin.

"Why?" he asked, making her blink rapidly.

"What? What do you mean?"

He tilted his head and studied her. Beneath the flawless makeup, he saw the hint of the same fatigue he carried. "Why? Why do you care so much?"

"B-because it's my job. I'm paid to care, Pulse, and I do my job damn well."

Her words said one thing, but the brief shadow clouding her gaze said another. This was personal for her, and he wanted to know why. Years working as an investigator gave him an overactive sense of curiosity he rarely got to satisfy. And he wouldn't get to today either. Talia might have piqued his interest, but he had too much of his own shit to deal with to worry about anyone else's.

"Right," he said with a dip of his chin. "I'm going to talk with Curly. I'm really not interested in dragging this out. I want to put last night behind me."

She pressed her lips together as though pinching off a retort before finally saying, "And if this becomes a pattern? If someone else accuses you of assault?"

The DEA would do that too. They would keep pinning crimes on him until one of them stuck, or he would grow so tired of the game that he relented and gave them what they wanted, which would never happen. He had to come up with a plan to keep his club safe and his life from going to shit. He started over from nothing once and didn't relish the thought of doing it again, not now that he had his club brothers and their women in his life and a job he loved.

"Then I'll deal with it."

"We'll." She rested her hands on her hips. The position thrust her tits forward. Damn, they were nice. She seemed oblivious to the fact that every male within viewing distance would be checking her out.

"What?"

"We'll deal with it. Not just you. That's what I'm trying to tell you, Pulse. I'm on your side, in your corner, or however you want to say it. Just keep that in mind. Okay?"

He nodded. Trusting outsiders wasn't easy. Hell, it wasn't something he did. And trusting someone with the secrets of his past? That was out of the question. But he said, "Okay. Thanks."

She nodded once. "Great. I have more people to meet, so I'll get out of your hair."

She turned from him, but before she could take a step, he said, "Hey, Talia?"

"Yes?" She spun back.

"Thank you. Don't think I said that last night. Thanks for getting my ass out of there so fast."

Her smile transformed her face, erasing the fatigue and lighting her up. "My pleasure," she said with a nod, then turned and strode across the yard to where Liv and Spec stood wrapped up in each other.

Each step caused her ass to swish in the most enticing way. She had more than enough to overflow his hands. Fuck, it had been a while since he'd grabbed onto a thick ass as he pumped into a woman. Groaning, he stared up at the sky.

He knew what he had to do, and unfortunately, it didn't involve Talia's ass. It did involve a very uncomfortable phone call to the one person he'd stayed in contact with from his old life if one text a year counted as in contact.

His brothers were absorbed in conversations with their women and others invited to this grand opening, so he could easily slip out the backyard's side gate. As soon as he was away from prying eyes and ears, he pulled out his phone and thumbed through his contacts. When he found who he was looking for, he strode away from the house and placed the call.

Two rings, then a gruff voice announced, "I don't have any details for you."

"And yet, you knew I'd be calling. Dammit, Birdy." He

nearly ground his teeth to dust as he pinched the bridge of his nose.

"Two hours ago, Max. I found out two damn hours ago." Birdy was a hacker Pulse had befriended back in elementary school. They grew up together, and by the time they were in their late teens, Birdy was tall and slender with the delicate bone structure of a bird and had been playing around in government agencies' computer systems. No one caught him.

Ever.

Birdy knew things that even the president didn't. He was a paranoid sonofabitch who could bring down the world with all his knowledge. His loyalty to Pulse went back to the moment they met when Pulse saved him from an ass-kicking by the school's biggest bully. He'd provided invaluable intel when Pulse had been an agent and was the one responsible for crafting Pulse's new life after he walked away from his former one years ago. They weren't exactly friends, but Birdy was the only one he could count on outside his club.

"I'm working on it, man. I promise. Something shady is going down, and I don't like it. I'll call you the second I have this shit worked out."

Pulse sighed. It was a long shot to assume Birdy would have been able to tell him exactly what was going on already.

"All right. Thanks."

"Watch your back, man, okay? Don't get lazy. Like I said, something shady is going down, and I don't like it. You seem to be at the center of something ugly."

Great. If Birdy was worried, then things were worse than he'd feared. "Will do. Same goes for you. Don't you go getting your ass caught."

He hung up to the sound of Birdy's offended snort. It made him want to smile, but his lips wouldn't obey.

Hopefully, Birdy could figure out what the fuck the DEA was up to and why they wanted Pulse. It was the only way to keep his club safe and him out of a body bag.

Chapter Six

Talia closed her laptop with a sigh. Her neck ached, and as she rolled her head from left to right, her stomach let out a loud, inelegant rumble.

A glance at her watch reminded her she'd planned to leave her office four hours ago, and, as usual, she'd lost herself in her cases and worked straight through dinner.

Long past dinner.

None of her colleagues would be surprised to hear she was once again the lone person in the office well after closing time.

"There's a chance you need a life," she muttered as she began to pack up her things. At least her favorite local restaurant would be open for another hour, so she could order some delivery and have it arrive around the same time she'd return home.

Perfection.

She pulled her phone out to open her favorite delivery app only to freeze mid-swipe as a noise that sounded suspiciously like the main door opening caught her attention. Her office wasn't too close to the entrance, but the door scraped the floor—something they'd been meaning to call a repairman to fix—making a distinctive screech whenever someone came in the office. During the day's hustle and bustle, they rarely noticed it, but at night alone, the sound was akin to nails on a chalkboard.

Talia frowned, setting the phone on her desk. "Hello?" she called out. "Margo?" Maybe her boss had forgotten something and returned to retrieve it. This wouldn't be the first time.

When she didn't get a response, the hairs on the back of Talia's neck rose, and a prickle of unease rippled across her skin. It was the kind of itch that said something was off. Call it women's intuition or a gut feeling, but she knew on a cellular level that whoever came into the office wasn't there to bring her a gift.

Instead of drawing more attention to her location, she swiped her phone to open the keypad. The local police station was less than a mile away. Could they get to her before—

"I'm just here to talk."

She jolted so hard she dropped the phone. It landed on her carpeted floor with a soft thump she could barely hear over her hammering heart.

Her gaze flew to the door where a man with olive skin, dark, gelled-back hair, and a well-fitting suit stood with his hands extended in a pose probably designed to put her at ease.

It didn't.

"Who are you?" she asked.

"Five minutes. To talk. Nothing more than talk." He had the barest hint of an accent, almost as though he'd worked to Americanize his speech. "May I sit?" he asked, pointing to the empty chair opposite her desk.

"No." Talia stared him down with as much menace as she could inject into her gaze despite how her insides quivered like a child scared of the boogie man. No matter what happened, this man would not see her fear.

His lips quirked in the barest of smirks as he stepped into

her office. He had a tan file folder tucked under his arm.

"Who are you?"

He placed the closed file on the desk and slid it in front of her with one finger, though he did respect her wishes and remained standing. "Please take a look through that."

Talia narrowed her eyes. Following orders wasn't her specialty. No one would ever accuse her of being a pushover, and she wasn't about to start now. "Who. Are. You?"

"Someone who wants to help a client of yours make a smart decision."

Talia stilled.

Part of her wanted to shove the file across the desk, hell, onto the floor, and tell this guy to kick rocks. But now he had her curious, and she'd spend every night for the next three weeks staring at her ceiling, wondering if she'd made the wrong decision if she didn't investigate the file.

The asshole still hadn't told her who he was.

They could stay in this stand-still stare-off for the rest of the night, or she could open the damn file and move this charade along. With a heavy sigh, she flipped the folder open to find a high-resolution photo that had her heart stopping dead in her chest.

"What the fuck is this?" she whispered as she flipped to another photo. If she'd been hoping the first was a prank, she was sadly mistaken to find the second photo containing the same damning evidence as the first.

A clear picture of Pulse in a black jacket with white letters on the back.

DEA.

In one photo, he wore dark glasses covering his eyes while holding a walkie-talkie in front of his mouth in a clear position of authority as he spoke to other agents.

A million questions ran through her head, but she felt too sick to open her mouth.

Is he an undercover agent assigned to the Hell's Handlers Motorcycle Club?

What is his angle?

What did this have to do with his arrest?

Who was this damn man standing before her?

Mind racing, she flipped to the next document, which wasn't a photo. It was a termination of employment record. She scanned the file as fast as possible and learned Pulse had been a DEA agent until he walked away around five years ago.

Thank God.

What was happening here?

She flipped to another page where the words blurred before her eyes. Instead of reading, her analytical brain ran in a million directions, trying to parse the purpose behind this little ambush.

And then the lightbulb flicked on.

She lifted her gaze. "You're a fed."

It wasn't a question.

"I heard you were intelligent."

She leaned back in her chair and folded her arms as her fear melted away and annoyance took its place. Compliments wouldn't win this guy any favors. She wanted nothing to do with whatever mess this man brought to her office. "So, what, you're here to tell me he's deep undercover with the MC, and the arrest served a purpose, and I fucked you over by getting him released so fast? Is that what this is? You want me to suck at my job next time so you can pull him back into the fold?"

The thought that Pulse could be deceiving his MC family made her want to vomit.

"No." The agent slid into the seat opposite her despite her refusal.

She bit her lip to keep from snapping at him. Whether or not he sat wasn't the issue.

"He really resigned five years ago. Max Vargas spent four years undercover with the Del Rios Cartel. The takedown went to shit, somewhat, and he walked away from the DEA without so much as a goodbye. He walked away from his entire life."

Her eyes widened. Holy sit, the Del Rios Cartel. That was big business. The destruction of that cartel had been the top headline on every news outlet for weeks. Ridding the world of that one cartel drastically altered the drug trade in the United States. Fentanyl deaths dropped by almost a third within three months. If Pulse was responsible for those arrests, he'd done an amazing thing for the country.

So, how did he end up in an MC?

Talia set her hands on the desk and pushed the folder back toward her visitor. "Okay, so he burned out after years of undercover work with no gratitude from the country he served, and he left. None of that explains why you are here now."

"We want his help."

She narrowed her eyes. "The Handlers don't deal drugs, nor do they do business with those who do. What could he possibly help you with?"

Shrugging, the agent said, "Maybe not, but they still know plenty of players in the game. And they're still one percenters. Don't try to pretend there aren't mountains of illegal activities behind that clubhouse's walls. Their enemies have gone missing or ended up mysteriously dead. That alone is enough to pull *Pulse* in." He said the nickname as though it tasted rotten on his tongue. "The federal government has had it with these motorcycle gangs—"

"Clubs," she muttered.

"*Clubs*." That time, he didn't bother to keep the mockery from his tone. "We're taking out as many as possible, and we want Pulse's help."

They wanted his help to take out his own club. This was worse than she thought.

"Ah, now I know who was talking to him after his arrest. The prostitute never named him, did she? You orchestrated that entire thing to get him alone so you could... what? Present him an offer? How much did you think it would take for him to sell out his club?"

The smile that spread across the agent's face had a chill running down her spine.

"It's not that kind of offer. Either he helps us, or he ends up in jail for what he did to that poor hooker, and his club finds out about his past. And if we can't get him on this assault, we'll get him on another one. You know how those bikers are. Hot tempers and all. There are so many ways they break the law."

She narrowed her eyes. "You're a federal agent, and you blackmailed a civilian with false imprisonment. How do you know I'm not recording this?"

He shrugged. "Like I said, you're intelligent." He stood and walked toward the door. "Convince him to work with us." He spun back to face her when he reached the doorway. "It's in your best interest."

"A threat?" she asked, tilting her head. "I'll have you know I don't respond well to those."

"No threats. Just facts."

"I won't do it."

For the first time, a flicker of irritation crossed his face along with something else. Something darker and more sinister. It had her fighting to keep from squirming in her chair.

"I'm sure we can convince you," he said, and with that bomb, he slipped from her office. A few moments later, the familiar screech alerted her he'd ventured out in the night.

Talia sat in her office for a long time, staring at her empty doorway and replaying the shit show she'd just taken part in.

The DEA had orchestrated Pulse's arrest so they could have a discreet *chat* with him. Chat being a euphemism for blackmail. They asked him to spy on his club, or they'd jail him and reveal his past to Curly, which could end with him six feet under. Did they know her secrets? Is that what the agent meant when he said he could convince her to comply? Of course, they did. They were the federal government. Why wouldn't they know her father had been Curly's defense attorney back in the day? One who got rich as hell on that case while working behind the scenes to screw over the client he'd been hired to defend.

Talia slumped forward, letting her forehead thump against the desk. Would there ever come a time when she felt she'd made reparations for that debt, or would she spend the rest of her life doing self-appointed penance for her father's sins?

"Go home," she whispered against her desk. Nothing would be determined tonight. She was too tired and emotionally charged to make any rational and professional decisions about how to handle this situation.

She hauled her body upright and out of her chair with the heaviest of sighs. Then, she spent the next five minutes straightening her desk and gathering the rest of her belongings. Her heels echoed in the quiet hallway as she strode toward the exit she'd be sure to lock the next time she found herself alone in the office at night.

The drive home would take her about thirty minutes at this time of night. She lived further inland, past the suburbs but not quite in rural land. There weren't gated communities, and the houses were spread out and older than those closer to town. Peace, quiet, and space were important to her. She'd rather have a longer commute and a large piece of property than live in a crowded area close to her office. Podcasts and audiobooks did wonders for making a drive fly by.

But not tonight. Tonight, as she cruised down the highway, she kept the car quiet. Her brain was whirring loud enough. Any additional noise would overwhelm her senses.

She flicked on her turn signal as she glanced in the rearview mirror. The car behind her was also taking the upcoming exit for the single-lane road leading her the rest of the way home.

Given the late hour, the miles flew by with ease. She couldn't see any cars in front of her, and the only one behind was the vehicle that had exited after her.

"Dude, back off," she muttered as she glanced in the rearview mirror again. The driver had crept up on her and was tailing close behind.

Too close.

She'd be rear-ended if a deer ran out and she needed to slam on her brakes.

"Jackass." She huffed as she signaled right and drifted toward the shoulder lane so the car could pass. "What the hell..." They stayed right on her bumper, also shifting into the shoulder lane.

The same ill-at-ease gut feeling she'd had earlier in the evening flared with a vengeance.

They were following her on purpose.

"Shit." Was it the agent? Some thug he'd sent after her to *convince* her as he'd threatened?

She wasn't going to wait around to find out.

She jammed down on the gas pedal and shot forward, moving back to the center of the lane.

The car sped and stayed right on her ass. From what she could tell, the dark, plain vehicle seemed about the size of a sedan. Its headlights prevented her from getting a good view of the license plate. She couldn't make out the state, and there was no way she could determine any of the numbers.

An engine rumbled louder. She spared another glance in

the mirror. "Shit, shit, shit."

He was even closer, practically kissing her taillights.

Talia zoomed past the turn she'd usually take to get home. No way in hell would she bring this asshole right to her house, even though they probably already knew where she lived.

Sweat coated her palms, making the steering wheel slick. She clenched the wheel tighter to keep her hands from sliding. Her knuckles ached from the force of her grip. Another glance behind her showed the car inching even closer. Heart in her throat, she pressed harder on the gas.

The speedometer snuck toward ninety.

Trees whipped by so fast they blurred.

They were in a fifty-five-mile-an-hour zone. Hell, she'd gladly take a whopper of a ticket if it meant a cop could end this.

"Come on," she whispered. A few more miles and they'd hit a small town. She'd pull into the first open business she could find. Maybe a well-lit gas station or convenience store. Anything that contained another human being she could use as a witness.

A screech of metal on metal assaulted her ears at the same time her car lurched forward. Talia shrieked and stared in the mirror, mouth agape. He'd hit her.

"Oh my God." A loud sob flew from deep in her gut. She blinked to clear her vision as tears flooded her eyes. She pressed hard with her foot until the gas pedal hit the floor. "Go faster!" she shouted at the car as though it would do a damn thing.

When the car bumped her again, she flew forward with a shout. The seat belt stopped her from smacking the steering wheel as it locked in place with a painful snap across her chest.

The next hit came so fast and violently that her hands

slipped off the steering wheel. The seat belt cracked across her chest with another agonizing jolt. Her neck snapped back then forward, rattling her brain, and her hair fell into her field of vision.

She screamed as the loud screech of crushing metal reverberated into the night. She felt like a ragdoll being tossed around by a careless child.

Something hit her cheek with a biting sting. She tried to grab it, but the momentum of the crashing car kept her from reaching for her face.

The last thing Talia saw before the world went black was the steering wheel rushing toward her face, followed by a massive cloud of white before impact.

At least my airbags work.

Chapter Seven

"Hey, Gabe, room twelve is asking for pain medication."

He glanced at his smart watch before looking at the nursing assistant assigned to his room. "Thanks, Sharon. He's due for some. I'll grab it now."

When he left the DEA, he started using his middle name, Gabriel, as his first name. No one called him Max anymore. At work, they called him Gabe, but everyone else called him Pulse, the nickname given to him by the club due to his profession. Hearing the cops call him Max the other night had fucked with his head.

He logged off the computer where he'd taken a minute to catch up on some of his charting. It'd been a busy shift so far. This was the first time he'd sat down in the past four hours, and it had lasted a whopping six minutes.

After taking care of the pain medication request, he started an IV in room eleven and answered a call from surgery, who had a room prepared for the patient in ER room ten. They were sending transport down to have the patient wheeled up for an emergency appendectomy.

Never a dull moment in the emergency room.

As he attached room ten's IV pole to the transport gurney, the pager clipped to his name badge beeped.

"Trauma coming in?" Sharon asked.

He nodded as he read from the pager. "MVA with one victim. You'll let Amy know?"

"Of course."

"Thanks," he called as he jogged toward the ambulance bay. As the primary nurse on trauma call for this shit, he was expected to respond to every incoming trauma. That meant he had fewer ER patients to care for during his shift so that others could cover for him during traumas, but it still made for a hectic, sometimes highly chaotic shift.

He fucking loved it.

The adrenaline rush, the life-or-death spur-of-the-moment decision-making. Pulse thrived on his work. Long before he'd gone the federal agent route, he'd wanted to be a trauma surgeon. Unfortunately, he'd let other's opinions sway him, and by the time he'd come to his senses and left the DEA, he felt he was too old to take on the time commitment and debt of becoming a surgeon. Critical care nursing was the next best bet, and he loved every second of his job.

The rest of the trauma team had assembled at the ambulance bay by the time the ambulance rolled in. Connor and Leslie, a paramedic team he knew well by now, lowered a gurney from the back of their rig and jogged toward the waiting team.

"What do we have?" Pulse asked as they reached him.

"Thirty-two-year-old female involved in a single car MVA, though she claims she was hit and the driver of the other car took off. Unconscious at the scene but has since come around. She's alert and oriented times four. No agitation. Positive for headache and nausea. No vomiting. Significant bruising on the sternum from the seat belt. She has about a three-inch laceration on her forehead. Bleeding is under control. She said no allergies or major medical conditions."

"Thanks, Connor."

The woman on the gurney had her head secured to a

backboard as per spinal injury protocol. Once they were confident she didn't have spinal involvement, that could be removed. The paramedics taped a bulky wad of gauze to her forehead to help control the bleeding and keep the wound clean.

Pulse moved to the head of the gurney to talk to the patient and get some more information while they wheeled her toward a trauma room for evaluation. "Hey there, ma'am. I'm Gabe, one of the nurses here at the hospital. We're going to take good care of you, okay? Can you tell me your name?"

He glanced down for the first time and almost swallowed his tongue.

"Talia?"

Her eyes were dazed and pain-filled, but they widened at the sight of him. "Pulse?" she whispered with a tremor of obvious fear. "Am... am I..."

"Shh, shh, shh." He picked up her hand and squeezed gently. "You're gonna be all right, hon, okay? Promise we'll get you all fixed up."

She couldn't nod because of the head restraint, so she whispered, "O-okay."

"Are you in pain right now?" he asked as he wrapped a blood pressure cuff around her arm.

"Yes, m-my chest hurts, and my head. My face."

"Okay, the paramedics gave you some medication through the IV to help with that, but I'm going to bump it up, okay?"

"T-thank you."

He winked, maintaining his usual calm and friendly expression. Patients in shock or panicking responded best to him if he was almost playful when talking to them. This helped distract them from their fear and pain.

"Okay, Talia, don't mind me here. Promise I'm not getting fresh," he said as he held up a handful of sticky pads. "While the docs are checking everything out to make sure you don't have any obvious injuries, I'm going to get you hooked up to an EKG so we can monitor your ticker. Is it okay if I unbutton your blouse?"

Despite everything she was going through, her face flushed. "Uh, yeah. That's fine."

"After we're done here, we'll get you up to radiology for some head and neck scans. Easy stuff. You won't have to do a thing but lie there and answer a few questions," he chattered as he slipped the first button of her silky blouse through the hole.

Then the next.

And another.

When he had them all free, he parted the fabric, and there were her tits. Right in front of his face, full, lush, and encased in a bright pink lace bra.

Never, not once, did he have a physical reaction to a patient in this kind of situation. Hell, he barely looked at his female patients as women. They were just parts he needed to assess for damage. Ninety-nine percent of the time, someone could offer him a million dollars five minutes after evaluating a patient, and he'd never be able to recall what color bra they wore. There was nothing sexual or attractive about trauma care.

Never.

But, of course, someone had drummed up that stupid phrase *never say never* for a reason.

And goddamn, those were some phenomenal tits.

His dick twitched beneath his scrubs.

A single tear leaked from the corner of Talia's eye. The sight of it shocked him back to reality faster than a slap. He hardly knew the woman, but his gut told him she'd deny that tear to her dying day if anyone asked. Talia was not the type of woman who wanted to show an ounce of what she would consider weakness.

"Hey," he murmured, taking her hand in his. Her palm was clammy and cold despite the seventy-five-degree night. "We got you now. We'll get you fixed up good as new."

"I'm s-sorry," she said, sounding like she was fighting sobs. "I'm j-just a little nervous."

Nodding, he squeezed her hand. "Understandable. But I promise we're gonna take the best damn care of you. Is there anyone you want me to call?"

She bit her lower lip and then sighed. "No. There's no one."

Why did those words have him wanting to press her hand over his heart?

Focus on your damn job. He refused to think of her as anything other than a patient. This was work. Same thing he'd been doing for the past few years.

He cleared his throat. "The paramedic said you got a doozy of a gash on your head as well, so after your scans, we'll get that all stitched up for you." He placed the electrodes for the EKG with quick, clinical precision, having done it countless times. Once he clipped on the wires, a familiar beep sounded as her cardiac rhythm registered on the monitor.

"O-okay."

"Gabe, radiology transport is on the way." He nodded at the nursing assistant before focusing on the telemetry monitor. Everything looked good. Her blood pressure was elevated but not to critical levels and not unsurprising due to the circumstances. The EKG showed a normal heart rhythm, and her oxygen saturation was within normal limits, which meant she was breathing normally and hopefully hadn't broken any ribs in the crash.

"Vitals are stable," he announced, receiving a nod from the physician.

"Abdominal ultrasound shows no signs of internal

bleeding." The physician moved up to Talia's head. "I'm Dr. Ragusa," he said with a gentle smile. "We'll get this off your head and let you sit up as soon as we are sure you don't have any spinal cord involvement or bleeding on your brain. Okay, ma'am?"

Her eyes widened, wary with fear. "Okay."

The physician pulled off his gloves. "Radiology is here. Gabe will help get you on your way, and I'll see you when you return from the CT scan. I'll be the one to stitch up your head."

"Thank you."

Dr. Ragusa smiled his customary warm grin that helped set patients at ease. He could be a prick when stressed, but most of the time he was a great physician to work alongside. After patting Talia's shoulder, he exited the room, leaving Pulse alone with her.

"I'm going to unclip the EKG leads but leave the sticky pads on. It's standard procedure. If we need them again later, we don't need to reapply them."

"Makes sense," she whispered.

He nodded as he unclipped the leads and then pulled a blanket up over her exposed chest. He didn't bother to button her blouse up again—radiology would only undo it. If she were anyone else, he'd help remove it entirely and slip her into a hospital gown, but he'd already had an unprofessional reaction to her. Seeing her bare tits might put him over the edge. They could take care of her clothing situation upstairs in radiology, though he'd probably get an earful later for sending her up unprepared.

"Why are they calling you Gabe? I thought your name was Max?"

A sour taste filled his mouth. "Gabe is my middle name and what I prefer to go by."

"Oh." She frowned. The woman was too damn perceptive

and would probably have questions about that later.

"All set," he said when he'd finished his task. "It'll just be a few more seconds." He rested his arms on the bed's side rail and then stared down at the woman who was terrified, bloody, and hurt yet still managed to look beautiful. "Wanna talk about what happened?" he asked. "Sometimes talking helps you get over the shock of it all."

"Um... yeah." She tried to nod but could only tilt her chin. "I do need to tell you about it. Are we alone?"

He frowned. "Yeah... just us." Why did that matter? Unless she was embarrassed to tell him she was giving her boyfriend roadhead when he crashed or something equally awkward.

Why did that idea make his skin feel too tight?

"Pulse, I-I was run off the road."

He froze. "What?"

"I was followed from my office on my way home. I worked late tonight and didn't leave until around ten. The exit I take off the highway to get home is fairly rural. A car followed me as I exited and rode my ass the entire time, then they hit me. More than once."

What the fuck?

He swallowed what felt like a spiked ball. "You're sure?"

"Yes. I kept going faster, and I even tried to pull over, but they followed every move I made. Then, they hit me multiple times until I lost control."

He'd call Curly to relay this information as soon as he left this room. "Who... fuck, do you have any idea who it was? A pissed-off client, maybe? Someone who didn't like the verdict in their trial? Has anything crazy happened at work?"

She bit her lower lip but didn't respond. The longer the silence lasted, the more unsettled he became.

"Talia..."

"Hey, Gabe. This our patient waiting to head up to

radiology?"

He jolted and then looked up at Ricco, a transport tech he met on his first day of hospital orientation. "Yeah. She's all set, Ricco." He looked back down at Talia, whose eyes were heavy from pain and medication. "We'll talk about this more later," he murmured. He couldn't resist the urge to cup her cheek.

"Wait..." She grabbed his hand. "I had a visitor, Pulse. Before I left the office."

The way she stared at him, straight in his eyes despite her obvious exhaustion and discomfort, told him all he needed to know.

And it made him angry enough to kill.

They weren't alone anymore, and she was about to be wheeled out, so the hundred questions he had would go unanswered for now. But when she returned, he'd do whatever it took to carve out a few minutes alone to get some answers.

Ricco unlocked the casters on her bed and then wheeled her out of the room. Pulse stood staring after her until he was looking at an empty hallway. *Fuck!* He mouthed, though he wanted to scream it at the top of his lungs. He gripped his hair and paced the length of the empty room. "Fuck, fuck, fuck."

The DEA had gone after Talia.

What the hell did that mean? Did they want something from her? Was this to get at him? He barely knew the woman. Hell, he didn't know her. Why would they think injuring her would get to him?

Yet there he stood, his heart pounding and the fire of rage heating his blood, wanting to go to war, not because the DEA wanted him back but because they dared to involve Talia.

"Gabe, you okay?" Sharon appeared next to the open curtain at the mouth of the trauma room.

"What?" He dropped his arms and rolled his shoulders. "Yeah, all good."

She eyed him with pursed lips before shrugging. "Okay, room eleven's IV is finished, and he needs his next dose of antibiotics hooked up."

"Okay, thanks. I'll head in there now."

After casting a final concerned frown his way, Sharon nodded and left the room.

Pulse sighed. He still had hours on his shift, and they would drag by slower than a mile-long line at the Department of Motor Vehicles.

He cracked his neck side to side and shook out his hands. Years of undercover work meant he could act his ass off when necessary. Tonight, it was more than necessary. He had to fool the entire emergency room into believing he was fine and not pissed as fucking hell.

You got this.

As he strode from the room, pushing all concerns but work out of his mind, one rogue thought shot itself to the forefront of his mind.

Just what had Talia's *visitor* told her? Did she know exactly who he was? And at what point would she call Curly to inform him one of his men was a former federal agent?

He'd be back in this room the second Talia returned from testing.

Chapter Eight

She never got another chance to speak with Pulse.

Everything moved quickly after she returned to the ER from imaging. Thankfully, she didn't have any spinal cord issues or brain bleeding, but they did diagnose her with a moderate concussion due to a severe headache. She also vomited in the radiology suite, which was both painful on her sore chest and humiliating.

The staff acted like it was no big deal. They probably saw and dealt with worse every day, but as someone who prided herself on independence and competence, being the center of attention while at her weakest sucked.

Along with the scans of her head and neck, they'd X-rayed her chest and ribs. Thankfully, she didn't have any fractures, only extensive bruising that seemed to grow a deeper shade of purple by the hour.

By the time she returned to the ER, she was struggling to keep her eyes open. Someone had informed her there'd been a shooting in downtown Tampa with multiple victims, which meant Pulse was back in action and not assigned to her room. Her nurse ended up being a beautiful woman originally from Jamaica who kept her distracted while the sadistic physician shoved a needle in her forehead to numb and then stitched the laceration.

A potent cocktail of pain medications kept the headache at bay and her chest pain to a minimum but made it impossible to stay awake no matter how hard she fought sleep. At one point, she lost an argument with her nurse about being admitted overnight. She used every trick up her sleeve and every tactic she'd learned as an attorney to plead her case and prove she was well enough to go home and sleep there.

She lost.

Nurses were fierce as hell.

That was how she found herself in the drabbest room in America, staring at four white walls with a hideous wallpaper border. It had a geometric print that was popular in the eighties when it was installed. She didn't have to look at it for long. About five seconds after her floor nurse introduced herself and performed another assessment, Talia passed out cold. She woke every time they came into her room to check her blood pressure and give her medication, but she always fell right back out.

By morning, she was cranky from interrupted sleep and groggy from the damn medication.

She still hadn't seen Pulse.

Which was probably for the best, considering she didn't want to have a serious conversation while under the influence of narcotics. Somewhere around four in the morning, she'd refused anything stronger than ibuprofen. It didn't eliminate the headache as well as the strong stuff, but she hoped she'd feel clearer as the day went on and the opioids flushed out of her system.

"Good morning." A tall woman wearing light blue scrubs with French-braided blonde hair strode into the room with a sunny smile. "I'm Mindy, and I'll be the nurse taking care of you today."

A glance at the clock told Talia it was shortly after eight in the morning.

"Morning."

"How are you feeling this morning, sweetie?" Mindy asked, making Talia chuckle. The woman had to be five years younger and about a thousand notches perkier than Talia had ever been.

"I'm all right."

"How's the pain?" Mindy scanned her badge to log into the computer and then pulled up Talia's chart with a few mouse clicks.

"I have a mild headache. My sternum is very tender to touch and hurts like hell when I move, but it's okay when I'm still like this."

"Okay." Mindy click-clacked away on the keyboard, documenting everything Talia reported. "Have you been out of bed at all?"

She nodded. "Walked to the bathroom a few times and up and down the hallway once."

"Great. Well, your doctor should be stopping by for rounds in a bit. If he's satisfied, we can get you home this morning."

"Oh, thank God." The idea of being in her own space worked better at easing her discomfort than any painkiller could. "No offense, but I hate it here."

Mindy laughed as she stepped away from the computer and over to Talia. "None taken, I promise. I hate it here sometimes too. Let me have your arm so I can take your blood pressure. The quicker we get through everything, the quicker you can go home."

She'd let them shave her head if it would get her home faster.

Everything moved at a surprisingly rapid pace after that. The doctor came by, checked her forehead stitches and her bruised chest, and ran through a quick neurological assessment since she had a concussion. After she passed all those tests, he pronounced her free to go. Of course, she couldn't hop out of bed and stroll out the door. They made her call Margo for a ride home and promised someone would stay with her for forty-eight hours. She lied through her teeth when she assured them Margo would be by her side for the next few days. Nothing sounded worse than having her friend hover like a mother hen. Talia wanted to be alone in her space where she could be free to finally let out the emotions of the past fifteen hours by sobbing on her couch.

By eleven in the morning, armed with a brown bag of medication, a nursing assistant wheeled her out the door to where Margo waited in her brand-new Mercedes. She let her friend fuss over her but fell asleep as soon as they hit the highway.

"Are you sure you don't want me to stay?" Margo asked after she'd helped Talia into her house. "I can cancel court this afternoon."

Settled on her couch with a blanket and a hot tea, Talia shook her head. "No, you can't do that. That case has already been delayed twice. Go. I'm fine. I'm going to drink my tea, nap, watch some trashy TV, then probably nap some more."

Margo studied her for a moment as though having an internal debate on whether she should leave. She'd worn coral wide-leg pants with a white silk camisole and stylish black blazer, ready for the busy day of work Talia had interrupted.

"Go. I'm fine. I promise." Talia yawned, tossing in a mouth pat and heavy blink to show her friend and boss how tired she was. If she was a bit dramatic, so be it.

"Okay, fine. But I'm coming back with some dinner later, okay?"

"Kay. Thanks, Marg."

"And you are not to do anything strenuous, you hear me?" She pointed an accusatory finger Talia's way, knowing full well that sitting still wasn't Talia's strong suit. She was as good at relaxing as she was following orders.

"I hear you."

"I can't believe you didn't call me until this morning," Margo muttered as she swiped her purse off the couch. "I bet you never would have called me if the hospital hadn't forced you. You were planning to take an Uber, weren't you?"

Ooh, the lawyer you-better-not-lie-to-me stare. "Um…"

"That tells me all I need to know." Margo rolled her eyes while shaking her head, but her affectionate smile told the truth. Talia's stubborn streak forever amused her. After she slipped her feet into her nude pumps, she strode over and kissed the top of Talia's head. "Call if you need anything."

That would never happen. Margo had already wasted enough of her busy day on Talia's nonsense.

"Will do."

Margo snorted. "No, you won't. You do know it's okay to lean on people occasionally, right? You do not always have to be the strong one."

Ugh, this again. "I know," she said because it was the expected response.

A half hum, half snort was Margo's only reply. She knew pursuing this conversation was pointless.

Thank God. Talia didn't have the brain power to think about her mountain of issues just then.

"Bye, Tal. Be good. Love you!" Margo waved over her shoulder as she disappeared through the front door.

Any other time, Talia would have locked it behind her friend, but her limbs weighed three hundred pounds each, and her eyes were already sliding shut. The house was quiet and peaceful. The pain medication kept her headache at bay, and the pile of pillows Margo shoved behind her back kept her chest comfortable. A soft blanket negated the chill of the air conditioning, and within seconds, Talia slipped into unconsciousness.

Knock, knock, knock.

Talia startled, wincing at the pain that lanced through her chest. She blinked. "Wha…"

Knock, knock.

The door.

Frowning, she dragged her legs over the side of the couch. "Coming," she called out. "Oof, that hurts." Going from a reclined to a seated position pulled on her chest muscles. She felt like she'd been kicked by an elephant, or at least how she imagined it would feel being hit by one of those giant feet.

Knock, knock

"Coming!" she called louder this time. Who the hell was it? Maybe Margo couldn't make it for dinner and had ordered her some food.

By the time she shuffled to the door, she was tired again. And in pain. She was due for some pain medication. Her head throbbed where she'd received ten stitches, and her bruised sternum was beyond sore. Wincing, she reached for the knob and pulled open the door, only to find a very attractive man in jeans, a black T-shirt, and a Hell's Handlers' cut. His scowl didn't cancel out his appeal, but it did have her frowning.

"Pulse."

His gaze immediately went to the cut on her forehead before traveling up and down the length of her body.

She ran a hand over her hair as heat rushed to her face. Rarely did she go out in public with her hair down, and never in lightweight joggers and a simple ribbed tank top. She always secured her hair in a neat bun or similar professional style, wore a full face of makeup, and dressed to impress. Nothing overly fancy or flashy, but it was her armor.

Standing before Pulse in her loungewear with a scrubbed face and loose hair, she might as well have been naked.

Yes, she needed therapy. And no, she hadn't gone yet.

Getting someone as unwilling to lean on others as Talia to go to therapy was worse than pulling teeth. Just ask Margo. She'd said it at least a dozen times.

So now there she stood, skin prickling at the notion of being exposed and vulnerable with a gash on her head and no shields while a gorgeous man stood in her doorway, glowering.

"Uh, what... what are you doing here?" God, she was a respected attorney who'd taken down countless men in the courtroom with her sharp tongue and quick thinking, and here, she could not form a simple sentence without floundering.

"Seriously? You didn't lock your door after what happened last night?"

His scolding had some of her usual fire returning until she tried to raise an eyebrow and ended up grimacing as pain shot across her forehead in a fiery arc.

With a huff, she turned and strode into the house—time for some pain medication.

"Come in, why don't you? I was hoping someone would show up to yell at me. This day hasn't been shitty enough."

The door clicked shut, followed by the snick of the lock before heavy footfalls trailed her into her kitchen.

She didn't bother to turn and look at him until she'd swallowed four ibuprofen with a large gulp of water. When she turned, she found him still staring at her, but his anger had changed to concern.

"I fell asleep," she said and could have kicked herself. Since when did she explain her actions to a random man she didn't know? And yet, her mouth kept moving. "I was completely wiped out when I got home and passed out within seconds. Otherwise, I would have locked the door."

He frowned. "I'm surprised they let you come home alone."

She smirked.

"Ah," he said, shaking his head.

How long had it been since a man stood in her space?

Ages.

They stared at each other across her kitchen.

So long, she'd apparently forgotten how to act.

"Uh, can I get you anything? A drink or..." She shrugged.

"What? Fuck no. You should be resting, not fucking serving me."

He had a point. "Uh, okay. Then back to the couch, I guess." She gestured for him to leave the kitchen before her, but all he did was step to the side so she could pass by. She frowned as he followed her back to the living room, hovering close as though worried she'd keel over at any point.

"Sit anywhere you'd like." She returned to her favorite spot on the couch beside the armrest and pulled the blanket over her lap. It wasn't her clothes, but it worked as substitute armor in a pinch.

Pulse sat too. Next to her. Right next to her. So close he was *in her bubble*, as her coworker's daughter said when a boy at school had pulled her pigtails all day. Her breath caught. God, he was close. And what was that scent? He smelled woodsy, warm, and cozy, like a human blanket she wanted to burrow in.

What the hell?

That concussion must be worse than she realized.

"So I'm guessing you're here for a play-by-play of what happened last night?"

"How are you feeling?" he asked instead of answering. "The stitches look great."

"Oh." She pressed a hand over her forehead where they'd stitched her up and left the wound open to the air. They'd cleaned it as best they could, but she probably needed to rinse it in the shower, which they said was fine, just no soaking. "I feel like I was in a car accident."

He grunted.

"I assumed we'd talk at the hospital. I'm sorry you had to come all the way out here... wait, how did you find out where I live?"

He grinned, and damn, he was attractive when he smiled.

"Right." They probably checked her hospital records. Either that or his club had some hacker extraordinaire in the club who knew everything from when she lost her first tooth to what she bought at the grocery store last week. They fell silent. The weight of what she'd learned last night settled between them like a ticking bomb ready to blow.

He was too close. She couldn't smell anything but him. All she could feel was the heat wafting off him It, combined with the warmth from the blanket, had her sweating. Or maybe it was the upcoming conversation that made her sweat.

She wasn't one to beat around the bush. A problem solver, that's what Margo called her. Unresolved issues drove her insane, and she'd rather jump into an uncomfortable chat if it fixed an issue. So why was she hesitating now?

Get it together.

She cleared her throat. "So, do you want to tell me why the DEA sent someone to run me off the road and give me a concussion?"

His eyes flared, and he reared back as though she'd smacked him. Whether it was from her blunt delivery or the information itself, she couldn't tell.

The way his jaw ticked and his fists curled on his thighs spoke to his rising anger.

Maybe she should have softened the delivery.

"Sorry. I didn't know how to bring it up."

"You're sure it was the DEA?"

His gaze burned with emotions she couldn't decipher.

"As sure as I can be." Talia sighed. A dull throb settled

between her eyes. Unfortunately, she'd had all the medication she could for the moment unless she wanted to pop open the few narcotics the doctor prescribed.

And she didn't.

"I worked late last night. I was the only one left in the office, which is not uncommon."

His eyes narrowed as though he disapproved.

Talia shrugged. "I'm a bit of a workaholic."

Understatement of the year.

"Anyway, the main entrance makes this annoying squeak we're constantly meaning to fix, but I secretly like it because it lets me know whenever someone comes into the office. I heard it last night, and a man came into my office a few seconds later. He never gave me his name. He—"

"Describe him."

"Uh...." She closed her eyes and conjured an image of the unwelcome visitor. "I was sitting, so I'm not totally sure how tall he was. Six-footish, I'd guess. He had tanned skin and black hair, all smoothed back with a lot of product. No facial hair. No wedding ring. His nails were nice like he'd had them manicured, and he wore a suit that fit him well. He wasn't overly muscular but not skinny either. Medium build, I guess." She opened her eyes. "Is that helpful at all?"

His lips pressed together in a grim line. "No, unfortunately, that could be a hundred agents."

"He wanted me to talk you into working with the DEA again."

He arched an eyebrow at that.

For a moment, it seemed he wouldn't spill his secrets. He glanced away with his shoulders so bunched and tense that her fingers itched to dig in and loosen him up. But that'd be highly unprofessional, and they were already crossing lines here.

After a few drawn-out moments of silence, he looked back

at her. "I was an agent for a little over a decade."

Was an agent. Past tense. Did that mean her visitor was right, and he was no longer working for the government? Her instinct had been correct, and Pulse wasn't a plant in the MC.

"I did a lot of undercover work. A lot. For my last case, I spent four years with the Del Rios Cartel posing as a high-ranking official."

Talia blinked. "He mentioned that. Pulse, I remember those headlines. That case was insane."

He nodded.

"I remember it well," she said as she shifted to face him better. "I was in my last year of law school. We studied the trial extensively in real-time as it was televised. That was you?"

"That was me. My final case. Walked the fuck away when it was over and haven't spoken to anyone from that world in more than five years."

The relief shouldn't have been so substantial, but she'd spent half the night worrying about him destroying the MC from the inside out. For whatever reason, maybe it was the DEA coming after her, she believed him when he said he'd left that life behind. There were so many blanks to be filled in.

"What happened?"

He rubbed a hand across his chin, stubbly with a day's beard growth. When he met her gaze, his eyes were deep with pain and regret. "I was under for four years straight."

"That's a long time." How did someone survive an operation that long without losing themselves?

"It is. Too long. We kept getting so close, but not close enough to take them down so my assignment was extended over and over. I don't regret taking them down. The Del Rios Cartel was a violent, evil place most of the time. They did unspeakable things to innocent people and were responsible for hundreds of deaths, be it directly or indirectly, through the drugs they brought into our country. They needed to go away, and I'm proud to have been part of that."

"But..." She tilted her head, studying the handsome man whose expression grew bleaker by the second.

"People don't understand what being undercover in a situation like that does to your head. You spend years with people you hate, but not every second is spent taking them down. You also laugh, hang out, and celebrate holidays and birthdays. You get to know the people behind the evil deeds, and to their friends and family, they are often just people. They love them and treat them well. It fucks you up." He shrugged. "At least it did for me."

"They liked you."

He nodded once, then shrugged. His shoulders moved slowly as though the weight he carried made the movement difficult. "I did my job well and became one of the family. So well, I was permitted to date the cartel leader's daughter."

Talia sucked in a breath. "Wait..." She straightened. "She died in the DEA's raid. The day they arrested everyone. She was killed. Oh my God, Pulse."

Pain twisted his features. "They fucked up. She wasn't supposed to be there. I made sure. Booked her at the spa that afternoon, but the DEA moved the time up, and no one told me. She showed up, saw me and her brother in cuffs, drew a gun..."

Talia swallowed around her thickened throat. This poor man. She reached for him, resting her palm on his forearm. "I'm so sorry, Pulse. Did-did you love her?"

He shook his head. "No. She was a means to an end. But I liked her, and I tried to treat her well. She had no part in the family business, though she knew who her father and brother were and benefited from their money. I know that makes her guilty by association, but she didn't deserve to die. Not that way. Not that day."

"Of course not. God, I'm so sorry." She tugged on his arm, and he turned into her so she could wrap her arms around him. He buried his face in the crook of her neck, sending a ripple of goosebumps down her arms. His scent overwhelmed her, erasing any discomfort the position caused.

They stayed that way for a few moments, both lost in thought. Her air conditioning whirring to life was the only sound besides their breathing.

"I walked away that day," he eventually said against her skin. "So many fucked-up things happened during that time, but Camila's death was the final straw. I couldn't do it anymore, so I resigned and left that life behind."

And at some point, he'd gone to nursing school to begin a new career. She'd loved to ask him what drove him toward his current job, but it wasn't the time. They needed to focus on the issue at hand.

"Want to know the most fucked-up part?"

She ran her hands up and down his back. The patches on his cut tickled her palms and reminded her of what the DEA agent wanted in the first place—Pulse spying on his club.

"What's that?"

"I missed it," he whispered against her skin. "Missed them. The way they were with each other. The way I became part of the family."

The pieces fell into place. She nudged him back by his shoulders. Their gazes locked, and her breath caught.

"That's why you joined the MC."

Chapter Nine

He'd have been more comfortable if someone carved him open and let his insides spill out all over the room. Four years undercover, never talking about his true feelings and thoughts, followed by five years of keeping himself emotionally removed from everyone in his life, meant he was severely out of practice talking about his shit.

Sharing his secrets with Talia, secrets he'd never voiced, made his body prickle as though thousands of needles were dancing along his oversensitive skin. His clothes felt too tight, near suffocating. Her arms around him felt intoxicating and torturous.

Her tits pressed into his chest, and her soft skin against his own soothed as well as aroused. He was as out of practice with physical intimacy as he was emotional. Sure, he fucked on occasion, but that's all it was. The sixty seconds of hugging Talia was more meaningful than a single sexual interaction he'd had over the past five years.

"You needed a family," she whispered as she snuck a hand under his cut then continued rubbing his back. Without the leather and thick patches blunting the sensation, he might as well have been naked. The heat from her hand seared through his thin T-shirt.

"Yeah," he whispered back, though the admission nearly

killed him.

Talia's hand slid to his lower back, then stilled beneath his cut. She pulled away, only far enough so she could see his face. "And now the DEA wants you to spy on your family."

Did they? Something about this entire situation was off. After a decade of working for them, Pulse knew how the government worked. The alphabet agencies could be shady as fuck when they needed to be, but actively running a woman off the road to get their way? That wasn't their style. There were so many methods of putting pressure on a person that were more effective and subtle.

When he didn't respond right away, Talia frowned. "That's what they want, right? I mean, that's what they told me. And when I told the agent to suck on an electrical cord, he said he had ways of making me comply, hence the car accident." As though a lightbulb went off in her mind, her eyes widened. "Unless..."

He nodded.

God, she was so close he could see a moon-shaped speck of gold in her right eye.

"It's more in line with something a cartel out for revenge would do. Oh shit, I had the impression he was trying to downplay an accent."

Goddamn, she was quick. "Yes. I didn't think that at first, but given what happened to you..." He shrugged. "Something deeper is going on. Maybe a rouge cartel member we missed during the arrest who's now posing as a DEA agent."

She swallowed. Her throat rose and fell with the motion, drawing his attention. His lips tingled. She'd taste good, like sweetness and strength intertwined.

"Or maybe they feel the ultimate revenge is infiltrating the DEA."

Oh shit. She was right. He let his hands fall from around

her. They landed on her thighs. "Five years is the perfect amount of time to get someone in the door. They could have worked up to a solid position and been trusted by the entire agency by now."

"Yes." She nodded. "And they bring up this idea of delving into MCs as the perfect way to fuck with you and everyone you love."

"Fuck," he spat out as he tried to push off the couch.

Talia caught his hand, drawing him back down. "Pulse, wait." She kept a firm grip on his hand. "You have to tell Curly."

He reeled back as though she'd slapped him. "What? Fuck no." This time, he successfully ripped out of her grasp and leaped off the couch. "That cannot happen," he said as he paced away. "Worst idea ever. You have no idea the shitstorm that would bring."

She rose from the couch with a wince that had him feeling like an asshole.

"Talia, you should be sitting." He started for her, but she held up a hand, stopping him in his tracks.

"Listen to me. Curly is a good man. He will underst—"

"No." He stared at the ceiling as he inhaled. "There's nothing Curly hates more than cops. Feds are cops on steroids. I've been lying since the day he met me. He'll kill me. Hell, I'll be lucky if he kills me. Most likely, he'll sic Spec on me, and I'll be tortured for a few weeks before they kill me."

"He accepts Tracker's ol' lady, Jo. Maybe it would be the same for you."

Jo was a former cop in their town who'd quit the force due to corruption in the department.

"You know it's not the same."

"Pulse…" The pleading in her eyes almost had him giving in.

But he couldn't.

He shook his head. "I can't, Talia. I can't... do that to them."

The truth was he didn't care what they did to him. Joining the MC with his history always held an enormous risk—one he'd been willing to take. He'd gone looking for a family to replace what he'd had during his undercover time with the cartel. What he found blew that experience out of the water. He and his brothers were tight in a way he'd never experienced. He'd die for any one of them. Even as he held himself at a distance emotionally, he could be himself around them.

In all ways except one.

Talia studied him without speaking. What was she thinking? Would she announce that she planned to tell Curly despite his wishes? He wouldn't blame her. Curly paid her to represent the club. No one man was above the club. She'd be well within her rights to tell Curly everything they discussed. She'd be a fool not to.

"Okay," she said after the silence grew almost too heavy to endure. "We'll try it your way. For now."

"We?"

She nodded with a crooked half smile. "They say two heads are better than one, right?"

"I don't want you involved, Talia."

Her huff of laughter rang hollow. She reached for the stitches on her forehead. "I'm in it now. I don't scare easily, Pulse, and I've always fought for what I believed. It's important to me. You can try pushing me out, but I won't go easily."

His admiration for this woman, already high, grew with every word she spoke. "Okay. You can help me under one condition."

One eyebrow rose in what he recognized as her warning

signal. A skeptical watch-what-you-say cautionary look. It was sexy as hell and fierce as fuck—two phrases that described Talia perfectly. He couldn't help but smile in return.

He folded his arms across his chest. "You sit back down and don't get up for the rest of the day."

Talia narrowed her eyes. Her hip popped to the side as she rested her hand on it. "Are you telling me what to do?"

He had to bite the inside of his lip to keep from laughing. If he let this play out much longer, his mouth would end up bloody, but he couldn't resist having a little fun with her. He advanced into her personal space, stopping only when he was close enough, she had to lift her chin to maintain eye contact. Pulse might not be the tallest in the group at six feet, but he still had at least five inches on Talia.

"That a problem?"

Her mouth opened and closed. She blinked. A sound nearing a squawk left her. Pulse bit his cheek harder. He could feel the waves of indignation rolling off her and smacking into him. She was stuck. Her instinct was to tell him to shove his demand up his ass, but on the flip side, she knew she should be sitting and resting.

"It is," she ended up saying even as she turned and strode to the couch. "I'll sit. Not because you told me to but because it's the smart thing to do."

Well, shit. Why was that sass so hot? Would she be like this in bed? Would she fight for control and channel all that independence into passion? Would she try to run the show? Or would she go the opposite way and hand over control to give her mind a rest? Fuck, either of those would be fine by him.

He shifted as his cock thickened in his jeans. If she noticed, she'd likely castrate him.

Syringes.

Stethoscopes.

Bedpans.

That last one did the trick—nothing sexy about a bedpan.

Thank God she didn't have her glasses on because nothing could have deflated his cock in that case.

Talia sat down and lifted her legs onto the couch, resting her back against a fluffy pillow on the armrest. Exhaustion seemed to kick in as soon as she was off her feet. She deflated against the cushions, closing her eyes on an exhale. The line of stitches on her face served as a constant reminder of what happened last night.

Because of him.

Protective instincts he hadn't felt for years rose to the surface. Nothing else would happen to her. Somehow, he'd find a way to keep her safe. That would mean enlisting the help of his club, which would require some fancy maneuvering. He didn't relish lying to his club more than he already had, but he had to find a way to keep her out of the DEA or cartel's crosshair.

She'd kick him in the balls if she could hear him making plans without her approval.

He cleared his dry throat. "Can I… can I get you anything? Water, or do you need something to eat?"

She blinked, and a look of surprise crossed her face. "Oh. Um, don't worry about it. I'm perfectly capable of taking care of myself. I don't need you waiting on me."

Pulse snorted. "It's a fucking glass of water. I'm not offering white-glove service."

Talia chuckled, but it was stiff. "Okay, well, I guess I could use a drink, thank you. There's a pitcher of water in the fridge. And glasses in the cabinet next to the fridge. Thank you. This is really nice of you."

For real? Was she so unaccustomed to someone offering to do anything for her that a simple glass of water seemed like a huge deal?

That would change if she spent much time around his club. They were so intertwined in each other's lives, constantly helping and easing each other's burdens. He almost smiled as he imagined how prickly she'd be as she learned to let his family in.

He fetched the water—she had lemons floating in the damn pitcher—and returned to the living room. Their fingers brushed as he handed the glass over. Hers were so soft compared to his. He had the strong urge to slide his hand up her arm to feel her silky skin, but he resisted and pulled away to sit at the opposite end of the couch, near her feet—a much safer distance than before.

"Thanks again," she said as she lifted the glass to her lips.

Pulse glanced away. He couldn't risk watching her mouth with all these weird feelings messing with his head.

"So, uh... what's the plan, Pulse?"

Wasn't that the million-dollar question? He rubbed a hand over his chin. It itched as it always did if he didn't shave daily. "Don't have one yet. I've got a guy I need to call who can dig into this for us. I'll have more for you after I talk to him."

"Okay." She drummed her nails against the side of the glass. "Hey, do you think I'm safe? Here at my house, I mean. Do you think they'd come for me here? I mean, I can handle myself. I just want to be prepared."

The vulnerability in her voice punched the air out of his chest. It had to be killing her to voice concern. Of course, she couldn't admit she might be unable to manage this all alone.

"Should I get a big dog or something?" she asked with a forced laugh.

He grinned. "Yes, to the dog, but that's only half for protection. The other half is because everyone needs a dog."

That had her laugh sounding much more genuine. "Do *you* have a dog?"

"No. But that's because I'm in a tiny-ass apartment and have my heart set on getting a mastiff. As soon as I purchase a house, I'll get one, though."

"Nice. Growing up, I always wanted a big dog, but my father was allergic."

"Now's your chance."

"I'd love to, but I work so much. Plus, I don't think I'm the nurturing kind. I'm too Type A. A poor dog would probably hate living with me."

Pulse frowned. What a sad thing to think about herself, especially when the evidence proved otherwise. Hadn't she just gone out of her way to comfort him while he bared his soul? For someone who presented with such confidence, Talia needed someone to clue her into what a fantastic person she was.

He wasn't the man to take that on. Not when he was drowning in his issues.

"To answer your question, yes. You're safe here."

"You sound certain."

He shrugged. "I am certain."

Talia was way too brilliant to fall for bullshit. Her eyes narrowed to slits. "*Pulse*, what does that mean? How are you certain?"

He sighed. "It means someone from the club will be outside your house at all times until this shit is resolved."

"What?" she shot forward, then winced and cradled a hand to her sternum. "Okay, that was dumb."

He curled his fists to avoid reaching for her and helping her settle back against the pillows. No matter how much he hated watching her struggle, she wouldn't want or appreciate the assistance when she was trying so hard to prove she didn't need anyone.

"Save your breath," he said. "It's done." Or it would be as soon as he placed a call and lied about the reason she needed an eye on her. "We've got a couple of new prospects who need shit to do, and this is perfect."

"What will you tell them?"

He stood. Work started in a few hours, and he'd need to get this sorted before then. He also needed to leave before he did something stupid like agreeing to tell Curly about his past.

Or kiss Talia.

"That's for me to worry about."

Her frown told him how hard she was working not to argue.

"I gotta take off, but I'll get someone out here within the hour."

"Okay. Thank y—"

He held up a hand. "Do not thank me for keeping you safe when the whole reason you're in fucking pain is because of me."

"Pulse..."

No way could he listen to her try to ease his conscience. "Call if you need anything," he said as he strode to the door. The instinct to pause and kiss the top of her head rode him hard, but he ignored it, just as he ignored how good her breasts felt against him when she'd hugged him.

The second her door closed behind him, he rang Spec, who answered immediately. "Yo, Pulse, what's up, brother?"

"Hey, the club's new attorney was run off the road last night. Can we get a schedule for the new prospects to keep an eye on her until I can look into what's going on?"

Not a lie. He was sure as hell going to investigate it, but not the truth either.

"Oh shit, she okay?"

"Concussion and a nasty laceration on her forehead that needed a bunch of stitches. She's bruised as fuck, too, but nothing she won't recover from."

"Damn, yeah, I'll get a guy out there right away. Text me her address. I'll have Liv and the ladies stop by with some food for her too."

Pulse couldn't help but grin as he imagined Talia's shock at finding an army of nosy ol' ladies darkening her door with more food than she could eat in a month.

"Perfect. Thanks, man."

"Interesting that she called you when she got hurt, right?" Spec's voice was thick with innuendo.

Rolling his eyes, Pulse said, "She didn't call me, dipshit. I work at the hospital on the trauma team, remember? She rolled in on an ambulance in the middle of the night."

"Well, fuck you. That's not nearly as juicy. I can't give you shit about that. Thanks for ruining my fun, asshole," Spec said, sounding disgusted.

Pulse grinned. "Love you, too, brother."

He sat astride his bike and glanced back at Talia's home. She had a nice place. It was older but had been well maintained and updated and set in a semi-rural neighborhood where the houses had plenty of space between them. He didn't exactly get a tour, but he'd guess it had three bedrooms. From what he saw, Talia kept it neat and organized, with a modern yet cozy style—lots of neutrals and soft colors.

He liked his home the same way. Work was a constant adrenaline rush, often overwhelming and chaotic, like life at the clubhouse. Having a house full of bright colors and patterns didn't allow his brain to come down from that high.

As he drove off, he ran through his next steps. Another call to Birdy topped the list now that he had protection for Talia sorted.

What a shitty twenty-four hours.

At least he could work on this problem, knowing that Talia was safe, and his club would protect her.

Who knew what would happen if they found out why he was worried about her?

Chapter Ten

He hadn't been kidding.

For the past week, a scowling biker sat outside her house at all hours. In an unexpected twist—she spread her fingers, peering through the blinds on her office window—they followed her everywhere she went.

Work? A biker came along.

Grocery store? They were there too.

Nail salon? Yep, a biker sat in the parking lot while she pampered her toes.

Unfortunately, that was the extent of her outings ninety percent of the time. Whoever these poor guys guarding her were, they had to be bored out of their minds with her mundane routine. Again, she was realizing she might need to find herself a social life.

After Pulse left a few days ago, she passed out and woke to a knock on her door a few hours later. A horde of smiling women armed to the teeth with a ridiculous amount of food bullied their way into her home and took over her life for the next three hours.

She'd appreciated their company, but the headache and exhaustion kept her from truly enjoying herself. The rest of them, though? They had a blast laughing, teasing, and acting silly.

Following the car accident, Talia took three days off work to allow her brain to rest, as ordered by her physician. Then she got back to real life—well, real life plus a babysitter.

And plans for the night. Liv had invited—ordered—Talia to join them at the clubhouse for a Friday night barbecue.

When was the last time she'd gone to a barbecue? She was mortified to admit it had been years. Occasionally, she hung out with Margo, but her friend was a partner in a busy law firm, had three kids, and had a husband who owned a small business. Her life was jam-packed with insanity. The rare occasions Margo could sneak away were spent on Talia's couch, drinking wine, relaxing, and watching reality television. They always invited Talia for holidays, but she tended to pass on the offer, feeling like an outsider in their family unit.

The MC was a family as well. One full of happy couples and people who loved and liked each other more than most blood relatives.

Fear of feeling like an interloper had her on edge all day. That and the fact she hadn't heard a peep from Pulse in the seven days since he'd showed up at her house.

"Girl, this is the fourth time I've walked past your office today and found you staring out that window. There better be a sexy man out there, or I'm gonna start worrying about you."

Talia jumped and yanked her hand from the blinds. "Shit, Margo, you scared me."

Her friend snorted. "I called your name three times." She propped a hip against the door. She wore a trendy power suit in her favorite coral shade.

The way Margo always looked so effortlessly put together reminded Talia of Liv.

"What the hell is going on with you, Tal? You've been off since you came back to work. Is it your head? Did you come back too soon?" Concern had Margo's forehead wrinkling.

Talia bit the inside of her cheek. She hadn't told Margo the entire truth about the car accident. Margo thought the club was overprotective since Talia was their attorney, and a random person ran her off the road. As much as she trusted her friend and knew Margo could take a secret to the grave, Pulse's story wasn't hers to share, and doing so felt like a betrayal.

"Nothing is going on. I'm just…" Ugh, she felt like the uncool high schooler who someone swung an invitation to the football party. Her shoulders sagged. "I was invited to a barbecue at the MC clubhouse tonight, and I'm stressing about it."

Margo's face lit up, and she stepped into the office. "You were? Why didn't you tell me sooner? This is fantastic." She clapped her hands like an enthusiastic kid instead of a high-powered attorney. "I'm so excited."

"Really?" Talia raised an eyebrow. "This is why I didn't tell you," she said as she waved a hand toward her bubbly friend. "You get all weird whenever I have plans."

"Pfft." Margo rolled her eyes. "What's weird is a thirty-two-year-old woman who hides behind her work and avoids socializing because she's terrified of having a feeling."

"Hey!" Ouch, that one hurt. She refused to acknowledge how accurately Margo hit the nail on the head. Denial had served her well for this long—no point in changing things up now. "I am not afraid of having a feeling."

Liar. It didn't even sound convincing in her head.

"I have feelings all the time. I feel hungry. I feel tired." She aimed a pointed look at Margo. "I feel annoyed."

Margo laughed as she came over and hugged Talia. "Oh, honey, you need so much therapy."

"Everyone needs therapy," she muttered against her friend's coconut-scented hair.

Margo drew back, still chuckling. "True, but some of us aren't as stubborn as you are, and we are willing to admit we need help and accept that help." She put her hands on Talia's shoulders and steered her toward the small sofa in her office.

"I'm not stubborn," Talia mumbled.

"Sure, sweetie. Just like I don't have an online shopping problem and didn't buy three pairs of shoes before I came in here." Margo gently pushed her onto the couch. "Now, tell me why this has you stressed."

She opened her mouth to tell Margo to forget about it, but that's not what came out. "They're all so close. In my whole life, I've never been as close to anyone as these people are to each other, not even my family." Especially not her family. "And they aren't even related. I just... it makes me feel..."

"Yes?" Margo rolled her hand as though encouraging Talia to continue. "You feel? Come on, T, use your big-girl words. You can do it."

She scowled at her friend.

Of course, Margo wasn't fazed in the slightest. She ate furious prosecutors for lunch, then went home to a pack of hungry children.

"You feel..."

"Ugh, shitty, all right?" she said with a huff that rivaled Margo's twelve-year-old daughter's. "It makes me feel shitty. Like I'm broken or something."

"And why do you think that is?"

She threw her hands up. "I'm sorry, did you get a degree in psychology while I was off?"

A finger wiggled back and forth in front of her eyes. "Don't get snarky with me, missy."

"Margo, I'm not one of your kids. I don't need you to teach me a lesson."

"All right, look, I'm teasing you." Margo grabbed her hands. "Mostly." Her rueful smile erased Talia's annoyance.

"First of all, you are not broken, far from it. Talia, you are an amazing person. It's okay to let other people see that. It's okay to go out and have fun. It's okay to want more and want what the people in that MC have. Ard it's okay to stop punishing yourself for something you had no control over. Something your father did more than fifteen years ago."

"That's not what I'm doing."

Was it? She frowned.

"It is, but we can talk about that another day. It's okay to trust. Not everyone, but you have a good head on your shoulders, T. You need to trust yourself first, then allow yourself to let others in. Once you do, you can have those close relationships you refuse to admit you crave."

Margo's kids were so lucky to have her as their mother. They'd never grow up fucked in the head and unable to connect with people.

"I have no doubt you can do this, and tonight is a great first step. Feeling nervous and unsure is okay, but you must stop holding yourself back."

She cupped Talia's face and stared at her with an expression too close to pity for comfort.

"You can't keep letting your fear keep you from connecting with people. You deserve to have a full life. One where you aren't lonely."

"I'm not lonely. I have you," she said, but it sounded weak even to her ears.

Margo's only reply was a small, sad smile.

Every time they had a conversation like this, Talia's stomach soured, and she fought violent waves of nausea. She'd been smack in the middle of a battle between her fears and her desires since before she understood what it meant to have daddy issues.

You're such a cliché.

"Repeat after me."

"Margo…"

"I will go to the barbecue."

Talia glared, which resulted in her friend clearing her throat and cupping a hand around her ear. "I can't hear you."

"I will go to the barbecue," she mumbled.

Margo nodded. "And I will smile and have fun."

"And I will smile and have fun. Margo, this is stupid."

The comment earned her a harsh glare.

"Yikes, no wonder your husband is terrified of you."

Margo's lips twitched, but she managed not to laugh. "I will talk to people and be friendly."

"Hey, I'm friendly."

Margo raised an eyebrow.

"I will talk to people and be friendly."

"And I will tell at least two people something personal about myself that has nothing to do with my job."

"And I will—" She froze as Margo's words registered.

Her friend's fierce glare transformed into an expression of patience.

Talia sighed. Her shoulders sagged. Why was this so hard for her? People meet other people and form relationships every day. They share stories, experiences, and even traumas. They become friends and intertwine their lives. Sometimes, those friendships become as close as family or turn intimate.

Why did the thought of it turn her blood to ice?

"And I'll tell two people something personal about myself."

"That…"

"That has nothing to do with work."

"Good girl." Margo hugged her. "Now go home and change into something cute before the barbecue."

She glanced down at her olive, wide-legged slacks and camel-colored blazer. "This is cute. What's wrong with my outfit?"

"Nothing at all if you're at work. Everything if you're at a barbecue full of bikers. Put on a cute pair of denim shorts and a tank top. A tight one."

"But it'll be dark around six. I'll be chilly."

Margo shrugged. "Guess you'll have to find a biker to lend you a hoodie." She tapped her lips. "Like maybe that sexy one you bailed out of jail the other night."

"Margo! He's a client."

"He is also tall, dark, and handsome with a good job, a sexy voice, and those dark eyes that smolder." She shivered and winked.

Yes, he was. He was all those things and more—protective, kind, and caring beneath a rough exterior.

Still a client.

"Yes, he's a good guy."

Margo snorted. "He's more than a good guy, and you know it. Keep him in mind when you're picking out an outfit. Make sure your top is tight. You've got great tits. No babies have destroyed them."

Her face heated. "Margo, you can't possibly be encouraging me to pursue a client."

She shrugged. "Normally, I would not, but it's you. You're too serious. You need someone to shake your life up a little, and I think Mr. Sexy Biker Nurse might be just the guy to do it."

Guilt over not sharing the truth about Pulse wormed its way under Talia's skin, but she couldn't say anything. On top of not feeling comfortable sharing someone else's secret, Margo would worry herself sick. Besides, this entire conversation was ludicrous. Even if she didn't have massive intimacy issues, she wouldn't go after a client. It was unprofessional and the kind of thing that could ruin her reputation in law circles.

"I'm not starting anything with Pulse."

"Oh, his name is Pulse? Is that because he makes yours race?"

"Oh my God." She swatted a laughing Margo's arm. "You have problems. Serious problems."

Her friend's laugh turned into a cackle. "Come on. I've been married to the same man for more than a decade. Give me something to live vicariously through."

"Please. I've seen the way your husband drools whenever you're around. You probably have a better sex life than most honeymooners."

Margo's eyes went dreamy. "Yeah. We really do."

After that, the conversation shifted from Talia's issues to Margo's family—thank God. They chatted for another twenty minutes before Margo ushered Talia out the door and to her car with strict orders to send a picture of her outfit for approval before heading to the barbecue.

That wasn't going to happen.

She'd find something sensible and modest to wear that wouldn't draw unprofessional attention.

But as she stood in her closet an hour later, she couldn't help but remember the feel of Pulse pressed against her last weekend. His heat, scent, and those eyes Margo correctly described as smoldering. Before she knew it, she found herself reaching for the pair of denim shorts Margo claimed made her ass look like a snack and a hunter-green ribbed tank that fit her like a second skin. Nothing fancy or flashy, but tight enough to be considered sexy.

Hopefully.

Chapter Eleven

"She's here! I'm so glad."

Pulse glanced from where he was flipping burgers to Liv, who smiled and waved toward the side of the clubhouse. He followed her gaze only to halt mid-burger flip.

"Who's here, babe?" Spec wandered over, beer in hand. "Oh, that's Talia, right? I liked her. She seems badass."

"I like her too. And she's super badass. I don't know why, but I get the feeling she needs us in her life." Liv accepted a kiss on the cheek from her ol' man, who chuckled.

"My little savior, always collecting strays." He slid his arm around Liv's waist and tucked her into his side.

No matter how often he scolded himself, Pulse couldn't stop the uneasy itch at the base of his spine when Spec came near him. It started after his arrest and worsened after he confessed his past to Talia. Spec would figure it out. It was only a matter of time before the DEA got annoyed enough to drop a hint. The club's enforcer was intelligent and tenacious. Spec would run with whatever morsel they fed him and uncover Pulse's deep, dark secret.

He'd spent the last week trying to act normal around the man while in a constant state of heightened anxiety.

Liv stood near the grill with a platter of open hamburger buns, ready for Pulse to deposit the cooked meat. "What can I say?" She hip-checked her ol' man. "I want everyone to be as happy as I am."

"Well, I'm not sure that's possible. I mean, there's only one of me and one of my dick, so unless you want to share, no one can ever be as hap... oof!" Spec laughed and rubbed his ribs where Liv's sharp elbow made contact.

Pulse let their flirty banter fade to the background as he focused on the woman walking toward them from the clubhouse. Christ, what the hell was she wearing? Those damn shorts should be criminal. Any man who stood behind her would be helpless to look anywhere but at her ass. What the hell happened to her conservative professional outfits?

It's a barbecue, idiot. Did you expect her to show up in a suit?

The skintight tank top had him fighting off a damn stiffy like a fucking horny teenager.

Who told her dark green was his favorite color?

The only thing that kept him from actively drooling was the wariness in her gaze. She hadn't walked so stiff and tense even the day she'd come to the shelter's grand opening without knowing anyone. Her shoulders were so bunched they nearly hit her ears, and her eyes held a wariness he wouldn't have expected from someone who regularly faced hungry prosecutors in court. Talia was uncomfortable as hell, and he was most likely the reason.

Fantastic.

"Dude, that burger is seconds from going up in flames."

Pulse jolted. "Shit." He scooped the charred burger no one would dare eat and tossed it over the grill. Ray would sniff it out in a few minutes, and that dog wouldn't mind a crunchy burger.

"Here, take this." Liv handed the platter off to her man. "She looks ready to bolt. I'm going to go say hi and get her a drink to loosen up." She darted off to intercept Talia.

Pulse blew out a breath. At least he had a few more

minutes to get himself together before he had to talk to her.

"See something you like there, brother?" Spec asked, waggling his eyebrows.

"What?" Pulse flipped the last of the burgers, then shut the grill. "What are you running your mouth about?"

"I'm talking about how that pretty lawyer with the banging body makes your eyes bug, and your tongue loll out like a cartoon character."

His lolling tongue was the least of his problems. His dick getting rock hard every time she came within one hundred yards of him was the real issue.

The stitches on her forehead might as well have been a beacon flashing in the night. They were there because of him. Because someone thought it'd be a good idea to fuck with her to get at him.

That thought deflated his cock instantly and had his blood boiling with a rage he hadn't felt since he'd watched Camila's lifeless body crumple to a dirty warehouse floor.

"Fuck off," he snapped at Spec. "She's the club's attorney. Seeing her reminds me I was arrested on bullshit charges last weekend."

Spec sniffed the air. "Speaking of bullshit." He snickered at himself. "Oh, here they come." He leaned in and mock whispered, "Want me to find out what she thinks about you? I could pass you a note later on."

Pulse scooped the first of the finished burgers off the grill. "I want you to fuck right off," he said as he slid it onto a bun and then went back for another.

Of course, his comment only made Spec laugh. "Hey there, Talia," he said as she and Liv reached them.

Liv had her arm linked through Talia's and appeared to be tugging her along as though to her doom.

"Glad you could join us." Spec slapped him on the back. "Pulse here told us more about your accident the other night.

Glad my man was working and could help take care of you."

For fuck's sake. Spec had no idea the minefield he'd just stepped in.

Talia's eyes bugged wide as they locked on him. He gave her one subtle shake of his head. Fuck no, he hadn't shared any details of her accident. At least not anything that would land him in a body bag.

She blinked. "Oh, uh, yeah. That was a rough night."

"Are you feeling okay?" Liv asked.

"Yes. Feeling great. Back to normal." She reached up to the stitches on her forehead. "Well, almost normal. Still have another week of these, unfortunately."

"They're barely noticeable," Liv said, which made Talia snort. "Okay, they're noticeable, but it looks like it's healing well."

"Uh, yeah," she said, touching it again. "I'm trying to take good care of it so it doesn't scar too badly."

Liv's expression turned sympathetic. "Some decent concealer and no one will ever notice it."

"Talia, you look like you could use a drink." Spec slid his free arm around his woman's waist. "I'll grab you one after I drop these burgers at the food table. Anything in particular you want?"

"Oh, thanks, but I'm good. Liv already offered."

"Ah, come on," Spec said. "You had a shit week, and it's a party. Live it up."

Talia chuckled and sighed. "Okay, I guess I could use a drink or ten. Beer works for me, thanks."

Liv wrinkled her nose, but Pulse nearly swooned. There was something super sexy about a woman drinking from a long-neck bottle.

"Let's go grab one for her, babe," Spec said as he guided Liv toward the outdoor bar they'd set up.

"Wait, but..." Liv's gaze flicked between Pulse and Talia

before she nodded. "Oh..." Her lips curved in a knowing grin. "Good idea, Spec. I'll definitely help you with that. Be back in a few, Talia." She allowed Spec to lead her away.

"Did she just squeal?" Talia asked as Liv practically bounced to the bar.

He grunted. "Probably. Liv's nuts, but in the best way."

Talia chuckled, but it was stilted and awkward, as was the silence between them.

He turned off the grill and then faced her. "You look good," he said as he folded his arms across his chest.

"Oh, thanks." She shifted under his assessing gaze.

Silence again. This time, it was so thick he could almost feel it.

Talia glanced over her shoulder and then cleared her throat. "Thought I'd hear from you before now. The last thing you said was that you had to make some calls and to expect an update soon. Unless you've been on hold a long-ass time, I'm guessing you have some answers and have been avoiding me."

Damn, he admired the way she went after what she wanted.

No one was in earshot, but he stepped closer anyway. Her clean and sweet scent had his head swimming. So did the sight of her in that outfit. How something could be so casual yet so hot would always amaze him. But what had him fighting to keep from putting his hands all over her was that confidence.

"I'm risking a lot for you, Pulse," she whispered. "Do not jerk me around. I am not the type of woman who'll be led around on a leash and sit when she's told."

Christ.

A wave of white-hot lust rolled through him.

Everything about her, from her stance to her expression to her stiff laugh, spoke to how out of her depth she was in the middle of a biker barbecue. Yet she looked him right in the eye and demanded what she deserved.

H-O-T.

Sure, he was a dick for avoiding her this past week, but now that she gave him a glimpse of her fire and spirit, he couldn't regret the choice. This woman would be a firecracker in bed, though he had a feeling a man would have to work damn hard to earn a spot there.

"You're right." He spoke low even though his brothers were wrapped up in their own shit. "But this isn't the spot for this discussion. Tomorrow?"

She blinked as she drew back, and he couldn't stop his smirk. She assumed he'd argue or toss a bunch of excuses at her. "Sure. Tomorrow works."

"I'll come to you. I'll bring breakfast."

"Right. Uh, okay. Good." She nodded once but didn't say anymore because Liv bounced back over with two drinks.

"I brought you a gin and tonic with lime," she said, grinning. "Brooke mentioned you drank one when she stopped by the other night."

Brooke and Talia had been hanging out?

"By the way, I'm pissed I wasn't invited." Liv mock pouted as she handed over the drink. "Anyway, I thought you could use something stronger than beer. Also, beer is gross."

"Babe, some people like beer." Spec rolled his eyes.

"I think you're all lying," Liv said with a shudder.

Laughing, Talia accepted the glass from Liv. "Thank you. For the record, I do love beer, but you're right. I could use something stronger. The last few days have been crazy at work since I missed the beginning of the week."

She'd gone back to work already? Shit, what good was having a bodyguard if he was going to let her do stupid shit?

"Shouldn't you have taken the whole week off?"

She raised an eyebrow as though daring him to challenge

her ability to make intelligent choices for herself.

"Take it back. Take it back," Spec whispered as he took a dramatic step away from Pulse.

Liv laughed. "Oh, Talia, I think you are the perfect addition to our insane family."

"Oh, no, I'm not part of—"

The rest of her protest disappeared beneath more of Liv's laughter. "Come on. Let's leave the men to do whatever weird stuff they do. We need some girl time." Liv towed her away to where the other ol' ladies were chatting while they destroyed a bowl of chips and guacamole.

Pulse had to fight to keep from staring at her ass as she walked away.

Before Spec could add more of his two cents, Pulse grabbed the platter of burgers and added them to the rest of the food.

"This the last of it?" Curly asked as he pointed to a space on the table for Pulse to set the platter.

"Yep, everything is ready to eat." They had ribs, chicken, and burgers, along with a ton of sides. They had enough food to feed three times as many people as were present. Then again, his brothers could eat.

"Someone say meat?" Jinx asked from a few feet away. He grabbed his junk and smirked. "Because if there's not enough, I have this huge sau—"

"Nope!" Harper stretched onto her toes and slapped a hand over her man's mouth. "No one wants your sausage, so please don't whip it out, or offer to add it to the table, or put it between two buns, or whatever vulgar suggestion you were about to make."

Pulse snorted—typical Jinx.

The big guy's eyebrows drew down to an annoyed V. Harper slowly removed her hand an inch, hovering as though prepared to remuzzle her ol' man at any time.

"Baby, what the hell?" he whined in a pitiful tone. "I thought you loved eating my sausage."

Harper's face went beet red, but what caught Pulse's attention was the strangled laugh that came from about twenty feet away. Talia stood there, eyes twinkling as she bit her lower lip.

Shit, he liked this woman. He needed to nip it before it became a problem.

The usual chaos ensued a second later. Everyone booed Jinx and threw heaps of insults about the guy's manhood and lack of sexual prowess. Typically, Pulse would have joined in and thrown a few verbal jabs, but he couldn't tear his attention away from Talia.

She let her lip slide between her teeth, and then she smiled. The full, wide, teeth-revealing smile transformed her face from serious and wary to open and happy.

Absolutely mesmerizing.

He reached for the table as his knees went. His head swam, and his heart sped. If a patient reported these symptoms, he'd have them lying down with a blood pressure cuff around their arm in seconds. Unfortunately, his diagnosis was more along the lines of a smitten storybook character than something he could pop a pill for.

He needed to get laid and fast. Someone, anyone who could get him off and shift his focus from this inappropriate attraction to his club's fucking attorney.

"Thank you, Harper," Curly said as he held Brooke's hand in front of the food table. "I think you saved all our appetites."

"Hey!" Jinx flipped two birds and waved them at everyone.

Curly spoke again once everyone's laughter died. "I know you're all hungry, so I won't talk long, but I've got something important to say."

122

The laughter and chatter disappeared. Every man and woman in this club loved Curly and owed him for making them a part of his found family. This club had saved them all in some way, Pulse included. The respect and loyalty they had for their president was unmatched.

"Well, shit," Curly said. He plucked at the front of his T-shirt, fanning himself with it. "Didn't realize I'd be this fucking nervous."

Nervous? Pulse's stomach flipped as a murmur went through the crowd. Did he have bad news?

Curly dropped Brooke's hand as he turned to face her. Concern scrunched her face. "What's wrong?" she asked.

Curly stared at her for a long, charged moment.

Then he dropped to one knee.

Someone gasped. Someone else—Jinx for sure—shouted, "About fucking time."

Curly reached into his pocket and pulled out a black velvet box.

"Oh my God." Brooke's trembling hand went to her mouth. Her eyes were glassy with unshed tears. Pulse had a feeling she wouldn't hold them back for long.

"I'm going to keep this simple because I'm a simple man," Curly said, gazing up at Brooke with so much love and adoration that Pulse had to look away.

Of course, his gaze landed on Talia, who stared at the couple with an open mouth and a look of wonder. Curly continued speaking, and though Pulse listened, he watched the pretty lawyer he was fascinated by.

"I've had nothing. I've been no one. I've lived in fear, without hope or dreams. I lived in darkness for so long that I didn't dare dream of seeing the sun again. I would do it all again in a heartbeat just to spend one minute with you, Brooke. You are everything. *My everything*."

A single tear rolled down Talia's cheek. She wiped it away

with an almost angry slap that had Pulse's lips twitching. She didn't handle these types of emotions well.

Hell, who did?

"I love you, Brooke," Curly continued. "You know how seriously I take those words. I love you and want to make you mine in every way possible. Will you marry me?"

A bird squawked from the trees behind them. It was the only sound besides the anticipatory breathing of the entire club.

Pulse turned back in time to see Brooke nod. Tears fell freely now, rolling down her cheeks and over her smiling lips. "Yes, Curly. Fuck yes, I'll marry you."

"Hell yeah!" someone shouted as cheers and whoops replaced the silence.

Curly stood in time to catch Brooke as she hurtled herself into his arms. They kissed.

And kissed.

And kissed as everyone clapped and shouted their congratulations.

When they finally came up for air, both were smiling so large their grins looked painful. Brooke hadn't even checked out the ring yet but didn't care about the jewelry. Curly could have wound a paperclip around her finger, and she'd be just as ecstatic.

"You lunatics enjoy the food," Curly shouted as he swept Brooke off her feet and into his arms. "I've got something to take care of first."

"Give it to her good, Prez," Jinx shouted.

Curly strode toward the clubhouse, his mouth back on Brooke's.

"All right, let's eat!" Spec shouted over the cheers and applause.

Pulse chose a seat on the opposite side of the table as Talia. He ignored Spec's raised eyebrow when he sat.

Damn, coupled-up people were always trying to pair off their friends.

Talia was his attorney. That's it. The fact that she was a gorgeous woman who made him hard didn't matter.

What mattered was what time he could escape and find a willing and random woman to suck his cock.

Chapter Twelve

The fourth drink had been a mistake.

She should have passed on the third one too.

But watching two people so obviously in love get engaged had her requesting the third drink and then another.

How did they do it? Curly and Brooke made it look so damn easy. It hadn't been all hearts and Cupids for them, but to watch them now, one would think they'd been specially designed for each other—two perfectly fitting puzzle pieces. They made being in a relationship look like the most natural thing in the world.

Talia genuinely didn't understand it. The idea of merging her life with another sounded impossible. What would happen to her independence? Her job? What about her personality? The things she loved? Wouldn't they all disappear or be dwarfed by her partner's wishes and desires?

It had happened to her mother, leaving the once beautiful and successful dancer a shell of her former self. Granted, Talia's father had been more of a colossal asshole than most men, but at one point, her mother had thought he was an incredible man. She'd looked at him once the same way Brooke looked at Curly. Then it all went to shit. Talia never found the risk worth it. That didn't mean she wasn't happy for her new friends, but she had little faith they'd be as happy in a few years as they claimed to be today.

Still, it would be nice to have a man want her. To gaze at her with love and lust like Curly did with Brooke. How long had it been since a man had that look in his eyes? The one that said he wanted to tear her clothes off and throw her on the bed?

Too damn long.

She needed to spend some quality tension-relieving time with her silicone boyfriend later. With the way Pulse looked tonight in a snug T-shirt that accentuated his firm, tattooed arms, she had plenty of fantasy fuel to carry her through a tension-relieving orgasm.

That thought had her giggling as she walked—staggered— down the hall toward the restroom.

"Shit," she whispered as she bounced off the wall for the second time. "I think I'm super drunk." She burst into a fit of giggles.

When was the last time she'd let this happen? It had been ages since she'd felt comfortable enough around people to let down her hair and pick up a drink.

Or four drinks.

It felt good to let loose and have some frivolous fun for once.

She made it to the bathroom without incident, took care of business, and then stumbled out of the restroom. As she shoved open the door with too much force and burst through with the grace of an elephant, she smacked into a hard, nicely scented body.

"Oh, shit! Sorry," she said, snickering so hard she snorted. She slapped a hand over her nose and mouth. "Sorry," she said again, muffled this time.

"No worries."

The familiar, amused voice had her head whipping up.

"Pulse," she squeaked.

Of course. Of-freaking-course.

He gripped her upper arms, steadying her. His hands felt so damn nice on her skin—warm, strong, yet gentle.

She shivered.

Pulse sucked in a breath, having caught the involuntary tremor.

Their eyes locked.

The air thickened.

"You smell so good," she muttered as she rose onto her tiptoes and inhaled his scent at the base of his neck. The aroma was more intoxicating than the gin. It went straight to her head and between her legs.

"Talia…"

She couldn't tell if his voice held a warning or a plea. The alcohol had soaked through her rational thinking and flooded her reasoning. Thoughts of going home and touching herself to the memory of his hands, smell, and how he looked obliterated the last of her good sense.

Her pulse thrummed heavily through her veins, making her whole body throb. Her breasts felt heavy, and her lips tingled. She licked the lower one, then inhaled him again.

She was so drunk. Drunk on alcohol, drunk on Pulse.

And it was so lovely.

Forget thinking. Forget good sense. She spent all day every day focused on those things. Tonight, with the mixture of alcohol and Pulse coursing through her veins, she only wanted to feel. She planted her hands on his chest and shoved.

His back hit the wall with a surprised grunt.

"Tal—"

She kissed him.

Not a shy, you're-attractive-and-I-want-to-explore-something kiss, but a full-on fuck-me kiss—open-mouthed, tongue, teeth, and aggression.

He froze as though stunned by her behavior. But it didn't last long. His arms closed around her, and he stole control of the kiss. Soft lips moved with hers—sure, confident, and hungry—while his arms held her flush against him.

She had the illusion of control, having trapped him against the wall, but five seconds of his lips on hers, and she was putty in his hands. He chased her tongue with his, not giving her a second to catch her breath. She whimpered, and his fingers flexed against her back.

She wanted them to move. To touch and stroke her all over.

How long had it been since a man kissed her? Too long, and not nearly as long as it had been since a man kissed her *this* way. The way that obliterated every thought in her head except one.

More.

Talia was an assertive woman, one who worked hard for what she wanted and refused to let the steep slope of a mountain deter her from scaling it. She never let fear stand in her way and bowed down to no one, particularly no man. But she also had enough trust issues to fill a swimming pool and never made herself vulnerable to others, physically or emotionally.

So, the fact that she was kissing Pulse like her life depended on it and the aggressor was out of character.

Insanely out of character.

She nipped his lower lip—something she'd never done—and he let out a guttural groan. His pecs flexed beneath her fingertips. That sound. She could live on it. Heat flushed every inch of her skin. She felt crazed. Out of control with desire. She wanted to do things to him. She wanted him to do things to her. Things she'd never done or even wanted because they'd give him power over her.

The thought of it terrified her, yet as a hardness ground against her stomach, it thrilled her just as much.

She pressed closer and widened her stance as he continued to ravage her mouth. One of his thighs slipped between her legs. He flexed the strong muscles against her pelvis. She gasped into his mouth as a riot of pleasure shot from between her legs through her body.

Pulse dragged his hands down her back to her ass, where he squeezed and rocked her on his thigh. She moved against him, finally getting pressure where she needed it.

Yes.

More, she needed more. She rocked against him, shameless in her need for friction.

So damn good.

God, I can't believe he's a client.

A wave of ice crashed over her.

Her eyes flew open, and she went rigid in his arms.

What the hell am I doing?

Pulse stilled as soon as she stopped humping his damn leg. He released her immediately.

She jerked away so fast and hard that she crashed into the wall opposite him.

They stared at each other across three feet of space. It wasn't nearly enough physical distance. His eyes were dark and wild with lust. His chest heaved, and his nostrils flared as he panted. He curled his hands into fists at his sides.

Talia breathed just as hard, trembling with unfulfilled need. Her body didn't understand why it felt so damn good one second, only to have those sensations brutally ripped away without satisfaction.

"I'm sorry," she whispered, shaking her head. "That was entirely inappropriate of me."

"Tal—"

"No." She held up a hand as she pushed off the wall. "I shouldn't have done that." She stumbled a few backward steps down the hall. "It won't happen again," she said as she turned and staggered away. The least the universe could give her was a graceful escape, but the damn alcohol had her unsteady, and the aftermath of his kisses left her weak and trembling.

Why did you do that?

It wasn't often she regretted her actions. Talia overthought and overanalyzed everything. Acting on impulse wasn't her, even with alcohol soaking her brain. And yet tonight, she'd gone and thrown that out the window.

"Hey." Brooke caught her as she bumbled her way toward the exit. "You okay, Talia? You're not looking too good."

"Um…"

No, I'm not okay. I just kissed the hell out of a man for the first time in years, and I was two seconds from begging him to tear my clothes off and do all sorts of filthy things to me.

"You know, I think I drank a little too much." She pressed a hand to her forehead. "I'm a little shaky and fuzzy-headed. Would it be okay if I left my car here overnight so I can get a rideshare home?"

Brooke linked their arms as she guided Talia outside. The night air had cooled to almost chilly, which felt incredible on her overheated skin. Talia inhaled gulps of fresh, Pulse-free air. A mix of disappointment and relief flowed over her as his scent disappeared, replaced by the outdoors.

"Of course, you can leave your car here," Brooke said as she steered Talia right. "But there's no need to get a car." A beautiful, refurbished barn stood tall and proud some hundred feet away. "We have a bunch of apartments in there for that very reason. A prospect is staying in one now, and I think, given how many shots he's had, Jinx and Harper will crash in another tonight. That leaves two empty apartments. You're welcome to either.

As much as she wanted to be in her bed, she was getting to the point in her drunken journey of inevitable pass-out.

Stumbling a few yards to a soft, warm bed sounded better than an expensive, long car ride home.

"Are you sure? I really don't want to impose."

"No imposition at all." Brooke patted her hand. "In fact, I insist. Come on."

Together, they walked to the barn. Brooke led her in and directly up a long staircase to the second floor.

"The prospect is directly across from this apartment," she said as she stopped at a black door. "He's quiet and won't bother you at all. Jinx and Harper, on the other hand, will keep you up all night with their antics if you catch my drift." She winked, and Talia's face heated.

"Gotcha. Appreciate you putting me on a different floor. It's hard enough not to be jealous watching all you couples drooling over each other. I don't need to add to it with a nocturnal performance."

Laughing, Brooke used a key to unlock the door. "Man, I really like you, Talia. You have got to hang out with us more." She opened the door and gestured inside. "Here you go."

"Thank you so much. Oh," she said as she stepped into the studio apartment. "This is nice."

"Thanks, but I can take zero credit for any of it."

The space, decorated with simple, neutral colors, was clean, modern, and cozy. A small kitchenette stood opposite a queen bed. A large-screen television hung on the far wall before a plush loveseat—more than enough for her to get through the night.

"There are extra toothbrushes and toothpaste in the bathroom, along with some skincare items. The fridge is stocked with drinks and some basics... eggs, cheese, bacon, bread. That kind of stuff. Feel free to help yourself to anything."

"Careful, with this kind of service, you might never get rid of me."

Brooke chuckled. "I wouldn't mind in the least. Especially with the way you help take care of our guys. I heard you helped Tracker get out of a sticky mess with his business yesterday."

Talia waved away Brooke's gratitude. "Believe me when I say that was nothing. Just some legal red tape that was very easy to cut through. That stuff is the easy part of my job." Her eyelids drooped, heavy with alcohol-induced fatigue. Damn that fourth drink.

"You look like you're about ready to drop, so let me get out of your hair. Feel free to wander over to the clubhouse in the morning. Someone is always there hanging out."

Yeah, she wouldn't be doing that. She'd already spent more time socializing today than in the past six months. Tomorrow, she'd be hungover and need to recharge her batteries in a quiet, biker-free environment.

Or at least in a place she wouldn't risk running into Pulse and humiliating herself further.

God, why did I kiss him?

"Super glad you came."

"Me too. And I'm glad I was here to see you get engaged. Congratulations again." She'd said it earlier when Brooke and Curly returned from their *task*, but it bared repeating.

"Thanks, Talia. You have a good night."

"Thanks, Brooke. You too."

Brook hugged her quickly but tightly. "G'night." Then she slipped through the door. A muffled male voice, followed by Brooke's laughter, had Talia grinning. Brooke's new fiancé must have trailed them and grumbled at her for intending to walk back in the dark alone despite the club's property being the safest place in the city.

Alone at last, Talia eyed the bed. The light gray comforter looked soft and cozy. It called to her. She needed to brush her teeth and wash off her makeup. Instead, she kicked off her shoes, strode toward the bed, and flopped down face-first. Ten minutes. Just a ten-minute rest, then she'd get up and do some semblance of a nighttime routine.

It was her last thought before darkness stole the rest of her night.

Knock.

Knock.

Knock.

Talia groaned. If that was a solicitor banging on her door at some ungodly hour despite her 'no solicitation' sign, she was going to lose her shit.

"I should sue," she grumbled as she rolled to her back. Her lips made a sticky, slapping sound as she moistened them. Why did her mouth taste like she'd eaten roadkill last night?

It took a few seconds to peel her eyelids open, and the bright sun assaulted her brain when she did. "Oh God, wait..."

She shot straight up, wincing when her alcohol-shriveled brain bounced against her skull.

"What the hell?"

She wasn't home.

The night came rushing back with the force of an avalanche. Christ, she'd stayed on the Handlers' property because she'd been too drunk and tired to go home.

After she'd kissed Pulse.

"Nooo," she said with a groan as she flopped back down.

Knock.

Knock.

Knock.

She'd put ten dollars on that being Brooke at the door, worried Talia had kicked the bucket in here because she'd slept half the day away.

She forced herself out of bed and lumbered to the door like a roaming zombie. The chilly wood floor had her shivering in seconds. Her mouth felt disgusting, and she could only imagine how it smelled. Her day-old makeup must have looked like a hot mess. Poor Brooke was about to get the jump scare of her life.

Wonderful.

She pulled the door open with a resigned sigh. "Good morn... oh, shit."

Pulse stood in the doorway, freshly showered. He wore dark jeans, a white T-shirt, and his Handlers' cut. He held a cardboard carrier with two large coffees in one hand and a brown paper bag in the other.

He smirked as he gave her a once-over.

The urge to slam the door in his face and burrow under the covers for the next three hours crashed into her, but she couldn't be that much of an ass. Instead, she forced a smile that probably looked more like a grimace.

"Uh, hey." God, why did she act like this around him? She was great with words. As a trial attorney, half her job was using words in clever ways. But one glimpse of Pulse and the best she could come up with was, *hey.* In the short time she'd known this man, he'd seen her more vulnerable than she'd let anyone see her in years. It was as uncomfortable as a pebble in her shoe.

Yet she didn't want him to go.

"I come bearing caffeine and sugar," he said with a grin.

"Wow, thanks. That's really nice of you." Could she be more awkward?

"Can I come in?"

"Oh, yeah. Of course. Sorry." She widened the door and stepped out of the way.

He faced her as he came in, brushing against her and sending jolts of desire skittering across her skin. She sucked in a breath. How did he do this to her?

"Told you I'd bring you breakfast this morning. You made

it easier by being here."

Right. He had information for her. There she was, mooning over him like a smitten teenager, and he was there to discuss business.

Did that mean he didn't remember the kiss? Maybe he kissed a different woman every night. Perhaps she was freaking out over something he considered the same as a damn handshake.

As if she wasn't humiliated enough.

Hell, the man was gorgeous, had a good job, and rode a motorcycle. He probably had women flinging themselves at him from all angles. A random drunken kiss was just another Friday night for him.

Get it together and be a professional.

"Thank you. I need five minutes to undo some of the damage I did last night," she said as she waved at herself. There wasn't anything she could do about wearing the same clothes as yesterday, but a thorough toothbrushing and face wash should make her feel more human. At least she wouldn't be breathing dragon air his way.

"Take your time," he said as he set the food on the table.

Talia escaped toward the bathroom. As she was about to shut the door, he called her name. "Talia?"

"Yeah?"

"I'm sure you're not comfortable wearing the same clothes you had on last night, but I can't say I'm sorry to see you in those shorts again." He winked, then turned his back on her to unpack whatever was in the bag.

Talia shut the door, encasing herself in the tiny bathroom. She sagged against it, staring at the ceiling as Pulse's words curled her lips into a genuine grin.

This was bad.

This was so, so bad.

Chapter Thirteen

The room felt like a pressure cooker quickly rising to the blowing point.

They were attracted to each other and had been since they met.

Talia was his club's attorney.

She was the only person who knew about his history with the DEA and the current mess that history brought to his life.

There were so many complicated factors to sort through and organize. It would be better for all involved to ignore their attraction and move on.

But then there was that kiss.

Goddamn, she'd taken him by surprise with that kiss. There'd been a desperation to it. An underlying hunger that led him to believe she was starved for the things he could give her. The things he could do to her. He was just as greedy for it. Hell, if she hadn't come to her senses, he might have fucked her right there in the hallway against the clubhouse wall.

It'd been a long time since he'd had some action from anyone besides his own hand, and now that he'd tasted her, he couldn't think of anything else. He'd spent the entire night hard and imagined how she'd look coming on his fingers, his tongue, his cock. He'd jerked off three times and still could have pounded a nail through a two-by-four.

One glimpse of her this morning, even hungover and awkward, and his cock was back at attention. This woman went to his head faster than any drug.

He unpacked the muffins he'd picked up on his way over and set them on the table. One giant cinnamon crumble, and an equally colossal chocolate chip muffin sat side by side. Talia could choose. He'd eat either with a smile. Thanks to Brooke, who'd visited Talia multiple times while she'd been home recovering, he'd learned she loved oat milk brown sugar lattes, whatever the hell all that meant. Thankfully, the barista knew because he'd have been out of luck if they needed clarification.

Talia emerged a few moments later, wearing soft olive-green sweatpants and a beige ACDC T-shirt. She still had a stiffness about her, but with last night's makeup gone and her hair in a high ponytail, she looked fresh and fuckable.

Goddammit, his cock couldn't catch a break. Not that it mattered what she wore. She'd need a damn hazmat suit to keep from turning him on.

Squaring her shoulders, she walked straight to him. Her lips compressed, and her eyes sharpened in a look of determination that could only mean one thing.

"Look, Pulse," she said as she reached him. "I want to apologize for my behav—"

Nope, he wasn't having any of that bullshit.

He grabbed the back of her neck and yanked her to him, crashing his mouth to hers. She let out a muffled squeak, allowing him to slide his tongue between her lips.

Her minty-clean flavor invaded his taste buds. Fucking addicting.

She went rigid, arms hanging at her sides for about five seconds, and then she melted into him.

Fuck yes.

He kept his hand clasping her neck and splayed the other across her lower back as he plundered her mouth. Her soft moans made his cock ache. Strong hands gripped his cut at his sides. She clung to him, letting him have his way with her mouth. Imagining her grasping his bare skin the same way had him pulling her even closer. As soon as his rock-hard cock made contact with her stomach, she whimpered.

Shit, this was about to get out of hand.

He released her and ended the kiss. Talia still clutched his cut as she stared up at him. Her eyes were wide, pupils blown, and cheeks flushed.

He groaned. That kiss was a mistake because that sample taste wasn't close to being enough. He'd spend the day as hard and unsatisfied as he'd spent his night

"Wha—"

"Don't ever fucking apologize for kissing me."

It shouldn't have been possible, but her eyes flared even wider. She licked her lower lip, drawing his attention. God, that lip had tasted good. It would look good, too, spread wide for his cock.

"O-okay." Her voice trembled, and she panted as though having been interrupted mid-workout.

"You might have acted out of character because you were drunk, but I fucking loved it. I get it's complicated as fuck right now, but I just want it out there that I had no problem with it."

Talia blew out a breath. "Phew. Wow. Okay, that's, uh… that's pretty damn hot," she muttered as though he wasn't standing right there.

He chuckled. "Come on. Sit. Eat a muffin and drink some coffee. I'll fill you in on the shit I should have called you about a few days ago."

"Why didn't you?" she asked as she moved to sit at the table before the cinnamon muffin.

His gaze locked back on her mouth.

"Oh," she said on an exhale. She ran an unsteady hand over the top of her head and down her ponytail. After blowing out a breath, she picked up her coffee. "Thanks for bringing breakfast." She took a sip, and her face lit with pleasure. "Oh my gosh. This is my favorite drink ever. How did you know?" A pleased smile replaced her nervous expression.

"That would be Brooke."

"Ah, right," she said with a nod. "We had coffee a few times this week. Well, thanks. Please sit."

He did, then grabbed his coffee—black and a lot of it—the only way he could ever drink it. Nothing against Talia's sweet beverage, but he just wanted as big of a caffeine hit as possible and as fast, which plain black coffee delivered.

"Mm… this is good, too," she said as she broke off a piece of muffin and popped it in her mouth. "Yum."

Pulse groaned. He was helpless to do anything but stare at her lips as she licked a rogue crumb.

"I had no idea you had such a one-track mind." Her cheeks pinked, and she cleared her throat.

"Well, if you could see what I see, you'd be the same way. You gotta stop drawing attention to your mouth. Maybe face the other way while you're eating." It was time to get to the real reason he'd stopped by, and he never would if she kept doing sexy things like chewing.

She burst out laughing and slapped a hand over her mouth. "Chewing does it for you? Seriously?"

She continued chuckling, sparking a fire inside him, but different than the fire that burned when she'd kissed him. This one grew, smoldering at a low flame, and he wanted to keep it burning forever. Keep her laughing, smiling, showing a side of herself he guessed she didn't let others see often. How amazing would it be to know he was the man who could draw those expressions from her whenever he wanted?

Maybe even the only man.

It'd be incredible—a pleasure that would run deep and wide.

He shrugged. "What can I say? I like your mouth."

"All right." She pointed at him with a smirk. "That's enough outta you. I had no idea you were so much trouble."

He tilted his head, studying her amused expression. "Really? You met me in an interrogation room, and you didn't think I was trouble?" The banter was almost as much fun as kissing her.

"Not what I meant, and you know it. Now focus. You owe me some explanations, so start talking."

If only an explanation were all he owed her. She was in this whole mess because of him.

"I have a contact I've used for years. I helped him out of a bad situation when we were just kids, and he's been loyal to me ever since. This guy has some special skills he's been able to use to find out information I couldn't obtain otherwise."

"Wow." Talia snorted. "As an attorney, I've gotta tell you, there are more than a few holes in that story."

"I know." He set his coffee down and scooted his chair closer to her. "Talia, I've landed you smack in the middle of a clusterfuck you don't deserve to be involved in. The more details you have, the bigger the risk to you."

She pressed her lips together. Her brow wrinkled as she processed his words. "Is that the reason you went radio silent this week?"

Of course, it was. The thought of putting her in more danger enraged him. "It is." That and he wanted to rip her clothes off every time he looked at her. His club had enough reasons to hate him. Fucking their attorney would only make things worse.

"Hmm." She tilted her head as her spine straightened.

"You know I don't need you to decide what risks I should take?"

"I do."

If the situation weren't so volatile, he'd have laughed. Leave it to her to get spicy when he tried to keep her safe.

"This isn't my first go around, Pulse. I've been at my job for years and am privy to plenty of sensitive information. If I didn't know how to be discreet, I'd have been out of a job two days in."

"This has nothing to do with whether or not I trust you to keep your mouth shut. I trust you implicitly. It's about your safety."

"You do realize I'm a grown woman who is perfectly capable of taking care of myself?" Any trace of flirtation vanished, leaving the fierce attorney he'd trust to defend him any day.

"I do."

"And you realize I don't need some man making any decisions for me, no matter how they might affect me?"

"Yep."

"And yet, you're deciding what I do and do not need to know."

"That's correct."

Oh, man, her eyes were spitting fire now. His cock twitched. The bastard had never learned good timing.

She huffed. "Why?"

"Because fuck your reasons."

"Excuse me?" Her voice rose, and she hopped up, fury flying all over the room. "What gives you the right—"

He stood, too, snagged her around the waist, and yanked her to him, kissing her with all the pent-up fear, anger, and desire he'd been growing over the past week. It only lasted a few seconds but was a hard, fierce kiss, not another frenzied exploration. This was a claiming.

"That gives me the fucking right," he said as he ripped his mouth away.

"Pulse…"

"No, Talia. This is not about independence or what I think you can or can't handle. This is about your goddamn safety, and I'll be fucked before I let someone hurt you again because of me. If that means I act like a Neanderthal, so fucking be it."

He shoved away from her and stalked across the apartment. This place was too damn small, and he reached the opposite wall in under twenty steps. He should have gone out the door.

"Pulse, I…"

He whipped around so fast that she stumbled back a step even though fifteen feet of space separated them. Her eyes were wide and radiating a mixture of anger and sympathy. She held her hands wide as though approaching a wild animal.

"I'm not scared."

"You should be. You really should be." Memories of Camila's lifeless body lying in a pool of her blood assaulted him. She hadn't been afraid either, and look where he'd gotten her. "These people want revenge, and they don't care about who they have to destroy to get it." It was as much an admission of the cartel having infiltrated the DEA as he could give her right then. Even that was too much.

"If we work together, we can figure this out."

"They're monsters, Talia. I will not have someone take you away before I've even had the chance to taste your pussy."

Chapter Fourteen

His words hit her like a punch to the gut, expelling all the air from her lungs. Every inch of her skin erupted in flames as she imagined his mouth on her, bringing her pleasure.

She wanted that. She wanted it more than anything she could think of.

The entire situation was out of control. There they were, arguing about him deciding what she did and didn't deserve to know regarding her safety, and all she could think about was what his tongue would feel like between her legs. She was pretty sure he'd confirmed in a roundabout way that a powerful drug cartel had an agent operating from within the DEA. It was information that was vital not only to her safety and his club's but also to national security.

Would he be gentle and slowly drive her out of her mind? Or would he bring her to a brutal orgasm, aggressive in his goal to make her come?

Nothing else mattered but the answer to that question.

She tried to regulate her breathing, but her heart raced so fast that she had no choice but to pant to keep up with its oxygen demand.

Her hands went to the elastic of her sweatpants near her hips.

I'm about to do something foolish.

"And if I give you that chance?"

But it will feel so good.

He froze. "Excuse me?"

Talia slipped her thumbs inside her waistband and shimmied the fabric down a fraction of an inch. Just enough to make her point known. Cool air hit her hip points, making her shiver. "If I give you the chance to taste me, then what?"

Pulse growled, literally growled, and her pussy dampened.

Who was this needy woman, and what had she done with the shark of an attorney who never gave a shit about having a man? She had a lovely collection of vibrators that got the job done without ordering her around or making demands beyond battery replacement.

But right then, all she could think about was Pulse touching her.

He walked toward her with slow, sure steps. Her breath caught in her lungs. The gleam in his eye was nothing short of predatory. Another shiver raced across her skin, this time a mixture of nerves and anticipation.

She stepped back, then again. Not to escape him but to find relief from her internal swirl of emotion. Her back hit the small refrigerator, ripping a gasp from her lungs.

Pulse smirked. He grabbed her wrist and tugged her hand from her pants, flattening her palm against the refrigerator. Then, he treated the other arm the same.

He stared at her, his gaze smoldering with so much intensity that it was almost impossible to maintain eye contact. Had a man ever looked at her with such raw desire? It was like he couldn't survive one more minute without having her. That look made her skin tingle and soaked her pussy. It left her heart exposed and defenseless—two things she'd fought hard against and the reason all her previous relationship attempts failed.

Pleasure was on its way, and she wanted it so badly, but

this was more than physical release. Could she survive the emotional vulnerability riding shotgun to the pleasure?

He replaced her hands with his own, slipping his thumbs into the waistband of her sweatpants. Talia didn't move her palms from where they pressed into the refrigerator.

"Yes?"

Her heart stuttered in her chest. It'd been hurt before, smashed to smithereens. The thick scars she'd developed prevented anyone from accessing it for years. Not family, friends, and certainly not men she hardly knew. The way it beat so hard felt as though it was preparing her to run, to flee before Pulse could damage it.

He stroked his thumbs over her hip points, and goosebumps erupted up her torso.

Her heart might be afraid, but her long-neglected body wanted this enough to defy caution. Then, her brain was stuck in the middle, and she was conflicted about which way to go.

"Tal?" Another of those sensual brushes of his thumbs had her trembling.

God, the way his eyes burned for her.

Suddenly, she couldn't stand another second without his hands on her.

Her throat had dried up, so she nodded.

"C'mon, counselor," he said, voice lower and rumbling. "You know how important words are."

Shit, he was right, and the fact that he wanted explicit consent made her stomach flutter along with the ache between her legs. "Yes. God, Pulse, yes."

He immediately dropped to his knees, taking the sweats and her simple black bikini panties down to her ankles.

Instructions weren't needed. She stepped out of her clothes and placed her bare feet back on the floor. Thank God she had a pedicure two days earlier.

Pulse rose high on his knees, putting his face in line with her sex. Another wave of thanks rolled through her, this time for the Brazilian she'd had after the pedicure. She wanted to look good for him. She wanted him to like what he saw. She wanted him to want her.

Maybe even more once this was over.

Terrifying.

His forehead hit her lower belly, and he inhaled her scent.

Heat flared from where their skin touched. It was such an intimate position. She'd have been mortified any other time with any other man, but all she could do was pray he wouldn't stop.

He gripped the outside of her hips, jerking her pelvis forward. Talia adjusted her feet and bent her knees to help him get his desired angle.

There it was again—the feeling of vulnerability, but this time, physically, along with her emotions. He met her gaze, and his dark smile promised mind-melting pleasure.

And then the man got to work.

Talia gasped as he kissed her right above her clit. Then, another on the side of her mound. And another. Little teasing kisses that had her pussy fluttering with need and made her groan in frustration.

"Pulse…" she whined, voice breathy.

He chuckled against her skin but still didn't give her what she wanted.

"Yeah? Something you need?" he asked as he nudged her with his nose, then blew on her sensitive skin.

Her face was burning. Hell, her entire body erupted in flames. "You know. Stop teasing me."

He glanced up with a wicked gleam in his eyes. "Make me."

Her breath caught in her lungs. Make him? How? Should she grab his head and shove it against her pussy?

Shit! Yes, I should.

He wanted that. He liked her strong and assertive. That's how she was in her everyday life. Only here did her insecurities and issues take over. But she'd been the one to kiss him, and he claimed to like that. The hardness she'd felt against her stomach confirmed it.

She peeled a trembling hand off the cool metal and sifted it through his short hair. Like a jungle cat's purr, a rumble rolled off him.

His soft hair slid through her fingers until she closed her fist, gripping the strands hard.

"That's right," he rumbled. "Show me what you want. Show me how you take care of yourself."

Before her stunned brain could find a shred of rationality, she yanked him to her pussy. Her damp thighs burned with the effort of holding a semi-squat against the fridge, but it allowed him easy access.

He sealed his mouth over her and speared his tongue inside without any warmup. Sharp pleasure, almost unbearable, had her curling forward. She held his head against her with a firm grip as she rocked her pelvis forward, fucking herself on his tongue.

"Oh my God. Oh my God," she chanted as that gifted mouth wreaked havoc on her nerve endings.

He pulled out of her pussy, dragging his tongue through her folds up to her clit where he licked with gentle flicks. For one second, she mourned the loss of his tongue inside her, but it felt so incredible on her sensitive clit that she could only moan and continue to thrust against his face. Her quads screamed for relief, and she fought to keep them working, but when he sucked her clit between his lips, she lost the battle.

"Pulse," she cried as her knees gave out, and she slid down.

The man didn't miss a beat.

He kept his head buried in her sex as he clutched her hips and helped lower her to the floor. Her ass hit the floor with a soft thump. Pulse scooted back effortlessly, never breaking rhythm as though he'd choreographed this entire dance.

He kept eating her out, and she kept clinging to his hair.

Her legs, which had turned to Jell-O, splayed wide. He cupped her ass, holding her against his ravenous mouth even as she kept him pressed there. The poor man probably needed a breather, but she couldn't command her fingers to loosen their grip.

Thinking became impossible. All she could do was slump there against the refrigerator as the hottest man she knew pleasured her with his mouth. Every lick, suck, and scrape of his stubble against her flesh had her insides spiraling tighter.

He held her ass so tight she'd have marks tomorrow. Yesterday, that would have been unimaginable, but now she wanted it and craved the bruises to remind her how this man had feasted.

She moaned as a wave of ecstasy washed over her. She was drunk on pleasure, suspended in a state she could live in forever, yet she wanted to come just as much.

How had she lived thirty-two years without this?

He guided his tongue back inside her, and her eyes nearly crossed. A flash of him working something bigger, thicker inside her came to mind, and that was all she needed to send her into the stratosphere.

Her back arched off the refrigerator as sensation exploded through her. She shouted, shook, and probably gave Pulse a bald spot as she lost control of her strength She squeezed her eyes shut and rode out an orgasm so powerful it eclipsed any she'd previously experienced. The waves seemed to go on forever and not nearly long enough.

Eventually, her muscles fatigued, and she sagged against the refrigerator in a sated, gooey slump. Then she realized she still had a hand in Pulse's hair, though she couldn't grip it tight any longer. Instead, she flexed and extended her fingers, running her nails through his scalp.

He groaned, then lifted his head, meeting her gaze.

Her hand fell away, heavy and weakened.

Pulse's cheeks were flushed. His eyes were heavy and satisfied. His hair stood on end, and his lips glistened with evidence of how much she'd enjoyed herself. He looked wrecked, even though she'd been the one to come her brains out.

Slowly, as though he knew his effect on her, he licked his lips clean. He hummed as though she was a treat he'd been dying for.

She owed him something. A thank you or praise—a return of the epic favor—but she was hypnotized in place by his stare. "Pulse... I..." What? What on earth did she say now?

I don't usually act like this.

Can you come back and do that to me every day?

It's been a while, but want me to suck your cock?

Please don't hurt me.

He pushed to all fours and crawled toward her like a jungle cat. Her breath caught as he brought his lips to her ear.

"You are the most delicious thing I've ever tasted."

His breath wafted over her ear's sensitive skin, eliciting a run of goosebumps down her neck. She'd just had a massive orgasm. How was it possible to already want more?

"Pulse." She turned her head, and their lips brushed.

He sat back on his heels and held out a hand. "C'mon, let's get off the floor. I think it's past time I fill you in on what I learned this week."

"Really? But what about... you?"

He smirked. "Next time."

She frowned. "Wait, really?" What man turned down an orgasm? And why? Did it mean he didn't really want her? Oh

God, did he get her off out of pity because she'd thrown herself at him last night?

"Stop," he said, eyes narrowing. Then he tapped the side of her head. "I can hear the gears grinding. Turn off that big, sexy brain."

"I just want you to feel good too."

Her face flamed. Had she really said that out loud? This was why she avoided men. Something about them made a typically intelligent, rational woman turn stupid. It was the climax. Orgasms that spectacular did something to the brain. They erased all sense of self-preservation and logic and turned her into a stereotype.

Gross.

And yet, she still wanted him to be happy with her.

"You think I don't feel good? Talia, I wanted a taste of your pussy, and I got it. I wanted to feel you come all the fuck over my tongue, and that's exactly what I got. I couldn't feel any fucking better right now."

Holy crap. No man had ever spoken to her like that before with such raw, honest sexual appreciation.

She loved it.

"Okay then," she said as some of her usual grit returned. "Guess you owe me some explanations."

Pulse grinned. "I'm ready to take the stand, counselor."

Chapter Fifteen

Two days later, Pulse could still taste her. Her flavor had seeped beneath his taste buds and embedded itself in his brain. Not that he'd ever complain. She was the most addictive damn treat.

However, it did make concentrating at work difficult, and by the time he left his shift at eleven o'clock, he was more than ready to go.

The idea of calling Talia tempted him, as did showing up at her place unannounced, but it was late, and she worked early. Plus, the next time he got her naked, he wanted to take his time and not worry about how tired she'd be the next day.

After he'd helped her get dressed, they sat on the couch and chatted about what he'd learned, which wasn't much. Birdy had confirmed his fears that the Del Rios family had inserted someone into the DEA. They were out for deadly revenge and coming after Pulse.

Unfortunately, Birdy didn't have much more than that. They seemed to be playing the long game, biding their time before making overt moves. Well, aside from running Talia off the road. It seemed they didn't want to kill Pulse but destroy his club and everything he cared about before ending his life. He'd asked Birdy to continue digging and get back to him as soon as he had something new to report.

He stowed his things in his saddle bags, then climbed on his bike for the half-hour trip to his apartment. He lived closer to the clubhouse than the city.

Like typical for a Friday night, the highway leading out of Tampa was quiet. Everyone traveled into the city for the restaurants, bars, and clubs. He was one of the few fleeing the crowds. He navigated the deserted highway with practiced ease, preferring to be on his bike to almost anywhere in the world.

Had Talia ever ridden a motorcycle? It'd be the sweetest torture to have her riding at his back—something to make a mental note about and revisit soon.

A flicker of light against the night sky caught his attention. He glanced at his side mirror, where a lit-up police car appeared about two hundred feet behind him. Not two seconds later, the whoop of sirens blared over the highway noise.

"Shit," he whispered, glancing down at his speedometer. It read sixty-seven miles per hour in a sixty-five zone. No way in hell were they on his ass for two ticks above the speed limit. It wasn't a registration or license problem either. He'd renewed the registration two weeks before and had never had his license suspended or a lapse in insurance. Sure, he'd been lost in thoughts about Talia, but he hadn't missed a stop sign or blown any lights getting on the highway.

That left two options—general harassment against the MC by the local PD, which happened more than he liked to admit, or they were after him personally, thanks to a crooked DEA agent.

Neither scenario boded well for him.

"Hey, Siri," he said to his helmet's Bluetooth. "Call Talia."

It rang four times in his ears before her groggy voice came across the line. "Hello? Pulse? Do you know what time it is?"

The cruiser closed in on him. Two additional sets of lights

in the distance flew toward him as well.

I'm fucked.

"Tal, this isn't a social call," he shouted over the wind rushing by. "I've got cops on my ass for no goddamn reason."

"Shit, Pulse." All traces of sleep vanished from her voice. "Pull over right now and do exactly as they tell you. They'll be looking for any reason, no matter how small, to bring you in."

He glanced in the mirror. He risked being run off the road if he didn't pull over now. "Pretty sure they're bringing me in no matter what I do. There are at least three cruisers on me now."

"Fuck," she spat amidst the sounds of rustling clothing. "I'll meet you at the station. If you get a chance, record the interaction."

"I'll try."

"Pulse… be safe."

The line went dead. He signaled right and began to slow his speed. He fucking hated this shit. What made it so much worse was how he used to be law enforcement. To see the system abused in such a way enraged him.

As soon as he came to a stop, he killed the engine and dropped the kickstand.

The cop car screeched to a halt behind him. Two seconds later, a deep voice boomed. "Off the bike. Hands in the fucking air."

He raised his arms in a position of surrender—so much for having time to record the interaction.

The squeal of tires announced the arrival of the second and third cruisers.

Pulse had lived through some scary shit in his life. Hell, he'd spent four years pretending to be a high-level cartel member. At any point, if he'd blown his cover, he'd have been killed in a nasty way. He knew fear. He understood the taste of it on his tongue and the sickness in his gut—the way it took over all the senses and made breathing a challenge.

He felt that now along with profound helplessness, and nothing pissed him off more than being helpless.

There was nothing to do but obey, so he swung his leg off his bike and turned to face the officers.

"I said hands in the fucking air," the cop shouted despite Pulse's hands being up by his head.

He couldn't make out who the officer was. Their headlights shined a blinding path from their cruisers. Others joined him, all positioned behind their open car doors with guns at the ready.

Fucking ridiculous.

"Turn around. Drop to your knees. Keep your hands up!"

There wasn't anything he wanted to do less than give his back to these untrustworthy assholes, but what choices did he have?

"Is your body cam on?" he shouted.

"I said, turn the fuck around!"

He did, slowly, so as not to give them the impression he planned to run or reach for a weapon. Then he sank to his knees, hands in the air. The road bit into his kneecaps beneath his jeans. Man, he'd had much more fun the last time he'd been on his knees between Talia's gorgeous legs.

"I gave you a lawful order. Turn around now!"

What? He'd already turned.

"We have given you a lawful order. If you continue to resist, you will be tased."

Fucking hell. So that's how they were going to play this? No way in hell did any of these cops have their body cams on —maybe the audio, but not the video. In court, they'd plead technical malfunction, then play this bullshit audio to make him look like a disobedient maniac.

"Last chance, asshole," a cop shouted. "Get on the fucking

ground."

This would be the perfect time for Spec or anyone from his club to appear. But they wouldn't because he'd been keeping secrets from the men who had his back—secrets that would turn his people against him in his greatest hour of need.

On his knees in the dark, illuminated only by the shine of police cruisers, as the cops continued to shout about his disobedience, he tried to prepare himself for what came next.

The sharp barb embedded itself in his upper arm. They knew where to aim the taser. His leather cut would have prevented the darts from entering his skin.

The electricity hit like a viper's strike, sinking into his flesh with a sudden, merciless jolt. His muscles seized, locking in place as every nerve caught in a net of raw, crackling energy. The fire-hot rush of pain reached every corner of his body, penetrating his bones and holding him hostage.

He screamed through clenched teeth as time-warped, stretching each heartbeat to an eternity. Every second became a landslide of paralyzed weakness. There were no thoughts, no reasoning, just a primal, animal sense of survival trapped under the weight of pure voltage. His world narrowed to a buzzing cage of static and fear, an unrelenting throb that refused to let go. He pitched forward. The ground rushed toward his face at a furious velocity. Without control of his extremities, he could do nothing to stop his face from colliding with the rough road.

And then, as quickly as it began, it released. Muscles slackened, and limbs sagged as heavy as lead on the side of the highway. Feet pounded the pavement as the cops rushed to him. He tried to push onto all fours, but the electricity left a profound fatigue and weakness.

The first boot to his ribs sent a shockwave of agony screaming through his side. He'd have fought if he could, but another kick had him retching.

"Still fucking resisting," one of the cops shouted.

"Get him cuffed," another yelled. "We'll drag him to my cruiser."

They yanked his arms behind his back without an ounce of care. He winced at the burn in his shoulders. His cheek scraped against the ground with a painful tearing sensation as they hauled him around. Cuffs were slapped on him next, so tight they bit into his wrists. If Spec got word of this, he'd lose his fucking mind and go on the warpath with his bloodthirst for vengeance.

But how would Pulse explain any of it?

"You have the right to remain silent, motherfucker..."

He zoned out during the Miranda warning he knew by heart. It meant nothing to these cops beyond a formality. A check in the box so he couldn't claim they never mirandized him. Not that it mattered. None of this would ever see a courtroom. Most likely, they'd hand him over to the DEA, and he'd fall off the face of the earth from there.

The cops hauled him to his feet by his aching shoulders. Thankfully, he could get his feet under him and remain standing without support.

"Not so tough without your little bike buddies, are you?" Officer Newton, a cop he'd dealt with before, sneered. "Nothing more than a buncha fucking thugs. We're gonna take you down one by one."

Newton was older than Pulse, at least he looked it, but probably not by more than a decade. Years on the job driving around in a patrol car, meeting at the local cop bar, and most likely chowing down on donuts each morning had him on the heftier side. If it wasn't for the gun and five other officers, Pulse could have outrun him with ease. Instead, he was ushered to the car and *guided* into it. Newton smacked Pulse's head on the door frame as he tossed him into the back seat.

"Now's when the real fun begins, asshole," Newton said as

he filled the door frame with his ruddy face. Running the fifty feet from his squad car to where he'd tased Pulse took a lot out of the man.

"You seem a little winded. Might wanna hit the gym once in a while, Officer Newt. You know, to work on that cardiovascular endurance. Wouldn't want people escaping their unlawful arrests, would you?"

"*You* didn't escape."

Touché.

"What'd you do to piss off the feds?" Newton asked. "You'll be our guest tonight, but tomorrow, we got a suit from DC coming to claim you. You'll be their problem then, and there'll be one less biker polluting our town."

Pulse mashed his teeth together. Talia warned him to cooperate. She was the only reason he didn't blast this asshole the way he craved.

To think he and Newton had once been on the same side made him sick, though they'd never really been on the same side. Newton was a dirty piece of shit who didn't deserve to wear the uniform. Pulse had never gone against his oath to serve and protect. Well, not until the day he told them all to fuck off and walked away.

Newton chuckled. "Keep your secrets. Don't matter to me none." He slammed the door and then shuffled around to the driver's side. "Think I'll take myself out to a nice steak dinner tomorrow night," he said as he stuffed himself into his seat. "Oh, shit, sorry. That was kinda cruel, huh? Seeing as how you won't be eatin' one of those anytime soon." He laughed again as he started the squad car.

Pulse turned away, staring out the window at the short, slender cop strolling their way—Newton's partner. She pulled the door open and dropped into her seat. "Nice work, partner," she said as she held out a fist to Newton, who grinned and bumped it with his own.

What a load of horseshit.

Pulse shut his eyes. After a few attempts to further insult him, they got the message that he couldn't be baited and finished the drive in silence. Thank God. His face stung, and his left ribs ached like a son of a bitch. All he wanted was a stiff drink and a soft bed.

Maybe one with Talia in it. Yeah, he could get behind that. Her soft, warm, and sated while they lay entangled, sharing a whisky between them.

Damn, that'd be nice.

Too bad for him he'd be sleeping on a prison cot tonight and possibly in a pine box after that.

Chapter Sixteen

She'd never appeared so unprofessional in her career, and she couldn't have cared less.

Talia barged into the police station wearing gray cotton sleep shorts, an oversized black hoodie, and flip-flops. Her hair was piled in a sloppy bun, and her face didn't have a stitch of makeup. She had only her keys, wallet, and phone stuffed in her kangaroo pocket and enough blazing fury to burn the building to the ground.

A familiar face sat behind the front counter—Officer Blasetto, the annoying desk jockey who'd previously given her the runaround. Just what she needed—a misogynist cop to make this night worse.

Her flip-flops slapped against the linoleum as she marched over to the desk. "Excuse me," she said when she arrived.

Blasetto wrenched his gaze from whatever had him riveted to his computer—probably another rousing game of solitaire or an Andrew Tate YouTube video.

"You again," he said as his mouth twisted into an ugly sneer. "Always a pleasure."

"Likewise."

His eyes narrowed.

Direct ego hit.

"What can I do for you, Miss Attorney?"

"You can direct me to—"

The front entrance opened. "Get the fuck inside," a deep, angry voice shouted.

Talia whirled. Her mouth dropped open as she witnessed Pulse being escorted into the station by a large officer with *Newton* on his nametag.

Pulse looked like shit. His cheek was scraped and bloody, his clothes were filthy and torn, and he held himself stiff as though walking pained him.

Her stomach plummeted. What had they done to him?

"What the fuck is she doing here?" Newton growled, yanking Pulse to a stop by his elbow.

Pulse snorted even as he winced. "Did I forget to mention it? I called her before I pulled off the highway."

"Excuse me," Talia asked, marching forward. "*She* is his attorney, and *she* is here to be his legal counsel as is his constitutional right. I think the real question here is why the fuck does my client look like he's had the shit beat out of him?"

"He resisted arrest," Newton said with a smirk.

"Did he now?" She folded her arms over her chest. "Why am I finding that so hard to believe?" If it wouldn't land her in cuffs right alongside Pulse, she'd smack the smirk right off Newton's cocky mug.

"Don't know." His jowls shook as he nodded. "He put up a real nasty fight. Had no choice but to tase him."

Her chest ached. They tased him? She swung her attention back to Pulse, whose face was a mask of controlled rage. She had to look away. Seeing him hurt and angry twisted her insides and brought forth complex emotions she couldn't afford to show the cops.

"Take this into a fucking room," Blasetto barked from the front desk. "For Christ's sake, this is not the place for a scene."

"Probably smart," Talia announced, loud enough so anyone in the lobby would hear. "You don't want everyone hearing about how you assaulted my client, and the hell I'm going to rain down on this department." She stepped aside and gave Newton a sweet smile as she gestured for him to walk. "Please lead the way, Officer."

When she was younger and would make a face in frustration, her mother would say, "Talia, I hope your face doesn't freeze that way." She could confidently say she hoped to hell Newton's mug froze in that disgusted scowl.

Pulse winked and mouthed, "Dayum, that's hot," before Newton shoved him forward.

His ability to joke was encouraging, but she couldn't get in the same head space yet. How was he not vibrating with fury the same way she was? With as much confidence and authority as she could manage in her flip-flops and loungewear, she marched after Newton while imagining strangling him.

The slap of her sandals mocked her with every step. Would these old-school boys' club officers take her seriously without her professional attire? If she were smart, she would call Margo to take over. This became personal the moment Pulse put his hands—and mouth—on her. To be honest, it became personal long before that. She could no longer remain objective regarding him and probably everyone in his club. Hanging out with them had been a mistake. They'd crossed the line from clients to friends. How did she properly represent them when she couldn't step back and view their case without bias?

But she hadn't called Margo, and she wouldn't. Instead, she'd flown out of bed in the middle of the night with nothing mattering beyond protecting Pulse.

She followed the officers and Pulse into an interrogation room where a sergeant stood waiting. The sergeant instructed

Pulse to sit in the metal chair. Before he sat, Newton unlocked his cuffs. Talia only had a second to feel relief before they cuffed his hands to a metal ring on the table in front of him.

"Seriously?" she asked, going to his side. "Is this necessary?"

Newton grunted. "He resisted. Violently."

"Bullshit. I followed every damn order you gave me. What a fucking joke." Pulse shook his head.

"How exactly did he resist?" Her voice conveyed her disbelief.

"He got violent, like I said."

Talia glanced at the sergeant, whose expression was one of someone who'd swallowed sour milk as he observed their interaction. "Funny, isn't it, Officer Newton, that you and your partner don't seem to have a mark on you? Not a hair out of place, not a wrinkle in your uniform, not so much as a scratch, and yet Pulse looks like he's been through some shit."

Newton's eyes narrowed.

That's right, asshole. I don't believe a word out of your lying mouth.

"We tased him before it got physical. It's how we keep ourselves safe, miss."

Oh, the *miss* had her hackles risking. Condescending jerk. But she didn't let the annoyance show. She'd be damned if she let this guy know he got under her skin.

"I thought he was violently resisting. So, which is it? Was he violent with you, or did you tase him before he got violent? I'm just trying to get a clear picture."

"He was lashing out, screaming obscenities, and making violent threats. We—"

"Lies." Pulse's cuffs rattle against the metal table. "All fucking lies."

Talia rested her hand on his shoulder to quiet him. They

needed to let this lying officer hang himself with his words.

"We tased him to protect ourselves. It was a lawful traffic stop, and he resisted. End of story."

"Hmm. Pulse, could you explain to us what happened from your perspective?"

"Ma'am," the sergeant broke in. "Please let us take the lead here."

Ah, the pat on the head. *Shh, little lady, wait your turn.*

Pulse coughed, but it sounded like a poor attempt to cover a laugh. He understood she wouldn't appreciate the sergeant silencing her. Pulse had no power in this situation as the one under arrest, but he still could have spoken up. He still could have told the sergeant he was out of line or demanded he speak to her respectfully. But he stayed quiet. Maybe some would find his silence to mean he didn't have her back but viewed it the opposite way. It showed he valued her position and trusted her to handle the situation without backup. He respected her enough to try to assert himself in her domain. That meant more to her than any words he could have said in her support because handling misogynistic cops was her specialty.

She swung her gaze to the sergeant. "By all means," she said in a syrupy voice. "The floor is yours."

Talia sat in the chair next to Pulse. His leg bounced, tapping out an anxious rhythm with his boot. Beneath the table, she slid her hand to his thigh and gently pressed down. He stiffened for a beat but stopped fidgeting.

If it hadn't seemed suspicious, she would have left her hand there for the duration of the interrogation to feel connected to him. But one of the cops would have noticed, making this experience worse for everyone.

"Mr. Vargas," the sergeant said. "My officers pulled you over for going ninety-six in a sixty-five zone."

Pulse barked an ugly laugh. "Bullshit. I was doing sixty-seven. I checked as soon as you lit me up."

"Don't worry." Talia patted his arm. "This will all be on their dash cam recording. We'll be able to verify every word they say."

The sergeant continued as though they hadn't spoken. "Once you were stopped, you became extremely resistant, forcing my officers to take drastic action to subdue and detain you."

"Fucking lies."

"What are the exact charges?" Talia asked.

"Speeding more than thirty miles over the speed limit, which is a traffic misdemeanor in Florida."

"Thank you. I'm aware of traffic law," Talia said. "What else, since I'm assuming there's more."

"Obstructing official business and resisting arrest with violence. You'll be booked here tonight. Some federal agents would like to speak with you tomorrow and possibly transport you to DC. I am not aware of what the federal charges are or if there even are any. They are tight-lipped with their business. I just know they want you."

A chill ran down her spine as she turned and met Pulse's troubled gaze.

Nothing else mattered right then but getting him released as soon as possible. If she failed and he was allowed to be whisked away by the feds tomorrow, who knew when she'd see him again?

Probably never.

Something passed between her and Pulse, a nonverbal agreement to downplay anything related to the feds. They all knew the only reason he'd been pulled over in the first place was to hand him over to the government agents, but she couldn't let these officers find out how terrifying that prospect was.

"So, what we have here is your officers claiming my client

was speeding and violently resisting, and my client claiming that is a lie."

"I'm sure you're aware criminals lie all the time," the sergeant said in a condescending tone.

Screw him. "I wasn't finished speaking. The way I see it, this can be resolved in minutes. I'd like to see the body cam footage."

Newton, who stood by the door, froze. His eyes widened for a fraction of a second before he again schooled his features.

Busted.

The sergeant didn't have such an obvious tell, but even he shifted, and his gaze narrowed. "You know we do not have to produce that for you at this time."

"But you have it, right? I mean, there were six officers on the scene. You should have an abundance of footage showing how aggressive my client was and how he forced your officer's hand. How they had no choice but to tase him and, from the look of his clothes, kick him."

She swallowed down the bile that crept up at the thought of him being kicked by boots while defenseless from the tasing.

The sergeant cleared his throat. "Ma'am, I don't have to—"

"And, of course, there is dash cam footage documenting the extremely high rate of speed my client was traveling at. Well, gentlemen, it looks like there's not much I can do with such strong evidence of my client's unlawful behavior. I guess we'll be seeing you in court. We can review the footage there."

Newton mumbled something.

"I'm sorry. What was that?"

"There was an issue with the cameras."

"There was?" She snapped. "Oh shoot. Well, lucky for you, five other officers were on the scene. Unless…" She placed a hand over her chest and gasped. "Wait, you're not saying all the cameras had technical issues, are you? So, there's not a single shred of evidence beyond the bruises and cuts on my client to show what happened tonight? Oh, no. What rotten luck."

Pulse snickered while the sergeant compressed his lips and folded his arms across his broad chest as though his size and stature would intimidate her.

Please, she ate brutes like him for lunch.

"State your point, ma'am."

"My point, gentlemen, is that you clearly think I'm stupid if you plan to convince me all the body cameras stopped working at the same time, the exact moment of my client's arrest. More likely, your officers turned off their cameras because they didn't want any record of the abuse against my client. If he is not released at once, I will be filing a motion for adverse inference as well as a dismissal of all charges with prejudice. In case you don't know, it's a motion for the judge to infer that since the camera footage is magically unavailable, it would show something unfavorable toward your side. From there, dismissal would be almost guaranteed. After that, I'll be filing charges of unlawful arrest, assault, and infringement on my client's civil rights. Now, since the feds have not provided you with any charges, you cannot hold him based on their request to speak to him. My card is in his file. The federal agents may call me to set up a time to meet with us when they arrive."

No one spoke. The room filled with tension and rage, but finally from the cops instead of her or Pulse. She had them, and they knew it. They could push it and risk not only the case being tossed out but a lawsuit. One she'd be sure to win. Heads would roll if it went that far.

Ah, how she loved victory.

"Well, shit, boys, that's gotta be the sexiest thing I've ever seen. I'm feeling a whole lot better about this situation. How 'bout you?" Pulse grinned up at the cops.

Talia's face heated, but it had nothing on Newton's. He'd turned an unhealthy shade of purple and practically vibrated in his boots. If he were a cartoon, smoke would be rising from his ears.

"Officer Newton, please remove Mr. Vargas' handcuffs." The sergeant spoke through clenched teeth as though it pained him to give the order.

Talia bit her lip to keep from smirking. Pulse, on the other hand, didn't bother with restraint. He grinned as big as she'd ever seen him, taunting Newton and his sergeant.

The officer huffed and spluttered before he walked over, shaking his head. He unlocked the handcuffs with murder in his eyes.

"Mr. Vargas, you are free to go," the sergeant said. If you do not answer when the federal agents call you tomorrow, tonight will seem like a fantasy compared to what will happen to you."

"Threats, Sergeant? Really? I'm sitting right here." Talia batted her eyelashes at the man.

"Ms. Davenport, it will be on you if he doesn't take that call. And, no, these are not threats. Just a statement of fact."

"Of course, Sergeant. My client will be a good boy and cooperate with the feds."

There was no way in hell they'd be doing a damn thing the feds wanted which meant they needed to find a safe place to lay low for a while. But she could worry about that once they were out of there.

"We'll see." The sergeant glared for a few seconds, then stalked out of the room. "See them out, Newton," he called over his shoulder as he left.

Pulse stood, rubbing his wrist. "Well, I'd like to say it's been fun, but I think I'll go with *fuck you* instead." He rested his hand on Talia's lower back and guided her out of the room before Newton could respond. Warmth seared through her sweatshirt to her skin.

They'd most likely turned off the camera in the room, and she didn't want to stick around for a second more than they had to. Newton was pissed enough to do or say something stupid.

When he reached the hall, Pulse dropped his hand. An immediate and profound sense of loss pummeled her so hard she gasped.

Pulse shot her a concerned side-eye. She shook her head once.

Nothing, it was nothing—just a weird, fleeting sensation.

As they walked side by side toward the exit, the urge to take his hand had her curling her fingers into fists. She'd be a fool to show her cards to these cops. Besides, Pulse wasn't her boyfriend or anything ridiculous like that.

Then why did she suddenly feel like she wanted to rip his clothes off and touch him? Just hold him, breathe him in, and have him assure her he wasn't harmed. She rolled her shoulders and cleared her throat but couldn't shake the impulse. Instead, it grew with each step.

God, she wanted to feel him and be touched so badly that her knees wobbled.

What was happening to her?

Adrenaline crash?

Maybe, but adrenaline crashes were a familiar sensation that never accompanied a powerful urge to be near another person.

A man.

Then again, nothing had made sense since she first met Pulse.

Chapter Seventeen

What a fucking night.

Talia swooping in to save his ass from crooked cops had become a disturbing pattern.

Fresh air greeted him as he walked outside. Funny, he'd forgotten it was the middle of the night. That explained the fatigue clinging to him. Twelve hours in the emergency room followed by a tasing and dramatic arrest would exhaust anyone.

Talia had to be wiped too. He'd woken her up in the middle of the night to a shit show she had to sort out. And sort it she did. The woman was amazing. She'd had those cops shitting themselves with a few well-placed threats.

But now that they were headed for her car, her vibe was not reassuring.

"Thank you," he said as she marched toward her vehicle at a rapid clip.

"Not necessary. It's my job, and your club pays me very well to do it, including overtime for middle-of-the-night calls." They reached her car, and she went directly to the driver's side. "Am I taking you to your apartment?"

He frowned. What happened to the fire from moments ago? This Talia emitted icy waves. "Yeah, that's good. You okay?"

She smiled, but it didn't come close to reaching her eyes. "Of course. Why wouldn't I be okay?"

He studied her across the top of her car. She hadn't bothered to take the time to dress in work clothes or even brush her hair. Something about her throwing on the closest thing and rushing to the police station had his stomach tightening. Did she regret not looking professional in front of the cops? It might not have been professional, but she looked incredibly sexy in a tousled, recently fucked kind of way.

Precisely the type of thing that would set her on edge.

"Because tonight sucked. And it was only the beginning of the suck."

She shrugged. "Like I said. It's my job."

So, I'm nothing but a job to you?

He bit off the snarky reply. Tensions were too high, and nothing good would come of it.

"Well, you're damn good at it," he said before sliding into her passenger seat.

She joined him a moment later and started the car without another word. Complete silence ensued for the first five minutes, but it wasn't a comfortable quiet. Every twenty seconds or so, Talia glanced his way before focusing back on the road. She clutched the wheel so hard her knuckles stayed white, and her tension was so palpable it became a third person in the vehicle. Her neck and shoulders would be permanently bunched and full of tender knots if she didn't relax.

Two more minutes passed before he couldn't take the silent treatment any longer. "Talia?"

"Yeah?" She glanced away from the road. "You good?"

Could her tone be any faker? "There's a park on the left at the next stop sign. Pull in."

She peered at him with a frown. "Is something wrong?"

Too many things.

171

"Just pull in."

"Uh, all right."

She rolled to a stop and then made the left into the deserted lot.

"Drive to the end and park."

Her huff of annoyance had him grinning. Even flustered and off her game, she didn't respond well to commands. But she drove to the far side of the parking lot and pulled into a spot facing a lake no one should ever swim in. Gators owned it and most bodies of water where they lived.

"What's up?" she asked, facing him once she'd put the car in park.

"Come here." He patted his thighs.

"What?" Talia forced a laugh and looked everywhere but at him. "I'm not going to hop over the console and sit in your lap, Pulse."

"Talia…" He patted his thigh again.

She sighed, then finally lifted her gaze to meet his. He saw the same thing he felt. A jumble of emotions—frustration, annoyance, fear, and raw need. All things Talia would struggle to admit, but nothing that would drive him away or make him think less of her. Talia was pure strength and grit, but even the strongest needed a soft place to land now and then.

"Come here."

"Pulse, this is silly." Her voice wavered.

"Talia…" He gentled his tone, and she blinked rapidly.

Shit, was she about to cry? Why did the thought of it feel like a knife to his heart?

No, Talia wouldn't cry. That was a weakness too far in her mind. She huffed another strained laugh, then climbed over the console with much more grace and ease than should have been possible. Her knees landed on either side of him, wedged between his body and the car, and then she settled down on his lap. The second her incredible ass hit his thighs, tension bled out of him as though someone had released a pressure valve.

Talia's soft sigh had him grinning. He rested his hands on her hips. "Hi," he said as he squeezed.

"You're hurt," she whispered. "They hurt you." She cupped his face and gently turned him, so she had a better view of his scratched cheek.

It hurt like hell when it happened, but the discomfort had faded to a dull sting. Her soft hands took away the last of the pain. He couldn't feel anything but pleasure when she touched him.

"I hate that they hurt you." She stroked her thumb along his jawline beneath the extensive abrasion.

"A scrape and some bruises. Nothing to stress about. I had worse last month when I helped Spec chase down some meth dealers who were selling to kids in our area. They put up a helluva fight and busted my nose."

She didn't laugh at his anecdote, letting her hand drop as she bowed her head. "I think I'm losing my mind," she mumbled. "Something is wrong with me. I feel… crazy."

"How so?" He slid his hands around her back and under her sweatshirt. She whimpered when he encountered her bare skin.

This was precisely what he needed—her warm, soft skin in his hands. He stroked his fingers up and down her lower spine, soaking her in.

"I was frantic when you told me the cops had you," she admitted, staring at his chest.

If she would only put her hands there or anywhere back on his body.

"I didn't even put on real clothes. All I could think of was getting to you. I was so scared. And now.. " She swallowed. "Now I feel like I'm losing my mind. I'm anxious and frustrated. My skin is too tight and tingling, and I feel like the only way to make it stop is to have you touch me. Everywhere. I want you to touch me everywhere, Pulse. I've never felt a desire this strong before, and I don't know how to stop it. I feel so fucking needy, Pulse. How do I make it stop?"

"Shh." Her words went straight to his head and his cock. They were a drug, sending him soaring higher than the clouds. "Baby, it's okay. It's okay to need someone. It's okay to want someone."

She disagreed with frantic shakes of her head. "No, it's not. It's disgusting." She held his gaze, and the turmoil swirling in her eyes pierced his heart. "I'm not needy," she said, smacking a hand to her chest. "I'm tough and independent. Other attorneys hate going against me because I'm ruthless, and my record is so good. I don't rely on or need anyone."

"Sounds lonely."

"It's not. It's smart. I can give myself everything I need or want. I take care of me." Another slap against her chest. "I do it. No one else."

Though it wasn't what she meant, he couldn't stop imagining her caring for herself in a specific way. He saw her pleasuring herself with a thick dildo, making herself come until she shook. His dick hardened fast, and he had to fight to keep from grinding up against her.

Did she feel it?

Of course, she did. How could she not?

"Fine," he said, slipping his hands around to her belly. He stroked up until he reached her tits.

Oh fuck, no bra.

She really had run out of there as fast as possible.

He filled his hands with her tits.

Talia's eyes went wide, and she grabbed for his upper arms. "Pulse," she said on a gasp.

"You can do it all yourself. You don't need anyone. You

don't need this," he said, stroking his thumbs over her puckered nipples. Her desperate whimper had him nearly coming in his pants like a teenager who'd never touched a woman. "Christ, you're so sexy."

Her pupils eclipsed the chocolate brown of her eyes, and her breathing sped to a pant. Two seconds of playing with her nipples, and she was already squirming on his lap.

"You can do it all yourself, but guess what? I'm here, so you don't have to. I'll touch you all you want. All fucking night. But I think I know what you really need." He pushed his hips up into her, grinding against her. "I think you need a cock inside you. *My* cock. Filling you up."

"What?" She shook her head. "No, Pulse, that's crazy. I don't need that."

He pinched her nipples. Her head fell back on a long moan, exposing her throat. He licked up the side of her neck. "You need it, baby. Your body is begging for it. Why are you fighting so hard?"

"I-I'm scared."

How much strength had it taken for her to admit that to him? And what had happened to make her so afraid of letting others in? Talia kept everyone at a distance from her body and mind. She'd already let him in, which threw her for a loop. He knew the deep, overwhelming loneliness of isolating himself and someone as beautiful and vibrant as Talia didn't deserve that soul-destroying solitude.

"It's okay to need it," he whispered against her ear as he tortured her nipples. "It's okay to need me. It's okay to want to be fucked. I know what a gift you're giving me, and I'll take care of you. It's just us here. Not a soul will ever know what goes on between us. I need you just as fucking bad."

Those last words seemed to tip her over the edge. "Please, Pulse."

"Please, what, baby? Tell me what you need."

She met his gaze with an openness he'd yet to see from her. "You. I-I need you. Please fuck me."

Victory surged through him, heating his blood to near boiling. If she'd denied him, he'd have released her immediately and suffered the awkward car ride home, but it would have hurt. Not only the blue balls, but he wanted more than her pussy. What did she describe? The deep-seated need she felt for him, that's what he wanted. He wanted this rigidly disciplined woman wild for him.

Because that's what he felt for her.

Out of fucking control.

No matter what happened after tonight, he'd make sure this woman never regretted showing him her precious, vulnerable side.

He released her tits and wrapped his arms around her, still under her shirt. He slid one hand up to her neck and drew her to him. Their mouths collided in a desperate, hungry kiss that curled his toes. Nothing was hotter than the way she fought him for control.

She gripped the back of his head and dueled her tongue against his. He nipped her lower lip which made her gasp and ground her pelvis against his rock-hard cock. If he lasted five seconds inside her, it'd be a damn miracle.

She whimpered into his mouth while rocking against him as though trying to ride him through their clothes. When the sting of her teeth sinking into his lower lip registered, he grunted and tore his mouth away.

"Get your fucking shorts off," he practically shouted as he went to work on his zipper.

Talia giggled and shimmied out of her shorts as best as possible in the confined space. They were a mess of arms, legs, and mumbles as they freed themselves. Her shorts landed in the footwell while he managed to pull his cock out and lower his jeans beneath his hips.

"Condom?" she asked as she straddled him once again.

"Shit. I fucking forgot." Jesus, he'd have fucked her bare if she hadn't said something. When had he ever been so careless? When had a woman ever had him so out of his mind for her?

He managed to reach into his back pocket and retrieve his wallet, where he kept a condom. Not that he'd needed one for ages, but there wasn't any harm in being prepared.

"Allow me." Her eyes sparked with a mix of desire and playfulness as she plucked the condom from his fingers.

"Fuck yes." Grinning, he interlaced his fingers behind his head and leaned against the headrest. "Do your worst."

Her smirk made his dick twitch. God, he'd love to strip her down and spend hours licking and studying every inch of her, but cops patrolled the park on occasion, so time wasn't on their side. Next time they'd be completely naked so he could see those tits he'd had his hands all over—see and taste them.

Talia's hands were steady as she ripped the condom open, but her eyes glowed with filthy promise. She bit her lip as she withdrew the condom, meeting his gaze. One day, he'd have her make that exact pose, and he'd photograph it because it was too gorgeous not to be captured.

"Get it on me so I can get inside you."

"Yes." The second her soft fingertips made contact with his dick, he hissed a string of curses. She rolled the condom down with sure hands, then positioned herself above him, staring down. He moved his hands from behind his head to her lush hips, squeezing the flesh.

Talia moaned, then together, they guided her down onto his rigid cock. Her eyes flared as the tip notched against her entrance. That much was enough to have him fighting to keep his eyes from rolling back in his head.

"Jesus," he whispered as her tight pussy swallowed him

inch by inch.

"Pulse…" Her voice wavered with a tremor of nerves.

"I got you, baby. So fucking tight. So hot. Christ, you feel better than anything I've ever felt."

"S-same." Their foreheads met as he continued to work himself inside her.

After a few moments, their bodies met as he seated his cock fully inside her. Talia trembled. The ripples had him clenching his teeth. Nothing should be allowed to feel this good, this hot. How was he supposed to go on without wanting this every second of every day?

She was tighter than he'd expected, so tight it took his breath away.

"You good? Is it too much?"

"No. I mean, yes. I'm good. So good. You feel so big inside me, Pulse. You're stretching me. It's incredible."

"Yeah?" He kissed the side of her neck, her jaw, her ear. "You like that big cock filling your tight pussy?" he whispered against her ear.

She moaned and started to rock on him. "I love it. It's never felt like this before."

Wasn't that the truth?

"You ready to ride me? Ready to make this perfect pussy feel even better?"

"Yesss." She kissed him as she rose and fell on his cock.

There wasn't enough room to fuck up into her as he wanted. He was a big guy, and her coupe wasn't made for fucking. His knees hit the glove box with every thrust, and her head bumped the top of the car more than once, but neither cared. He held her ass as she rode him, giving her extra leverage. He couldn't stop kneading the soft flesh beneath his fingers. If only he could see what his firm grip was doing to her skin.

They panted and moaned. It felt amazing, but he wished

he could fuck her as hard and deep as he'd fantasized.

"Pulse," she said as she ripped her mouth off his. "More. More. And harder."

Thank fuck she felt the same.

"Outside," she said around her ragged breaths. "Get out of the car."

Christ, he nearly blew his load right there.

"Too risky. The cops patrol."

"I don't care." She scrambled off him and shoved open the door. "I need it, Pulse. I don't give a fuck who catches us."

This woman would be the death of him.

She clambered out of the car shoeless and with her fantastic ass on display. Pulse followed less than a second behind her. She moved to the car's hood and turned her back to him. He spared precisely one second to ensure they were alone in the lot before pushing on the center of her back. As she folded forward, her hands hit the car's hood with a satisfying smack.

Now that beautiful ass was on display for him, illuminated by the moonlight. It stuck out like a target he'd never miss. He grabbed it, squeezing and kneading the way he'd done in the car, but now he could watch his handiwork. When he released her, she had red finger marks all over her skin.

Gorgeous.

"Do it, Pulse," she begged as she glanced over her shoulder. Her lips were swollen and red, her hair a mess. "Please. I'm too empty. Don't tease me."

He shoved two fingers inside her. She soaked his hand. Damn the condom. He'd give up his bike to feel this wet heat on his cock. Talia cried out and arched her back as he pumped his fingers in and out a few times. "More," she wailed, slapping the hood of the car. "Your dick."

He pulled his slippery hand from her pussy and clapped it over her mouth. Those cries of pleasure would alert anyone within a mile radius of how good he fucked her. Once she no longer announced their presence, he grabbed her hip with his free hand and slammed his dick inside her.

Talia shouted into his hand. She had to be tasting herself on his fingers, and the thought of coating her face in her arousal made him even harder.

Time was ticking, and the risk of being caught was high, so he hammered into her without mercy. Her pussy clung to him through the rough pounding. His balls were heavy and full as they slapped against her ass. He bit the inside of his cheek, trying to focus on the pain and slow the oncoming orgasm. Even with the risk of being caught, he wanted to cling to the mind-blowing feeling as long as possible.

Talia urged him on with muffled shouts. "Don't stop. Please, never stop," she cried into his palm as he powered into her. "Close, close," she shouted, or at least that's what it sounded like.

He skirted his hand around her body until he found her clit. Three quick strokes of the swollen nub were all it took for her back to bow and a tortured scream to vibrate against his palm. She stiffened, except for her pussy which rippled around him with strong contractions.

The intense pressure on his cock became too much to resist. He clamped his jaw shut and howled through clenched teeth as fireworks shot across his vision and his balls emptied. Every muscle went haywire, twitching while sparks skittered across his skin.

Eventually, he collapsed atop Talia, who lay limp against the car's hood. She grunted as she took his weight. He tried to push off her but only had the strength to lift his head and kiss the salty back of her neck.

"That was intense," she whispered.

He frowned. Good intense or bad?

The question had him worried enough to be able to stand

and draw her with him. He spun her, and she immediately sought out his mouth. The kiss was lazy and deep. He wrapped his arms around her and let her take the lead.

Good intense. It had to be, or she wouldn't have kissed him that way with appreciation and emotion.

"Come home with me," he said when they came up for air. "Sleep in my bed. Tomorrow's gonna suck, but I think I can bear it if I wake up next to you." He smoothed the flyaway hairs back from her face.

"Pulse," she whispered. She rested her head on his chest. "I don't even know what to do with a comment like that. It makes me want... things."

He wanted things, too, but first, they had to get the cartel off their backs, which meant making some hard decisions tomorrow.

"Is that a yes?" he asked, rubbing her back.

Her head moved against his chest. "Yes."

Damn. He grinned.

The rumble of an engine had Talia going rigid in his arms. "Oh my God," she whispered as her head whipped up. "Someone is coming. I'm standing in a parking lot with my everything out, and someone is coming."

She shoved him away so hard he stumbled back.

"Oh, shit, sorry! I didn't mean to push you so hard. Don't laugh. Your dick is out, so why are you laughing?" She fumbled with the door and then hurled herself into the car just as headlights turned into the parking lot.

It didn't take more than a glance to see it wasn't a cop, which was good because he couldn't stop laughing.

"Pulse! What are you doing? Get in here. You cannot be arrested again."

He snorted. "It's not a cop. Probably some teenagers here to have sex."

"Oh my God, who does that?" she asked, then groaned

and slapped a palm to her head. "Don't answer that."

He was still chuckling as he hauled his pants up and zipped. Then, casual as could be, he strode around to the driver's side. The car was parked in the center of the lot, far enough away that he couldn't make out the driver. As he'd told Talia, it was probably a group of teens looking to escape their parents and have a little privacy, but he wasn't going to stick around and find out if the cartel or DEA had caught up to him.

He pulled the driver's door open to find Talia slouched and struggling to wiggle into her shorts. Once again, he burst out laughing, which only earned him a glare he bet made people shit themselves on the witness stand.

It made his depleted cock twitch in an attempt to rally.

"Seriously, if you ever want what just happened to happen again, you will get your ass in the car and stop laughing at me." She tried to scowl, but her lips quirked.

Pulse slid into the car. "Please," he said as he buckled up. "Don't even pretend to threaten me, baby. You know you're gonna be begging for a repeat the second we get inside my apartment."

She opened her mouth, probably to blast him with that caustic tongue, but then she sighed. "Dammit, you're probably right."

Their gazes met, and they both burst into laughter.

He couldn't remember when he'd run through such a drastic range of emotions in one night. Fury, fear, hatred, lust, hilarity, and now, the night was ending with straight-up happiness.

Talia had done that. She'd taken his shitty night and turned it around.

He planned to hold onto whatever was happening between them, no matter how foolish or doomed, for as long as possible.

Chapter Eighteen

Mere inches separated them in Pulse's bed. Talia couldn't stop staring at his relaxed face as he slept. He could make millions as a model for men's cologne or underwear. Her lips quirked as she imagined his annoyance at a photographer trying to position him and snap hundreds of shots. He'd hate it. Pulse was born for a high-energy, high-stakes job. His ability to remain cool under pressure and not let his emotional side take over made him perfect for trauma nursing.

His hand rested on her bare hip, nearly cupping her ass as he slept. The small smattering of dark hair sprinkled on his chest tickled her as they drifted off to sleep, wrapped up in each other. Her fingers itched with the desire to stroke through it and trace his tattoos, but she wouldn't risk waking him. He'd worked a twelve-hour shift and then had a distressing night. The man deserved as uninterrupted sleep as he could manage.

How long had it been since she'd slept the whole night with a man? Years, close to a decade. Early in college, she'd had a longish-term boyfriend who'd cheated with a close friend of hers. It had taken until law school for that wound to heal. Not because she'd loved the man or even missed him much, but because the betrayal made her mountain of trust issues grow taller.

After months of pressure from her friends during law school, she'd accepted a date from a nice guy who worked at a lounge they frequented. Their date went well, really well, so she went out with him a second time. Then a third and fourth, and so on, until he asked her to be exclusive after two months.

She'd wanted to say yes. At that time, it felt like the man had singlehandedly healed her wounded heart, given her hope, and swept her off her feet. But growing up with a prominent criminal attorney as a father taught her more than how corrupt the legal system could be. It taught her never to take anyone at face value. It taught her wolves often hid in the softest, fluffiest sheep's clothing.

So she'd run a background check on the man she'd fallen hard and fast for. Not only was he married, but he sent his wife to the hospital on more than one occasion. He never found out she was the one to tell the cops where he'd be one night so they could serve his arrest warrant. That man was now serving time for aggravated domestic assault.

After that, she'd given up on anything more than the rare hookup and definitely no sleepovers.

Until tonight.

They'd gone straight to his bed when they got to his apartment. Pulse had stripped her down, kissing and touching everywhere before giving her another spectacular orgasm with his fingers this time. Then, he'd wrapped her in his arms, and they passed out, practically glued together. Unfortunately for her, sleep only lasted an hour or so, and now she was wide awake in the pre-dawn hours, watching a man sleep.

What was it about him that made her break all her rules for self-preservation?

Pulse's eyelids fluttered, then opened, and she stared into

the sleepy gaze of the man who twisted her up inside. He smiled, and foolish butterflies danced through her stomach. Didn't they know it never ended well?

And yet she couldn't help how her heart sped and hope flared to life.

"I'm so sorry," she whispered as she finally let her fingers reach for the warm chest they wanted to touch. "I didn't mean to wake you."

His grin didn't falter as he said, "Then you shouldn't have been thinking so hard and loud."

Talia grimaced. "Sorry."

He kissed her. She sighed into his mouth as she melted into him—just a little bit. Not enough to lose her badass-woman card, but she did melt.

"I'm teasing you." He tugged her in until their bodies were flush. It was then she realized their legs had been entangled all along. They'd slept as one instead of two separate bodies.

God, she was falling too hard and too fast.

"Can't sleep?"

She shrugged. "It's hard to turn my mind off after last night."

"Does that mean I didn't do a good enough job wearing you out?" he asked as he slid his hand down to her ass and squeezed.

Her smile came instantly. "No, you did a fabulous job. The best job ever. There's just a lot going on, you know?"

"I know." He opened his mouth as though to speak, then pressed his lips together.

"What?"

Pulse sighed. "You're not going to like this."

She drew her head back so she could see him better. "I'm not going to like what?"

He had a girlfriend.

A gaggle of kids.

He picked his nose.

Alarm bells blared between her ears.

"I think I need to tell the club about my past."

What? "Oh." She blinked as the words registered. "Pulse, you can't. You told me yourself that they'd..." She shook her head. She refused to put those words into the universe. "You can't. It's not safe."

He kissed her mouth, her forehead, and back to her lips.

Tears came to her eyes. He'd made his decision. There'd be no talking him out of it. Her gut told her it'd be a waste of breath trying to convince him otherwise.

"Why?"

"They deserve to know. What's going to happen later today when the cartel comes looking for me disguised as the DEA?"

"We'll hide. We won't be here."

"And where is the first place they're going to turn when they can't find me?"

Her heart sank. How could she not have thought of this herself? She was too close to think objectively.

"The club. They'll go after your club."

"I can't do that to my brothers. To their women. I can't put them in that kind of danger without at least a warning."

Her heart needed to slow so it didn't explode. His club was his family, his world, and he loved them. What would that be like? To have people in her life she'd sacrifice her safety and her own life for? To care for someone, to love someone that much?

Terrifying.

And yet, as she gazed at the handsome face on the pillow beside her, she realized she might know what it felt like.

And that was too frightening to deal with.

"When I patched, I took an oath. I made a promise to my brothers. We protect our own no matter what. No. Matter.

What. None of us are good men by society's conventional standards, but we all know the truth. Those men, my brothers, are the best goddamn men in this world. If I don't come clean now, I'm robbing them of the opportunity to live up to their oath. And I'm breaking mine. I've already broken mine by keeping secrets, but they can't deny I've been there for every one of them when they needed it. I've held their ol' ladies' hands. I've stitched their wounds. I've fought by their sides. Now, I need to warn them of the danger and ask them to return the favor, even if I don't deserve it. I need to trust in the oath we took and trust in my knowledge that they are better men than I am."

Her throat constricted until she could barely swallow. Damn him, why did he have to make so much sense?

"Pulse… I'm terrified for you." A tear slid down her cheek. Very rarely had she let a man see her cry, and she'd never thought it would happen again, but something about this man had all her shields crumbling.

He swiped the tear with a strong yet gentle thumb. "I know. And I need you to do something that's gonna go against every ass-kicking instinct that you possess."

Oh shit. She drew back. "What?"

"I need to ask you not to come with me when I talk to Curly."

"What?" She jerked her head back. "Are you out of your mind? Absolutely not. There is no way I'm letting you do this alone. What if they—"

He kissed her once, hard and fast. "Exactly. What if they… if this goes tits up? You can't be there, Talia. I won't put you in danger."

"Pulse, no." She shook her head so fast his face blurred. *"No."*

"Talia, I'm not asking."

A hysterical laugh bubbled out of her. "Excuse me? What

the fuck is that supposed to mean?"

His face changed before her eyes. Gone was the warm, generous lover she'd spent the night with and, in its place, the federal agent who'd taken down a vicious cartel. "It means you're not coming when I tell them," he said in a hardened voice.

"You have met me, right?" she asked, unable to keep the distraught edge from her voice. "Because the way you're talking makes it seem like you think I'm someone who takes orders. And most people figure out I'm not after spending about five seconds with me." She sat up, yanking the sheet up to cover her nakedness.

How fucking dare he think he could tell her what to do.

Pulse also sat, scooted close, and wrapped his arms around her. "It will kill me if something happens to you," he whispered in her ear. "I could be reading this all fucking wrong, and they might end me right there on the spot."

And he thought she'd allow that? That she could live with herself if she sat on her thumbs while he ran into the firing squad?

"That's why you need me there," she said with a choked sob. The idea of his club coming after him made her sick. "I could—"

"No," he said, kissing her shoulder. "Baby, we're a fucking outlaw MC. There's not a damn thing you could do. If it goes wrong, I don't want you to see. I don't want that to be your last memory of me. It'll break me."

"Pulse." The tears flowed freely now. She no longer cared about her pride or how she looked in his eyes. The only thing that mattered was keeping him alive. "You're playing dirty."

His lips met the shell of her ear. "When it comes to keeping you safe, I'll play as dirty as I fucking have to. I'll cuff you to this goddamn bed to keep you here if I gotta."

It wasn't an idle threat. Pulse wasn't the type of man to

make them.

Her heart sank, and she sighed. "Fine," she whispered as she turned to face him. "But I want you to promise me two things."

"Anything."

"Wait a few hours. You're operating on an empty tank right now. Sleep a little more. You'll need to be sharp and not fuzzy because we were up half the night screwing around."

A lazy grin curled his lips and made him look damn near irresistible. "No better reason to be fuzzy," he said as he leaned in and kissed her neck.

A shiver raced up her spine. She tilted her head to give him better access. What the hell was wrong with her? There he was, ordering her around, being an ass, and preparing to charge into danger, and she was ready to jump him.

"Pulse, this is serious," she said, pushing him off.

He sobered at once. "I know." His weary sigh had a twinge of guilt twisting in her stomach. "What's the second thing?"

"Call me the second you get there and the second it's over so I can tell you how stupid you are."

"Yes, ma'am." He chuckled. "I'd never deny you that opportunity." He tugged her back down with him. "Come on. You wanted me to sleep. Only way that will happen is if you're beside me."

They wiggled around until her back was to his front, tucked into the crook of his body with his solid arm holding her close. Physically, she'd never been so comfortable. Emotionally? Well, that was a tangled mess she couldn't begin to unravel.

Pulse's breath on her neck evened out within a matter of minutes, which wasn't surprising considering the night he'd had. Talia, on the other hand, stayed wide awake. She considered Pulse to have above-average intelligence, but maybe she needed to reconsider that with how easily he'd accepted her compliance. He wasn't the only one who would play dirty to protect the ones he lo—cared about.

She stayed that way, thinking and plotting until the sun began to show itself through his window. Pulse still slept like the dead behind her. He hadn't shifted once. His heavy arm still anchored her to him. Talia bit her lower lip and turned as slowly as possible to her back. Once she'd flattened, she worked her way to the edge of the bed one inch at a time, holding her breath to keep from moving his arm more than she had to.

When she'd made it about halfway free, he grunted.

Talia froze. Could he feel the pounding of her heart beneath his arm? Would that be what woke him?

He made a low snuffling noise and then rolled away from her to face the opposite wall. Talia remained as still as a statue, not daring to breathe for another five minutes before sliding out of the bed. Without a sound, she gathered her clothing and tiptoed from the room. Once she reached the foyer, she quickly threw her clothes on, slid her feet into her flip-flops, and slipped out the door like a shameful morning-after fleer.

When she got into her car, she pulled out her phone and texted Curly.

911. Need to speak to you and Spec ASAP.

She stared down at the phone. "Come on. Come on. Please be awake."

The reply came before her screen went dark.

Clubhouse. Now.

Thank God.

On my way.

Her car started without a sound, a benefit of having an electric vehicle.

Pulse would be beyond furious when he found out what she'd done. He might never speak to her again, and she couldn't say she'd blame him. As much as the thought of him dumping her felt like a knife to the heart, this was something she had to do.

If she had a fraction of a chance of keeping the club from viewing Pulse's past as a betrayal, she had to take it. She'd never be able to live with herself if they cast him from the club—or worse—and she'd sat at home like the good little lady as he'd ordered.

Fuck that.

Talia had spent the majority of her life trusting her gut. She'd been kicking ass for this long, and she'd be damned if she stopped now.

Chapter Nineteen

Talia stepped into the clubhouse to find Spec and Curly sitting at a round, four-person table with two cups of coffee in front of them. As she entered, they both moved to stand.

She held up her hand. "Not necessary, gentlemen," she said as she strode to the table. "Excuse my unprofessional attire. It's been a night."

Curly smiled, but it lacked its usual warmth and welcome. He knew she wasn't there for a social visit. "We don't give a fuck about formal or professional around here, do we, Spec?"

The enforcer watched her through narrowed eyes. His leg bounced beneath the table as though he was priming his muscles, ready to leap up and defend his president at the first sign of a threat.

"Good to know. May I sit?"

"Sure." Spec nudged a chair out with his foot. "Coffee?"

"No thanks. Despite being up all night, I'm jittery."

"Gotta admit, you got me wired as fuck, too," Spec said. "I just poured this to have something to do with my hands. Can we skip the small talk, and you tell us what the fuck has you texting 911 at six in the morning?"

"Fair enough." She placed her palms on the table and looked straight into Curly's eyes. "Before I begin, I feel I must inform you that I am recording this conversation. Should you feel the need to end our discussion in a... let's say, abrupt manner, you should know the file uploads to a cloud every fifteen seconds."

"What the fuck." Spec shot halfway across the table. His hands smacked the table with a loud slap. "Tell me you're not about to fucking extort us because you're fucking recording. I'll—"

Curly lifted a hand. "Brother, don't finish that sentence," he said, his voice cracking into the room like a whip.

"Fuck." Spec sagged back into his seat. He jammed a hand into his hair. "Sorry."

"No need," Talia said, though her heart had lodged in her throat. "I promise I pose no threat to you or this family you've built. I do, however, have some information that might be difficult to hear. Before I share it, I'd like some assurances from the two of you."

Spec turned to Curly. "You gonna agree to this shit?"

Curly leaned forward. "Talia, I already know."

Her mouth opened, but no sound came out. She blinked. He knew? "I-I'm sorry. You know?"

Nodding, Curly rubbed at a nick in the wooden table with his thumb. "I know who your father is. I know he was a defense attorney during my trial, and he took bribes to do a shitty job and overlook police corruption."

She leaned back. There were few times in her life she'd been truly stunned, and this was one of them. "I... how..."

"What the fuck?" Spec turned to his president. "You hired the daughter of a man who screwed you over?"

Curly ignored his enforcer and kept his gaze on Talia, who felt like she was upside-down on a massive roller-coaster loop. "You underestimated the strength of the background check I did before we hired you."

She was going to be sick, and they hadn't even discussed the reason she'd come to talk to them. "Is this about revenge?"

"It better fucking be," Spec muttered.

"No. I've been following your career, and it seems you've spent it trying to right your father's wrongs. You specialize in wrongful arrests and fighting for the underdog."

He had no idea.

"I do. And you hit the nail on the head. I'm here to pay his penance, but, um… that's not what I wanted to talk to you about this morning. It's different and more serious, I'm afraid. But I would love to revisit this with you."

"Great," Spec said, rolling his eyes.

Any other time, finding out Curly knew her secret and had hired her anyway would have been an enormous relief. Today, it barely registered. "Like I said, I need your assurances before I begin."

Curly tilted his head, studying her. "You're not here to harm one of my men or their ol' ladies."

"No. Quite the opposite. And I'm sorry to be so cryptic, but I need you to hear my terms and agree to them before I divulge more." If it weren't for the countless hours in a courtroom, her hands would shake, and she'd squirm in her seat. These men had stares that would scare the devil.

Curly's lips flattened into a thin line. He tugged on a curl— his namesake—as he thought.

"Where's Pulse?" Spec cut in. "You two have been all chummy lately. I'm assuming he has something to do with all this drama."

"He's at his house."

Spec's eyes narrowed. "He know you're here?"

"He does not. And to answer your next question, he would never have agreed to let me come here. I'm guessing he'll drop me faster than you can say throttle once he finds out I'm here."

"What are your terms?" Curly asked.

"You agree to hear me out completely. That means no flying out of here in a fit of rage until I have said everything I've come to say."

Curly nodded. "Agreed."

She looked at Spec. "And you?"

The poor man's jaw looked one more pound of pressure away from shattering. He spoke through clenched teeth. "Fine. Next?"

Here was the one that would throw them for a loop. She kept her hands flat on the table in front of her. It was the only way to keep them from trembling.

"I want your assurance, your promise, that no matter what I tell you today, no harm will come to Pulse."

The room fell so quiet she could hear the refrigerator hum from the kitchen.

Spec leaned forward. "Come again?"

This time, she was the one to spear him with a harsh glare. "You heard me fine the first time."

"Talia, I'm not in the habit of hurting my family," Curly said. His expression was one of concern and worry as opposed to the suspicion and doubt on Spec's.

"I know that. It's why I'm here, helping Pulse with a plan that would be suicide if it weren't for that fact. But I'm not stupid enough to come here without a backup plan."

"Fuck." Spec ran a hand down his face. "What has he done? Please tell me he did not beat that stripper."

That had her frowning. Of all the ways she'd imagined this going, Spec bringing that up hadn't crossed her mind. "Of course not. What's wrong with you?"

"Too much, darlin'. Too fucking much." His grin had a chill running down her spine. This was a very lethal man, and she was about to give him upsetting news.

Curly thumbed his lip before nodding once. "We agree."

"I want to hear it from him," she said as she pointed to

Spec.

"Damn, counselor, your balls are bigger than most men's." Spec huffed a mocking laugh. "You know, if I didn't admire that so much, I'd find you fucking annoying."

She smiled her first genuine smile in hours. "I'll take that as the compliment I'm assuming it was."

Spec grunted. "Fine. I agree to your fucking terms. Now talk."

In the hours she'd spent churning this over and over in her head, she'd decided this was the point to rip off the Band-Aid and tell them straight. She'd had no choice but to drop crumbs until they agreed to her terms, but the longer she pussyfooted, the more she ran the risk of losing their attention and cooperation.

She straightened her spine—the moment of truth.

"Pulse is a former DEA agent. He was single-handedly responsible for taking down the Del Rios Cartel about five years ago."

Both men stared at her as though she'd sprouted an extra set of tits from her head. She forced herself to remain still and calm under their stunned gazes.

Shocker, Spec reacted first. "I'm sorry," he said with an ugly laugh. "Can you repeat that? Because it sounded like you said my brother is a former fucking fed. But I know that can't be true because the Pulse I know is not a stupid motherfucker, and patching in as a fed would be the stupidest fucking thing he could do."

"Former," she said.

"What?" Spec spat.

"Former fed."

He seethed, so she turned her attention back to Curly. As the more reasonable of the two and the one with the power, she needed to appeal to him before his hot-headed enforcer. Unfortunately, his expression was as furious as Spec's, but at least he kept his temper in check.

So far.

"You promised to hear me out," she reminded the man. "And you promised not to hurt Pulse."

"You manipulated us. Fucking lawyers," Spec muttered.

Only years of experience in interrogation kept her from snapping at the angry enforcer. Like Spec wouldn't do whatever it took to keep Liv safe? Wouldn't he beg, borrow, steal, or manipulate whoever he had to if it meant ensuring Liv's safety?

Not that Pulse was on the same level as Liv. They'd slept together a few times, that's all, but she cared for the man.

Too much.

A muscle in Curly's jaw twitched. The man had self-control, she'd give him that. But then, who could survive more than a dozen years of wrongful imprisonment without commendable restraint?

"We're listening, Talia," he said in a voice that didn't match his rigid posture. "Tell us the story."

Spec huffed an irritated sigh.

Talia recounted everything Pulse had told her about his time with the DEA. The men didn't interrupt as she detailed his undercover operation with the Del Rios Cartel, his complicated faux relationship with Camila, and the ultimate demise of his career. She clearly emphasized how he'd cut all ties with the DEA and had nothing to do with any federal organization since then. She also highlighted his solitary life and the way the club had saved him from a life of isolation and depression.

"Well, damn, counselor," Spec said when she finished. "You are one impressive litigator. You almost had me falling for all that shit about him loving this club and how he'd rather die than hurt us. You must be a fucking shark before a judge."

She tilted her head and gave Spec the stare that humbled the most brutal criminals. "I am, Spec. Thank you for noticing."

Asshole.

She focused on Curly, who sat resting his chin on his steepled fingers. "Why are you telling us this now?" he asked.

"Ain't it obvious?" Spec asked. He rocked back on the chair's hind legs, folding his arms across his chest. "Dear Old Uncle Sam wants him back on the payroll."

"I'm sorry," Talia said, letting a bit of her cool façade slip for the first time. "Correct me if I'm wrong, but didn't you work for Uncle Sam for many years?"

"Not the same fucking thing." He leaned forward, and his chair legs hit the ground with a loud crack. "I defended my country," he said, stabbing his finger on the table. "He just—"

"He took out one of the deadliest drug cartels in history," she said, mimicking his pose. Her fingertip ached where she jammed it against the table, but she ignored the discomfort. Spec's attitude needed to be taken down a few notches, and she was happy to provide the service. "I know this club, and the Del Rios Cartel is exactly the kind of evil your club works to eliminate. You can't make me believe you think otherwise."

"This isn't about the fucking cartel." Fire shot from Spec's eyes. "This is about fucking liars."

"Spec, enough." Curly's voice remained calm and steady. "Talia, you're bringing this to us for a reason. I assume something happened, or Pulse would have probably gone to his grave with this information."

It became more challenging to keep her attention on Curly with each passing second. Spec's frequent scoffs and grunts of disbelief had her itching to reach across the table and slap him. "The police orchestrated Pulse's arrest for the assault on the prostitute at the DEA's request. They wanted to speak to him without any suspicion by the club. And yes, they asked him to spy on you and report to them, or they'd toss him in jail and out him."

"I fucking knew—"

"He very firmly told them where they could shove their offer." She raised her voice over Spec. "I arrived and got him released while I was unaware of any of this. A few nights later, when I was working late, a DEA agent visited me at my office. He threatened me if I couldn't get Pulse to work with him. That's the night I was run off the road and injured."

Finally, Spec's expression showed an emotion besides anger. Confusion wrinkled his brow. "The DEA's resorting to thug-level tactics now?"

"Or *someone* at the DEA is," Curly said.

Nodding, Talia pointed to him. "Pulse has one contact from his days with the DEA. This guy is not affiliated with any organization or government. He's independent and loyal to Pulse because Pulse saved his ass years ago. Anyway, due to some covert and, I'm sure, less-than-legal digging, he discovered that a Del Rios family member was able to get hired by and work their way up in the DEA."

"Oh fuck." Pieces were beginning to fall into place in Spec's head.

"Yeah, fuck."

"Jesus, the fucking feds can't do a goddamn thing right. So now we have a surviving cartel member with the power of a federal agency behind them out for Pulse's blood."

"That's the working theory, yes. We do not know if this is a widespread operation or if this agent is working alone. Last night, an Officer Newton pulled Pulse over, tased him, and beat him. They made up some bullshit story about him resisting arrest so they could jail him overnight. The DEA is supposed to collect him today and take him to DC. I was able to get him released with the promise that he would return to speak to the DEA today, which obviously will not fucking happen."

"Jesus Christ," Spec whispered.

Before he could say anything else, Talia plowed on. "Pulse is worried the DEA or rebirthed cartel will come after the club if they can't get their hands on him. He planned to come speak to you today and tell you all this information as soon as he woke up." She shrugged. "I beat him to it."

"Whoa, boy," Spec said with a laugh as he slapped his hands together once. "You were right about one thing. That man is going to hate your ass for this stunt. What'd you do, drug 'im?"

She glared at him. "Spec, I say this with all the respect I feel you deserve right now. Shut the fuck up."

"He—"

"Spec, I need you to put a lid on it for now," Curly said. He straightened. "I'm not going to lie, Talia, Pulse's past is going to be an issue for some guys in the club."

Spec snorted. "Some? Come the fuck on."

Curly shot him a look that had Spec's mouth snapping shut.

Wow.

Maybe he could teach her that trick. She had a potent glare, but Curly's was next level.

"I appreciate you coming to us with this. You've taken a great personal risk, which means you feel something for him. I made you a promise that no harm would come to him, and I stick by that." He glanced at Spec as he spoke. "It will need to be dealt with, but it sounds like our priority needs to be keeping our family safe and getting rid of what's left of the cartel."

The relief was so staggering she had to blink back tears.

Fuck.

These men couldn't see her cry. Not if she was the last

woman on Earth.

She cleared her throat. "Thank you. And yes, that's exactly why Pulse wanted to come to you."

"But you beat him to it," Spec said, shaking his head.

She turned her attention to him. "That's right." How could a sweet and kind person like Liv put up with this insufferable buffoon?

"The first step is to call a club meeting," Curly said as he pulled out his phone.

A series of pounding sounds came from outside. It sounded like boots on the steps.

All three of them froze. Talia's heart sank.

The door flew open with so much force that it slammed against the wall. A rush of warm air flowed into the building.

Talia closed her eyes with a sigh.

Pulse had arrived.

Chapter Twenty

Pulse woke with a brick in his stomach. He'd hoped for a few minutes of peace before he recalled what he had to do today, but no, his body remembered the instant he woke up.

Five minutes. He'd give himself five minutes to enjoy the feel of Talia against him before he got up and called Curly. Five minutes of losing himself in her soft, warm skin. He rolled over and frowned at the empty bed and cold sheets.

Had she slept at all? He sat up with a sigh. He'd most likely find her sitting at the table with a third cup of coffee as she stared out the window and ran through every possible thing that could go wrong today.

"Talia?" he called as he dragged himself out of bed. She didn't answer. His frown deepened. Could she be in the guest shower? Before emerging into the hallway, he tugged on some jeans and a plain black tee. "Tal?" he called again.

Maybe she'd fallen asleep on the couch. God, that would make him a dick. He'd slept on while she lay awake and eventually moved to the sofa alone.

But, no, she wasn't on the couch either. "Tal, where are you?" he called as he walked into the empty kitchen. He frowned. Hadn't she dumped her wallet and keys on the table when they'd come in last night?

On a hunch, he peeked out the window to the parking lot

behind his apartment.

Her car was gone.

Pulse experienced two seconds of confusion before the worst-case scenario hit him, and he knew without a doubt where she was.

"*Fuck!*" he shouted into the quiet apartment. "Goddammit." What a fucking fool he'd been. How the hell could he have fallen for her easy agreement to his ridiculous demand that she stay home? The Talia he knew would never go along with him ordering her ass around, especially if it meant leaving her on the sidelines.

"Fuck."

He jammed his feet into his boots, then sprinted toward the door. The cops towed his bike to the impound lot, but he had a truck for when he had to get to work on nasty days.

Christ, why had she done this?

He'd had this feeling once before—an out-of-control sick feeling that everything was crumbling around him. This guilt ate away at his flesh until nothing remained but a husk. It was the day Camila died. That had been his fault the same way this was. Talia could be hurt, and there wouldn't be anyone to blame but himself. If he'd thought Camila's death had destroyed him, he'd been dead wrong. If something happened to Talia, no part of him would be left to recover. What he'd felt for Camila paled in comparison to what he felt for Talia. Though he'd spent years with the cartel princess, he'd never experienced genuine romantic feelings for her. He craved Talia like a drug.

He floored the gas pedal and sped out of his neighborhood with his tires screaming against the pavement the way his brain screamed inside his skull. The fact that he didn't encounter any cops along the way was a miracle with how he weaved in and out of traffic at a dangerous rate of speed. Not that he'd have stopped for anything, but a high-speed police chase would have complicated the situation.

He reached the clubhouse in record time, screeching to a stop in front of the porch. He left the engine running and the door open as he charged toward the clubhouse and pounded up the three steps. With the roar of blood rushing in his ears, he threw the door open and came to a dead stop.

Talia, Curly, and Spec sat at a small round table. She had her back to him while his brothers sat opposite her, facing the entrance. All three froze at his arrival.

Too bad they didn't remain stunned for long.

"Pulse…" Talia stood and turned to face him with sorrow written all over her face.

On the other hand, Spec wore a murderous scowl, while Pulse couldn't decipher Curly's expression.

He focused all his attention on the woman who had him tied up in knots. "Why?" he croaked. His throat felt as dry as the Sahara.

She gifted him a sad smile. "I had to try."

Damn her.

The telltale click of a round being chambered had Talia stiffening. Pulse whipped his gaze to Spec to find his brother rounding the table with his gun leveled at Talia's head. His heart came to a standstill in his chest, which made no sense as his blood roared in his ears.

No, no, no.

This was why she was supposed to stay back. It was his worst nightmare come true.

"W-what the fuck are you doing?" Pulse shouted. He lurched a step forward, but Spec's voice had him freezing like a movie character immobilized in time.

"Don't fucking move!" his enforcer screamed. "You know I'm not fucking around."

"Don't do this." Now Pulse's heart hammered against his ribs so hard it fucking hurt. He could barely take a breath.

"Why?" he whispered.

"I made her a promise," Spec said, jerking the gun to indicate Talia. His eyes were wild with the same murderous ferocity he'd used to protect the club so many times. To see that hatred turned on himself was devastating. "I promised I wouldn't hurt you for your fucking betrayal. But I didn't make any promises about her safety, and I figure this might be the best way to punish you for your lies." He stared Pulse right in the eye and grinned in the cold, lethal manner he reserved for their enemies.

That's what he now considered Pulse.

"Spec, drop the fucking gun," Curly said, calm and rational as he could be. "This isn't the way we do things."

Talia stood steady, but the fear in her eyes broke Pulse's heart.

"Keep looking at me, Talia," he said, his throat thick. "I can't believe you did this, you stubborn, strong, wonderful, stupid woman."

He got a wobbly grin in reply. "I've never been any good at doing what I'm told."

"Yeah, I'm starting to get that."

"Spec, you do not want to do this." Curly inched a few steps closer to Spec. He kept his arms spread wide and unthreatening.

"I think I do, Prez. You've been fucking betrayed before. How are you not grabbing your gun?"

The longer Curly could keep Spec talking, the better their chances of escaping this without a bullet hole in Talia.

Spec was right. It'd be the best punishment imaginable. If he killed Talia, Pulse would never recover. He'd spend his life steeped in grief and guilt so powerful they'd destroy him from the inside out day by day until nothing remained but a living, breathing corpse.

"Because I know the world isn't black and white, brother,"

Curly said. "Our lives are all lived in shades of gray. Nothing is simple."

"Bullshit. There are lies, then there's the truth."

"We're all complicated, Spec. All square pegs trying to fit into round holes. You know that better than most. It's what brought us all together in the first place."

"Don't, Prez. Don't compare us. We're nothing alike. I would die for this club, and this motherfucker would hand us over to his buddies, the goddamn feds."

The kitchen door opened, and Liv burst into the room, barefoot and breathing like she'd run a marathon. Her hair was messy, she didn't have a stitch of makeup on, and she wore sweatpants and a tank top. Never before had Pulse seen her looking anything but put together and perfect in designer clothes with shoes and makeup to match.

"Spec!" she shrieked as she skidded to a halt. "Stop. What are you doing?"

Spec jolted as though he'd been slapped. "Liv, get the fuck out of here. You don't want to be here."

Brooke came in also but stayed near the kitchen entrance, staring with wide, terrified eyes.

Shaking her head, Liv continued toward her ol' man. "Scott," she said in a level voice. "Baby, please put the gun down. I don't know what happened, but Pulse is your brother, and Talia has done nothing but help the club."

"Liv, go. You don't understand. He was a fucking fed. This one came here to plead his fucking case." Spec vibrated with rage as he filled his ol' lady in with the bare-bones details.

Liv reeled back in shock. She turned her astonished gaze Pulse's way. With every telepathic power he didn't possess, he tried to pass his thoughts and intentions to her through his mind. She blinked, then switched her attention to Talia, who was now trembling. Something passed between the women, an unspoken bond and connection he'd never fully understand.

"You said *was*," Liv took another step toward Talia.

"What? Babe, back the fuck up."

Shaking her head, Liv took another step. "I can't do that, Scott. You said he was a fed. Not is. Jo was a cop, and you love her. Maverick's ol' lady was FBI and stayed at our house."

"He lied."

"Well, then punch him in the face or something, but don't do this. He's your brother." She kept walking closer.

Spec spat on the floor. "Not anymore." He'd gotten so lost in his anger that he didn't realize Liv had reached Talia.

Pulse held his breath as Liv pushed Talia behind her. She now stood at the business end of Spec's pistol.

He lowered the gun immediately. "Baby..." Anguish tinged his voice.

"This is not the way." She reached for his hand.

Spec sagged. He let the gun slip from his fingers into Liv's, who passed it off to Curly before wrapping her arms around her man.

Talia let out a choked cry and then sprang toward Pulse like a stallion shooting out of the starting gate. He threw himself toward her, meeting her halfway. She leaped into his arms, wrapping her legs around his back as she buried her face in his neck. He caught her with ease and held her against him so tight he couldn't believe she didn't squawk in protest.

God, she felt so good—warm, soft, alive.

She trembled and cried softly in his arms, which tore his insides to pieces. This strong woman should never be made to shed a tear. And it was all his fault. If Spec had hurt her—

Don't go there.

Liv had his gratitude forever.

Fuck talking to Curly or trying to work things out right then. Talia mattered most, and she needed to get the fuck out of there. Breaking down in front of others would upset her almost as much as being held at gunpoint. Pulse marched toward the exit with his arms full of Talia.

Before he reached the door, Brooke ran over. "Here," she said, holding out a key. "Take apartment four. I overheard the entire thing from the kitchen. The two of you will be safe there from the feds, and Curly will keep the club away until the dust settles. No one will bother you. You have my word. I also turned your truck off and put the keys in the apartment."

He searched Brooke's eyes and found nothing but sincerity and trust. "Thank you," he said with a nod as he accepted the key. Then, without another word, he slipped out of his favorite place in the world, but the place that now represented his most terrifying moment.

Neither spoke as he carried Talia across the property to the apartment. At some point, they'd need supplies to last them through more than a night or two, but that was a problem for later. Now, he needed to feel Talia's skin, hear her breathe, and hear her heart thump in her chest.

By the time he reached the apartment, Talia had stopped crying and quivering. She clung to him like he might vanish if she lessened her hold, but he'd never complain about being crushed in her embrace.

As soon as he closed the apartment door behind them—the same one she'd stayed in—Talia sighed.

Alone at last.

And still breathing.

"I'm going to put you down so I can lock the door. Okay?"

"Yeah." She unwound her legs from his waist and slid to the floor. Once she was steady on her feet, they released each other.

She silently waited while he secured the deadbolt. If it took him longer than usual, she didn't comment. He needed the extra time to get his emotions in check. To figure out whether he wanted to wring her neck for putting herself in danger or kiss her until she ran out of breath for wanting to protect him.

In the end, what he'd decided didn't matter. As soon as he turned back to face her, Talia took his hand and led him to the small bathroom. The determined gleam in her eye had him following without question.

She pushed him into the bathroom before her and turned on the shower. Steam filled the room within seconds, thanks to Curly's purchase of high-end tankless water heaters.

"I don't need a shower right now, Tal," he said as she returned to him. "We need to talk about what hap—"

"We both need a shower." She reached for his jeans and unbuttoned then unzipped the fly. He gritted his teeth as her knuckles grazed his dick. "We fucked multiple times last night, Pulse," she said with a sly grin. "We're pretty filthy."

Jesus. With her hands at his crotch and her dirty mouth, he didn't have a chance of preventing the erection. His cock swelled as she shoved his jeans over his ass.

"No underwear." She tsked. "Like I said, filthy."

"Talia..." The woman was playing a dangerous game. After the chaos of the previous night, realizing she'd run off that morning, then finding her under his brother's gun, he was riding the edge of sanity and control. It wouldn't take more than a nudge to tumble him over the edge.

"Shh." She sank to her knees and went to work on his boots.

His cock bobbed right in front of her fucking face like it was reaching for her damn mouth. He stared at the ceiling and counted to ten while he fisted his hands at his sides and prayed for control. "Step out." She patted his outer thigh as she stood.

"Talia, this is fucking nuts. You were just held at gunpoint." The word nearly choked him. "We need to talk. You need to break down or some shit. And I need to tell you how stupid it was to... oh fuck."

She nipped his lower lip—hard. His dick fucking loved it. Precum leaked from the tip and rolled down his shaft. Goddamn needy organ wouldn't let his brain run the show.

"What I need..." she said as she wrapped her hand around his cock.

His eyes slammed shut. "Jesus."

"Is for you to step in the shower so I can clean you off, then drop to my knees and suck you off."

Her words punched him low in the gut. He reached for the vanity to keep from hitting the floor.

"I want your cock in my throat, Pulse. So get in the fucking shower." She squeezed his dick until his eyes crossed.

He reached for the last vestige of strength to stop her and give her the comfort and assurances of safety she deserved when it hit him. This was Talia breaking down. She wasn't the type to curl into a ball and sob. She wouldn't want him to hold her and rock her while she lost her shit.

She wanted to take back her power. She wanted someone to control, and he was the lucky bastard to be at her mercy. Giving her this would help her get over what had happened better than forcing her to talk about how terrified she'd been. And when she was done exerting her authority over him, he'd turn the tables and eat her out until she was screaming, and not an ounce of anxiety remained.

"Yes, ma'am."

She released him, allowing him to enter the steam and warm spray. He shut his eyes and tried to regulate his breathing as he let the soothing water begin to unknot his muscles. His bruises would be sore for a few days, but he'd survived worse. After a quick rustle of clothing, Talia joined him in the shower. She frowned as she took in the purple welts marking his torso.

"I'm okay," he said. "Nothing more than some aches and

tenderness."

She nodded but still wore a frown of disapproval. Time to get her mind on something else.

"God, you're so hot. Gorgeous."

She stood before him, naked and without an ounce of insecurity. Water droplets speckled her tan skin, taunting him to lick them away. Her breasts were full and heavy, lighter than the rest of her skin, with rosy nipples he wanted in his mouth STAT.

Every move she made captivated him. The stretch of her side as she reached for the body wash. The way her arm flexed as she squeezed a large orange dollop onto her palm. How her breasts swayed as she lathered the gel between her hands. The scent of tangerines filled the small space, mixing with the lingering aroma of sex on their skin.

Instead of washing him as he'd expected, she first took care of herself, sliding her soapy hands across her chest, under her arms, over the swell of her stomach, and down between her sexy legs.

"Talia, let me touch you."

She shook her head, smirking. "No. And be quiet." Her eyes practically glowed with the high of being in control. And that's what it was—she got high off the power of owning him. "Switch so I can rinse."

He'd have walked straight into shark-infested water if she'd asked him to. They maneuvered around each other, her still stroking her hands over her body in the most erotic way imaginable and him with his fingernails digging into his palms so he didn't disobey her command and put them all the fuck over her. To add to the torture, he got to watch the suds sluice over her slippery body before they swirled down the drain.

Damn lucky soap.

When she finished the X-rated show disguised as washing

herself, she switched so he was back under the spray. "Your turn," she said with a mischievous smile as she reloaded her hands with the fragrant soap.

The ultimate test came next—Talia's warm, wet, soapy hands running all over him. She started at his chest, rubbing flat-palmed circles over his pecs and cleaning his chest hair. He groaned as her fingertips grazed his nipples—which had never given a crap about being involved before and which caused her to linger there playing for a few excruciating seconds.

His cock was so hard it fucking hurt, and combined with breathing in the thick steam, he was growing lightheaded. She walked around him, trailing her hands to his back, where she treated him to a quick massage. When her hands skimmed over his ass, he braced his hands on the walls of the shower to keep from collapsing.

She lowered behind him, taking care of his thighs and calves before rising again.

"I'm fucking clean," he growled, causing her to chuckle.

"Almost." She came back around to his front.

And then her hands were on his cock, and he was groaning long and low. This was not the light, clinical touch of someone trying to wash him. It was the caressing, squeezing strokes of a damn sadist getting off on his torment. She fisted him, sliding up and down with a twist at the end while her other hand kneaded his sac.

He kept himself propped up with his palms on the side walls, letting her play and wash away any evidence of their previous sex. Those hands on him felt like heaven and hell all at once. So good but not enough. His dick leaked so much fluid there wouldn't be anything left when she finally allowed him to come.

She watched herself work. He watched as she drove him wild with her hand. His breathing sped, and his stomach muscles clenched. The hunger in her gaze stroked his desire as much as her fingers. It would have been so easy to come right then. He could have unloaded all over those curious hands without much more effort, but she'd promised him her mouth, so he pulled his lip between his teeth and bit down hard to keep from coming.

"Fresh and clean," she announced in a cheerful, teasing tone that told him she was reveling in his torment. "Now, hold still."

She lowered to her knees on the tile floor. Never had Pulse seen anything sexier than Talia at his feet with wet hair and water plastered to her head as his cock dripped two inches from her mouth. Another drop of precum beaded on the tip as she licked her lips.

"I've been dreaming of this," she whispered.

You have no fucking idea.

She rubbed her cheek against his dick, ripping a gasp from him. Then, before he could get his bearings, she had him in her mouth, sucking the tip like her favorite damn lollipop.

"Mm," she moaned. The vibrations traveled straight up his dick to his overfull balls.

This was going to be over embarrassingly fast.

Talia grabbed his thighs and pulled him deeper into her mouth. Nothing beat the intense heat and suction of her mouth.

"Fuck, Talia," he said between heavy breaths. "You're pretty with your mouth full of my cock." And she was—eyes blissed, lips stretched, cheeks flushed.

Debauched and damn beautiful.

Her response was to suck him harder. When her throat muscles contracted around the tip of his cock, his hips bucked, and he reached for her head only to be slapped away by a determined Talia. She gripped his hips and pushed, anchoring him against the shower wall.

There'd be no stripping her of a single ounce of control.

Fuck, it was so hot watching her take her power back. He was more than happy to surrender to her ravenous need for dominance. As she continued to drive him mad with forceful suction and the hypnotic slide of her lips, he clenched his fist to keep from grabbing her head. It went against his instincts to let her immobilize his hips against the wall, but he resisted the urge to fuck her face and gave himself over to her command.

She tortured him with a gentle scrape of her teeth, teased the underside of his cock with her playful tongue before sucking him to the back of her throat again and swallowing. The onslaught of varying sensations kept him on edge and dying to thrust.

Sweat poured off his body, washed away by the rushing shower.

When she moaned again, the vibrations made his legs tremble.

She was driving him fucking mad.

On the next swallow, he knew it was game over. "Shit, I'm so fucking close, Tal. You gonna swallow it, baby? You gonna suck down all my cum when I fill that pretty mouth?"

She might have him at her mercy, but his words got to her. She whimpered as she met his gaze. The sight of her blissed-out from sucking him was more than he could take. He shouted as he arched off the shower wall, overpowering her hold on his hips. The movement jammed his dick down her throat. She gagged once before recovering in time to swallow his load as his balls erupted into her mouth.

"So fucking good. Baby, you're so fucking perfect." Wave after wave of molten pleasure pulsed through him, bucking his hips and spurting his soul through his dick. Talia gripped his hips, taking every drop he had to offer.

When he finally stopped coming, she shifted off her knees

and sat on the shower floor opposite him with a sated smile as though she'd been the one to have her brains sucked out of her body. Her lips were red and swollen from the stellar job she'd performed. Where was his camera when he needed it?

"That helped," she said with a tired smirk.

Pulse barked a laugh. "It sure as fuck did. But you know what will help even more?"

She arched an eyebrow.

"Coming as hard as I just did," he said as he lowered to his knees and sat back on his heels. The hard tile bit into his skin, but he ignored the discomfort as he reached for her. He took hold of her ankles.

"What are you doing?" she asked, her tone rife with suspicion.

It was his turn to smirk. "Returning the favor, of course." He yanked, and she slid across the slippery shower floor onto her back with a yelp.

"Pulse!" The fact she could laugh so shortly after such a traumatic event had to be a good sign. "What are you doing?" she half shrieked, half laughed.

"Told you already." He slid her toward him until he could reach her ass. He grabbed it in both hands and pulled her onto his bent knees.

"Oh shit." Her legs splayed wide around him, giving him the perfect view of her soaked pussy.

He was starving for a taste, but there wasn't enough room in the tiny shower for him to get in position to dive face-first into her pussy. He settled for sliding two thick fingers into her.

"Yes." She moaned and arched her back off the floor. She pumped her hips in time with his fast fingering, chasing the epic release she deserved.

"That's it, baby, work that pussy on my fingers."

He thumbed her clit, and she whimpered. That little

vulnerable sound after she'd owned him went straight to his head. He wanted more of it. More of the Talia no one else saw. The open, exposed Talia he wanted all to himself.

"Pulse…"

His body blocked most of the shower spray, keeping her from getting waterboarded as she writhed on the slick floor. "You love it, don't you? Love me working this needy pussy. Come on, baby, tell me."

"Y-yes… I love it. It's… oh, I'm gonna come."

He'd never considered himself a sadist, but he withdrew his hand.

"No!" Talia shouted. "No, Pulse. Why?"

He flattened his hand against her lower belly. "Tell me how much you want it. Tell me how much you need me. Beg me for it."

"Pulse…" she whispered. Vulnerability flashed in her gaze, along with indecision. This was hard for her. Taking over and driving him out of his mind was easy. She loved that. Thrived on it. But turn the tables, and she was so far out of her comfort zone she might tell him to fuck off, climb out of the shower, and finish herself off in the other room.

Her silence stretched. For a few agonizing seconds, he worried he'd pushed too far. Her body quivered, hovering so close to relief.

Let me give it to you. Trust me.

As though she heard his words, she met his gaze. "I n-need you, Pulse," she whispered. "You… just you."

Once she uttered the terrifying words, she seemed to regain her confidence. She locked her ankles behind his back and tilted her pelvis up with a sly smile.

"Make me come, Pulse. I know you want back inside me. I also know if I hadn't sucked you so good, it'd be your cock inside me right now."

There she was. Pride mixed with his desire. She's just

realized that despite being flat on her back begging for the pleasure she deserved, she still had all the fucking power.

He entered her with three fingers this time. It took less than five seconds to find her G-spot. He worked it until she was thrashing on the tile and mumbling nonsense.

"Pulse... Pulse..." Never had he loved the sound of his name like he did then. He could live on that sound for years to come.

It wasn't long before her incoherent words became nothing more than moans and whimpers. Her pussy gripped his fingers as though she never wanted him to leave.

"Close, close," she shouted as she arched her hips off his thighs, driving his fingers deeper. Her palms slapped against the wet tile, and then she was coming. What a goddamn gift it was to see this woman at her most vulnerable while she writhed with pleasure on his hand. Her pussy fluttered around him, soaking his fingers as it contracted.

"P-Pulse?" she said as she slacked against the floor, looking dizzy and tired.

"I'm here. You're so damn incredible."

A choked sob burst from deep within her. She scrambled off him, dislodging his fingers, and climbed into his lap. Immediately, she wound her arms and legs around him in a stranglehold. He returned the embrace, clutching her wet, naked body to him as tight as he could.

"I'm sorry," she whispered into his neck.

"Shh, it's okay, baby." He stroked up and down her back. He'd never been a touchy person, but he wanted and needed to feel her skin as often as possible. "I was scared out of my fucking mind, but I get it. I'm sorry too. I just wanted you fucking safe."

"Me too," she mumbled against his skin.

One of the many reasons he was falling hard and fast for this rock star of a woman.

They stayed there, wrapped up in each other on the shower floor until the water ran frigid, and they began to tremble.

Then Pulse carried her to the bed, where they spent the rest of the day.

Chapter Twenty-One

If Talia told anyone she felt the safest in a place where a man had held a gun to her head three days ago, they'd have her sanity evaluated. But that's how it was. Curly and Brooke came by the apartment that night, promising Spec would not be an issue or a threat to either of them. She must be going soft because she'd believed the man. More importantly, Pulse did, too, so for the past three days, they'd stayed in the apartment on the Handlers' compound. When she had to go to work, which she often did, a prospect tailed her. Pulse, on the other hand, went to work unguarded.

The DEA call had come and been ignored four times. Her home security cameras showed the local police and a government vehicle stopping by more than once. For some reason, they stayed away from the Handlers' property.

The reprieve wouldn't last. The Del Rios man who'd wormed his way into the DEA was not stupid. He had to suspect Pulse was on to him.

At what point would he make his next move, and would it wreak havoc on the Handlers' lives?

As nice as having a place to stay on the club's property was, today could mark the last time they were welcome to the apartment. Curly had wanted to let the dust settle before he brought the news of Pulse's past employment to the entire club.

Today was that day.

Church would begin in five minutes, and Pulse would be in the hot seat while she sat in the apartment working on an ulcer.

She hated being stuffed in the corner, even if she understood why she couldn't attend. She wasn't a patched member, and they had their ways of running things. Fine, she could play by the rules, but she didn't have to like it.

Typically, she'd dive into work to take her mind off her stress, but it wasn't working today.

"Ugh." She shoved her laptop across the table and flopped back in her chair. "This is pointless." If she kept forcing herself to work, she'd make a mistake that could harm a client's case.

Maybe a workout would help. Perhaps jog around the property, and if she happened to circle the clubhouse a few dozen times, so be it.

Knock, knock.

"Shit!" Talia jolted so hard she levitated off the chair. "Uh, I'm coming." She hopped up and covered the short distance to the door. Liv and Harper stood on the other side. They were dressed casually in denim shorts and simple T-shirts, yet somehow, Liv still managed to look like a supermodel.

Her insides seized. How much did Harper know? Liv knew it all, or at least Spec's version, where Pulse was a villain out to hurt the club, with Talia operating as his sidekick. They hadn't seen each other since Liv stepped in front of a gun, sparing Talia's life.

"Hey."

Liv opened her mouth, but no words came out. The two stared at each other across a chasm of charged silence.

Harper's gaze pinged between the two before she stepped forward. "We're here to take you to Brooke's. I have no idea what's going on, but I know it's serious. You belong with us for whatever is going on."

"Oh…" She glanced at Liv before focusing on Harper. "Thank you, but I'm not sure my being there is the best idea. I'm not sure how much you heard, but—"

"Nothing. I've heard nothing. No one has told me anything, and it's driving me nuts," Harper said with a humorless chuckle. "Liv said it's your story to tell. You're one of us, so we're here to listen and support you."

"I don't know…"

Liv stepped forward and pulled Talia into a huge hug. "I'm sorry," she whispered, her voice thick with regret.

"Are you kidding me? You pretty much saved my life." Liv had nothing to apologize for. Talia would never hold Spec's actions against her.

"I'm sure you were terrified." Liv still held her tight.

"Yeah, a little. Or so much I'm surprised I didn't pee myself." She tried for a laugh, but no one joined her. Guess they were going with acknowledging their real feelings.

Ugh.

They broke apart, both sniffling and watery-eyed. Liv shook her head. "Spec wouldn't have…" She shrugged. "He's —"

"It's okay, Liv." She gripped the other woman's upper arms. "He's supposed to protect the club, and he felt I was a threat. He was just doing his job."

"Yeah, well, that's not how things are done in this club. Curly was furious. I've never seen him so mad. He threatened to rip Spec's enforcer patch off his cut and shove it up his ass."

Harper snorted. "Jinx mentioned Curly had some creative threats. He just didn't know why they were being issued."

"Don't worry," Liv said. "I expect Spec will be much more reasonable today."

"What makes you say that?" Talia couldn't imagine the enraged man had softened his approach.

Liv smirked. "I haven't let him touch me in three days, and that includes sleeping his sorry ass on the couch the last few nights. The man is going through some serious withdrawals right about now."

Harper's eyes widened. "And you think that's going to make him behave better? I made sure to give my man the BJ of his life this morning so he's all happy and agreeable."

"I, uh…" Talia blinked. These women were nuts. "I have no words."

"You don't need any." Liv linked her arm through Talia's. "Just know my man is desperate to get some, and he knows that will not be happening anytime soon if he loses his shit today. I got your back, girl. Now, slip your feet into those cute sandals and come with us. You don't need to bring anything."

It had to be better than sitting around and pretending to work while internally freaking out.

"All right. Let me grab my phone." She hustled over to the counter, grabbed her phone, and then stuffed her feet into the cute sandals Liv referenced. Together, they walked out into the warm, late-morning sunshine.

"Want me to drive us over?" Harper asked. "I've got my car here."

"I have my car, too," Talia added. She might as well contribute somehow.

"Nope." Liv marched around the barn-turned-apartments. "I have a much better idea."

"Uh, Liv…" Harper hurried after her, leaving Talia no choice but to follow.

"We're taking these." Several ATVs were parked under an overhang alongside the barn.

"Oh, I've never driven one of them before." Today probably wasn't the day to start. Wrecking one of the club's vehicles would be icing on the cake she'd already frosted with crap.

"No worries. You can ride with me."

"Um… Liv, aren't you banned from driving these?" Harper asked. She stood with her hands on her hips, assessing Liv.

"Sure am. Spec told me I couldn't drive them anymore after he caught me racing one of the prospects." Her grin didn't hold an ounce of repentance.

"Okay, so…"

"Harp, that man is on my shit list. Until he's off it, I don't have to do a damn thing he says."

"Okay, now you're speaking my language." Talia laughed for the first time that morning, and damn, it felt good. Leave it to these women to pull her away from her anxiety.

"Okay," Harper said with a shrug. "It's your funeral."

"Nah." Talia shook her head. "It won't be your funeral. It might be your ass, though. I could see that man giving you a serious spanking after this."

Liv climbed on an ATV and then peered over her shoulder with a sassy grin. "All the more reason to go for a ride, wouldn't you say?" She winked and then faced forward. "Hop on, Tal."

"Well, if I'm going to get my ass thrown off the property, I might as well go out with a bang." She started for the ATV when Harper stopped her with a hand on her arm.

"It's gonna be okay. I don't know all the details, but I know this family. They can't be broken."

She was sweet, but Harper had no idea what her ol' man was learning right then. "Thanks, but I'm afraid I put some pretty big cracks in the foundation the other day."

"Cracks can be filled in. Our guys are experts at it. Have a little faith." Harper gave Talia a quick hug before climbing on her own ATV.

Cracks could be fixed, but if Spec's reaction indicated how

the meeting would go, she wouldn't hold her breath waiting for the welcome wagon to arrive.

THE VIBE IN the clubhouse was shit. There was no other word for it. No one spoke or ragged on each other like usual. Pulse's brothers sat there casting side-eyed glances his way. Spec and Curly were the only two who knew the details, but everyone else knew they were there for something serious involving him.

Being the center of attention sucked.

He might as well have a neon sign flashing over his head and blinking the word 'asshole.'

A phone chimed, breaking the thick silence. Jinx, who sat directly across the oval table from Pulse and who happened to be next to Spec, flipped his phone over. The big guy's familiar laugh boomed into the quiet room.

"Shit, brother, I knew you were in the doghouse, but I didn't realize your woman cut you off. No wonder you've been in a shit mood the past few days. Whaddya do?"

Spec sent Jinx a glare that would have incinerated most men on the spot, but not the club's resident jokester.

"Wait, don't tell me. Let me guess. You ran over one of her five-hundred-dollar shoes with your bike?"

The scowl deepened.

"No? Okay, you left the toilet seat up?"

Spec extended one middle finger into the air.

"Okay, that's not it either. Did you bring her the wrong Starbucks order?"

Tracker snickered. "How are your balls feeling today, man?"

That had Ty chuckling as well, and soon everyone was laughing and calling out ridiculous reasons Liv would be pissed at Spec. Now, it resembled the chapel before any typical church session.

For everyone except Spec, whose face was practically smoking, and Pulse, who couldn't unglue his tongue from the roof of his mouth to participate.

When Curly arrived and asked Pulse to tell his story, he'd probably open his mouth to speak and hurl all over the table. How had Talia had the balls to talk to Spec and Curly on her own?

She was so fucking impressive.

The worst part was the way his brain kept running to the worst-case scenario, which didn't even involve someone pulling out a gun and shooting him point-blank. No, the worst case for him would be seeing a table full of horrified and disgusted eyes staring at him as though they didn't know him.

Knowing his brothers saw his past as a betrayal would be a million times worse than any physical vengeance the club could dish out.

"Thanks, guys... sorry I'm late." Curly strode into the chapel and then shut the heavy doors behind him. "Had a call from Copper up in Tennessee."

"No worries, boss," Jinx said. "I was just telling everyone how I learned Spec's ol' lady cut him off because he did something dickish."

Curly's gaze landed on Pulse for a beat before returning to Jinx. "I'd expect nothing less from you, Jinx."

"You know me well, Prez." Jinx sat back in his chair, folding his arms over his chest with a satisfied smirk.

"All right, I don't wanna drag down the fun, but I gotta take shit to a serious place for now." Curly stood in front of his chair at the head of the table. All eyes focused on him. The man had the respect, loyalty, and love of every man in the room. Never had someone been more deserving of the president's patch on their chest.

"Before I turn this over to Pulse because it is his story to tell, I want to make a few things perfectly fucking clear, hear me?"

"Shit," Jinx muttered. His typical snark disappeared, replaced by a solemn nod. "We hear you, Prez."

"You asses stay in your seats, and your mouths stay fucking shut. We have a way of doing things in this club, and violence against a brother will not be tolerated. Is that clear?"

He stared straight at Spec as he spoke.

That's right, asshole, he's looking at you.

"Clear, Prez," Spec ground out through clenched teeth.

Such enthusiasm.

This was fucked before Pulse even opened his mouth.

"One more thing," Curly planted his palms on the table, leaning forward. "I wasn't going to say this at first because I don't want to sway anyone's opinion, but I think you can all speak your mind even if you disagree with me, so I'm gonna say my piece. I have Pulse's back, and I support him in this."

Oh shit.

His chest tightened to the point of uncomfortable. He wanted to thank his president, but his lungs wouldn't expand to draw in air so he could speak.

Across the table, Jinx frowned. "Think it goes without saying, Prez, that we all have his back too."

"Might wanna wait till you fucking hear what's going on," Spec muttered.

Jinx's expression went from concerned to downright panicked.

"We're ready to hear it," Ty said. "Whatever it is."

"The floor is yours, Pulse." Curly sat and reached for his scotch.

If ever there was a time for liquid courage, this was it. Pulse had been dumb to skip pouring himself a drink. Jinx must have sensed his unease because he pushed his whisky across the table. "Drink up, brother."

"Thanks." He slammed back the few swallows of whisky and then cleared his throat. "I appreciate you all hearing me out. I'm just gonna rip the Band-Aid off and say the shitty part straight-up. I spent about a decade, most of my twenties, working as a federal agent for the Drug Enforcement Agency."

The only sound was that of jaws hitting the floor.

Everyone stared at him as though they'd never seen him before and with varying degrees of disgust.

Fuck it. Getting shot by Spec had to be less painful than this.

"Wanna run that by us again?" Jinx asked. He stuck a finger in his ear and mimed cleaning it out. "Couldn'ta heard you right. Sounded like you said once upon a time, you were a cop."

Pulse's shoulders slumped. "You heard right. I was a fed. DEA for ten years. I worked undercover mostly, infiltrating the Del Rios Cartel."

The admission seemed to have stunned Jinx silent, which was no easy task.

But it didn't last long.

"Well, fuck me in the ass."

Chapter Twenty-Two

"Keep going," Jo said as Brooke refilled her glass. "After that news, I'm going to need all the help I can get. You know what, give me the whole damn pitcher." She motioned for Brooke to hand over the pretty glass pitcher with etched palm trees.

"Hell no." Harper shoved Jo's hand aside. "You think you're the only one who needs a drink after that? Top me off, Brooke."

"Screw this." Liv got up from her chair and hustled into the house, only to return twenty seconds later carrying three bottles of champagne.

"Yes. Now we're talking. Gimme one of those." Jo motioned for Liv to hand over a bottle."

Talia blinked. What the hell was happening?

"Here…" Jo filled her flute to the tippy top with champagne, then handed the bottle to Talia. "Drink from the bottle. You need this more than any of us, I'm sure."

"Um… it's eleven." How much were they planning to drink?

The ladies stopped moving and stared at her with affronted expressions. How was it that her refusal of day drinking earned her a more extreme reaction than the twenty-minute story she'd just told about Pulse's past and the current Del Rios threat?

Is this what Pulse was going through, or was his experience less surreal and more violent? Her stomach cramped each time she thought of him in there with his brothers. If even one reacted as Spec did, Pulse could be in serious trouble.

Why had she agreed to come?

"What did we tell you when we sat down, Talia?" Liv jammed her hands on her hips.

"Um…"

"We said it doesn't count as *drinking* if it's mimosas."

"Sure, but it's still—"

"Shh, it's best to just smile and nod." Kelsie, who seemed more subdued than the rest of these women, leaned over and whispered in Talia's ear. "Sometimes it's better if you just let her think she's winning."

"Heard that," Liv announced. "But she's not wrong."

Talia glanced between her empty glass and the chilled champagne Jo still held out.

"Oh, fuck it." The ladies cheered as she took the champagne and filled her glass.

Harper topped her off with about a teaspoon of orange juice. "See, mimosa."

"Sure it is." Everyone laughed, which only made the entire situation more confusing. "You guys did hear me, right? You heard what I said?"

"We did." Jo raised her glass. "Hence the extra drinking, remember?"

"Okay, so aren't you upset? I mean, don't you wanna cuss me out or something? I mean, Spec…" Maybe she shouldn't criticize one of the ol' men right to his woman's face.

"Spec acted like an ape." Liv sipped her drink. "Actually, I think a gorilla would have handled the news better."

"Here's the thing." Harper reached across the table for a

cheese cube as she talked. "Our men are fantastic. They treat us like queens, they're protective, they have great dicks…"

"Here, here."

"That's right, girl!"

"You know it."

She had to be in an alternate universe. It was the only explanation for these women.

"But they're still men," Harper concluded. "Very often, their little brain makes it hard for them to use their big brain." She pointed to her crotch and then her head with flair, as though in some strange one-woman show.

"That is the damn truth," Jo added. "I love Tracker, but the man can be a Neanderthal."

"This is not making me feel better about how things are going for Pulse right now."

Kelsie put her arm around Talia's shoulder and pulled her in for a side hug.

She had the craziest urge to bawl all over the woman's shoulder, but she shoved it down and tried for a smile that probably looked like she had gas.

Was Pulse okay?

"I don't want to speak for everyone…" Kelsie said, "… but I trust Pulse. The guy rescued me after a very bad… experience."

Harper reached across the table and squeezed Kelsie's hand. The women exchanged a sad smile.

"Anyway, I was in rough shape… injured, traumatized, scared, and in pain. Pulse checked me out before I went to the hospital, and he was incredible. His patients rave about how he's the best nurse they've ever had. That man is a healer, and there is no way to convince me otherwise. I don't believe for a second he has anything but the club's best interest at heart."

"We all love Pulse," Brooked added. "Most of us have wondered about his past because he keeps to himself more than the others. He's part of the group but stays on the outskirts. Now, I understand why. What a huge burden it must have been to carry this secret."

Jo nodded. "Not that I'm condoning secrets, but I understand why he kept quiet. They wouldn't have let him patch in if they knew." She shrugged. "As a former police officer, I understand the complexity of straddling both worlds, though it sounds like he's left that life completely behind."

Could it be this easy to have the women's support?

"Yeah, when he quit five years ago, he cut all ties. And they don't actually want him back. He made his feelings about them known. This is all part of a chess game orchestrated by the rebuilding cartel."

"Okay," Brenna spoke up for the first time. "This means they'll be getting serious about safety, and things might get sticky for a while. We're ready. We can handle whatever this cartel throws our way."

Jo polished off her mimosa. "Fuck yes, we can."

"You're assuming they won't vote to strip Pulse of his patch."

Or kill him.

"Nah." Jo waved away the statement as though it wasn't a concern. "They might be Neanderthals, but they won't turn their back on family. Pulse is family."

If only she had Jo's confidence.

"But Spec…"

"Look…" Liv sighed. "Like most of us here, Spec came to the club broken. He's been through things that would make most of us lose our minds. This club put him back together."

"And you, girl," Brooke said, smiling at Liv. "Most of it was you."

Shrugging, Liv nodded. "I do love that man, but some pieces are held together with chewing gum and a wish."

"I know how that goes," Kelsie muttered.

One day, Talia hoped she'd hear Kelsie's full story.

"I'm not excusing what he did the other day. And I never will. What he did wasn't right. But he has his reasons. He'll come around. It might take some time, but he'll see that Pulse belongs in this club."

"I understand, Liv. I really do. And thank you all. I'm used to going it alone, so your support is incredible and new for me."

"Ha, you'll never be alone again now that you have us. We're all up in each other's business all day long. It's what we call co-dependent in my professional world," Harper sing-songed. The mimosas were clearly going to her head.

"Hey, don't make our love for each other sound unhealthy," Jo called.

They really were a tight unit.

"Well, whatever you call it, I'm grateful. If you'd left me alone in that apartment, I'd have probably burst in on church and made everything ten times worse by now. So, thanks. And I'm sorry if I'm not much fun today. I'm just worried about Pulse and won't be able to settle until I see him. We've gotten… uh…" Oh my God, was she about to tell these women she was sleeping with Pulse? "Close."

"Yeah, you have," Jo said with a whoop. "Somebody's in lo-ove."

"What?" Talia practically shouted the word. Love? Hell no. Not love. Never love. She barely knew the man. What a ridiculous thing for Jo to say.

"Look at her," Harper fake whispered to Jo. "I think you broke her brain."

"No. I'm good. It's just… I'm definitely not in love."

"Mm-hmm." Jo saluted Talia with her glass. "Pretty sure we all said that at one point." She snickered as she reached for the champagne bottle.

Brooke, ever the mama of the group, shook her head. "Let it go, Jo."

Love. How silly. They were just close. That's all.

"*Let it go, let it go,*" Jo sang at the top of her lungs before frowning at her once-again full glass. This time, she hadn't bothered to add even a drop of orange juice. "I may have had too many of these."

"You think?" Harper asked, straight-faced.

And just like that, the tension burst, and everyone went back to laughing as though they'd met up for a fun brunch instead of waiting on their men to finish deciding Pulse's fate.

Talia tried to play along. She smiled and said the right things at the right times. She laughed when everyone else did and cooed over Brooke's adorable dog. She even shared a juicy detail when the conversation turned to bedroom activities.

But her heart wasn't in it today. It was across the Handlers' property in the clubhouse, enduring God knew what.

But that didn't mean she was in love. She merely worried about the man because he was a client and a good friend.

And if you believe that one, I've got an island to sell you in the Caribbean.

MAINTAINING EYE CONTACT with his brothers while he told his story was one of the most excruciating things Pulse had ever done. Seeing how their expressions changed from curiosity and confusion to anger to disgust had him fighting the urge to stare down at the table while he spoke. Hot shame prickled his skin like a full-body tattoo machine as he sat beneath their harsh stares.

"So, Talia and I have been staying here the past few nights. The DEA and the cartel must have an idea where we are, but so far, no one has shown up here. I can only assume they're planning something. So…"

Every man in the room gaped at him with varying degrees of shock and horror on their face. There it was again, the intense urge to avert his gaze. Strength didn't keep him sitting straight, nor did some internal sense of right and wrong. He kept his gaze up for one reason—his brothers deserved it. At the very least, they deserved to be told the truth with full respect and accountability.

Jinx broke the silence first. "So, uh... fuck, man, were you ever gonna tell us?"

Of course. Yes. Definitely. The lies could fall so easily from his lips.

"No. You might not believe me now, but that part of my life has been over for a long time. I don't associate with anyone from my time there."

"Mm." Jinx glanced at Spec. "And this is what's had you all fucked for the past few days?"

"Can you blame me?" It didn't seem Spec's hatred had cooled in the slightest. "He was a fucking fed. Everyone went through a background check before they patched in. A damn thorough one. If that shit wasn't there, he went through some serious fucking trouble to make it disappear. Bullshit, he doesn't still have fed buddies willing to suck his dick if he asks."

Jinx looked back at Pulse with a raised eyebrow as though asking for his response.

"I have one remaining contact from back then. Not a fed. Not affiliated with the government in any way. Quite the opposite. He's a hacker whose ass I saved back when we were in fucking elementary school. He's loyal to me, but I can honestly say his mouth has never been near my dick."

"Fuck you," Spec spat.

"All right." Curly lifted a hand. "Here's how this is gonna go. Any of you have questions for Pulse, you can ask them now. Then, we vote on whether or not Pulse stays in the club.

Majority wins. If he's in, this issue is squashed right now. As in fucking over, and you do not hold this shit over Pulse's head. Ever." He stared at Spec as he spoke.

"If it goes the other way..."

Pulse's heart thumped so loud he almost missed Curly's next words.

"He's out, but no harm will come to him. That's my final decision. You have a problem with it, you can follow him out the door." His gaze bounced from member to member as he spoke. His serious tone left no room for argument.

It was more than Pulse deserved.

Spec seethed in his chair.

No one would walk out if they disagreed with the vote. Pulse wouldn't let them. He'd quit before one of his brothers voluntarily left or their tempers got them kicked out of the club for something he did—even Spec. He wouldn't be responsible for screwing up his family more than he already had.

"How big a threat do you think the cartel is?" Ty asked as he rested his elbows on the table.

"I think they want to destroy the whole club. Since they've infiltrated the DEA, they have the power to arrest me for whatever the fuck they want. If they do, I'll disappear and never be heard from again. Then they'll dismantle the club with some bogus felony drug charges."

"Well then, I think the solution is simple," Spec said with an evil smirk.

Jinx frowned at him. "Really? You wanna hand your brother over to a drug cartel? You ever seen the shit they do to people?"

Shrugging, Spec folded his arms across his chest. "I survived torture. Maybe he will too."

"That ain't right, man." Jinx shook his head.

"What isn't right is him lying to us." Spec leaned forward,

practically snarling across the table at Pulse. "Give me one good fucking reason to believe you're not lying now."

What could he say?

Because you used to trust me.

Because it was a lie of omission.

I promise I'm telling the truth.

All his justifications fell flat.

"You can believe him because he's a good man," Ty said.

Spec scoffed. "You, too, VP? This is fucking insanity."

"He's never done anything to hurt his club, Spec."

"He—"

"I'm not done." Ty didn't often exert his authority, but his tone cracked like a whip into the room.

Spec shut his mouth.

"We started this club what, two, two and a half years ago? How many times has Pulse had our backs? How many times has he patched us up? How many of our women has he helped through—" Ty swallowed.

His ol' lady had suffered at the hands of human traffickers. She was doing well now, but it had been scary for a time, and those days would remain scarred in Ty's mind for the rest of his life.

He cleared his throat. "How many times has he helped our women through some serious shit? And now, the second his past might threaten this club, he's here willing to sacrifice himself."

Pulse's face burned. Ty made him sound like a damn martyr. All he wanted was to keep his brothers and their women safe. "VP, I'm not—"

Ty lifted his hand. "No, look..." He stood, his face fierce and dark. "I get it, Spec, you're butt hurt because this shit took you by surprise. But really fucking think about it. He didn't have to tell us shit. He came to you and Curly because he's worried about us and our ol' ladies. And he did it, knowing full well what you might do to him."

"Or he's in over his head and might as well see if we're willing to help his ass out. Or he's setting us up. There's more than one possibility, VP."

Ty shrugged as he sat. "Guess that's why we're voting then. So we can all decide for ourselves which possibility is most likely."

Christ, he couldn't take it anymore. "Look..." It was Pulse's turn to stand. "Regardless of how you all vote today, in my mind, you're my brothers. You can be pissed at me for as long as you need to come to terms with this shit. Bottom line, I'm not DEA any longer, and there isn't a goddamn thing they can say or do to make me go back."

"No?" Spec asked. "What if they get their hands on Talia? You saying you wouldn't give them exactly what they wanted to save her ass?"

He almost laughed. Spec didn't know Talia at all if he thought she wouldn't kick his ass worse than any outlaw biker if he did what Spec proposed.

"No," he said.

"Bullshit."

Fuck this. He'd taken Spec's anger and hatred for the past three days because he felt he deserved it, and it would keep the peace in the club. Everyone knew now, and the peace shattered. "I wouldn't have to." He leaned toward Spec, allowing his anger and frustration to flood his veins. "I'd turn to my club for help. The fucking club I pledged my life to. The club I've goddamn bled for. Same as you." He shouted the words in Spec's face.

They squared off across the table like two snorting bulls ready to lock horns.

Spec's eyes were wild in a way he'd only seen a few times from his enforcer. The time Liv's ex attacked her came to mind. He curled his fists as his nostrils flared.

One of those fists would no doubt be flying his way in seconds.

Pulse rolled his shoulders. Taking a hit was always worse if he tensed. He wouldn't fight Spec, but his brother probably had a punch that would send him flying across the room, and he wouldn't hesitate to throw it.

"Enough!" Jinx hollered. The man had a bullhorn voice without shouting. When he put force behind it, he could shatter eardrums. He put his hand on Spec's shoulder and shoved the man back into his chair.

"Sit your ass down," he barked as he pointed Pulse's way. "Both of you."

He dropped his ass into the seat as commanded.

"Ji—"

"No! You've said your piece, Spec, and we all get it. You're fucking pissed. Now we're gonna vote like the prez said. Then we're gonna put this shit behind us. I'll go first."

Pulse held his breath as Jinx turned his way. "You're my brother. You kept me fucking sane when Harper was in the hospital. I trust you, and I vote you keep your patch."

Spec scoffed while Pulse swallowed a lump of emotion.

"Same for me," Ty said. "After the way you helped Kelsie, I couldn't vote against you. I trust you too."

Pulse blinked. Christ, this was embarrassing as hell.

Tracker was next. He played with the new lip ring he'd gotten a few weeks ago, nodding. "I vote to keep you. We all got a fucking past. Your actions speak for themselves."

And around the table they went, each man stating their vote. So far, every single man had voiced their desire to have Pulse as a brother.

It was more than he could have hoped for and probably more than he deserved. When it was finally Spec's turn, the man looked Pulse dead in the eye. "I think you're an expert at going undercover to infiltrate an organization. I want you gone."

It hurt. A sharp ache stabbed through his chest even though he'd known which way Spec would vote.

No one said anything for a few seconds. Not even Jinx had an obnoxious quip to break the tension. After a few heavy moments, Curly stood. "My vote goes with Pulse, and that means the majority vote is that he keeps his patch. This is over. Fucking dead and buried. Now, we move on to the best way to keep this club safe and get off the cartel's radar." He swung his gaze Spec's way. "That means I need my enforcer on board. You gonna be able to make peace with this, Spec?"

For a moment, one of the worst of Pulse's life, he was certain Spec would flip off the room and storm out. Exhaustion swamped him. This one morning felt like it lasted an entire week. As Spec finally spoke, Pulse stared at a small nick on the wooden table.

"You can count on me, Prez." Spec said the right words, but his sarcastic tone did little to bolster Pulse's confidence.

"All right." Curly nodded, running a hand through his loose curls. "We got more to discuss, but I think we can all use a break."

"And a fucking drink," Jinx muttered.

"Everyone, take the day. I want you all here for breakfast tomorrow." He glanced at Spec. "No exceptions."

After agreeing, Pulse shot out of his chair and nearly sprinted from the clubhouse. The place that had been his refuge for the past few years suddenly felt like a cage whose walls shrank every few minutes.

He burst out on the gorgeous sunny day. It didn't seem fair to have dark storm clouds swirling inside him while the outdoors was picture-perfect. The day called for darkness and thunder. Mother Nature had decided to fuck with him.

He jogged down the steps and turned toward the renovated barn. He needed Talia in his arms, and he needed it now—the one good thing in his day.

"Hey!" Spec's voice had Pulse's spine stiffening.

He slowed to a stop and turned. Was this it? Would his enforcer lay him out flat and dance on his battered body?

Spec stomped down the steps and straight to Pulse.

He braced, ready for the hit.

But it never came, at least not in the form of a fist. Instead, Spec leaned close. "I won't kill you because it's what Curly wants. We can coexist in the club but stay the fuck away from me and stay the fuck away from my woman. Got it?"

Pulse nodded. "Yeah. I got it."

"Good. Now get the fuck outta my way."

Spec rammed him with his shoulder as he stormed by.

Pulse stayed where he was, watching his former friend peel out of the lot in a spray of dust and gravel.

He'd won. The vote went his way. Only one man voted against him. He should be celebrating.

Then why did he feel so defeated?

Chapter Twenty-Three

What the hell was taking so long?

Liv had dropped Talia back at the apartment five minutes ago with strict instructions to stay away from the clubhouse.

"Let the guys work it out their way," she'd said with a sympathetic smile.

"I don't like to be put on the sidelines," Talia had responded.

Liv had laughed at her. "Really? I hadn't noticed."

Right.

Well, subtlety didn't have to be everyone's strong suit. Talia was a problem solver. A fixer. She'd never apologized for it before and wouldn't today.

Once Liv left, Talia realized how much gratitude she owed the women for keeping her distracted over the past hour and a half. After five minutes alone, she was practically climbing the walls. If she'd been left to her own devices the entire time, Pulse might have returned to a pile of rubble where the apartment once stood.

Heavy footsteps outside the door had her stopping mid-pace. The door opened, and there he was. Pulse filled the doorway, tall, dark, and handsome, with a hint of danger and power that she'd always avoided. On paper, a man like him wouldn't mix with her. He was strong, assertive, a former fed, and a current outlaw biker. The type of man she typically bucked against on principle.

Yet the second she saw him, her breath caught, and butterflies filled her stomach.

She wanted him on a cellular level—wanted to be close enough to breathe his air, wanted to touch him, and wanted to do nothing but exist near him.

What was that?

"Hi," she whispered because she couldn't think of anything to say.

He started at her with an intensity that had her nipples hardening and her pussy fluttering.

"Um... are you... did they..." How did she ask the man if his entire life had been turned upside down?

"I'm not going anywhere." He stepped into the apartment. "Unanimous vote minus one."

Oh, thank God.

"Spec?"

He nodded.

"I'm sorry."

Pulse didn't respond. His steps lengthened, and in two seconds, he stood directly before her. The now-familiar scent of his fresh cologne had her inhaling like it was the last breath she'd ever take.

He gripped the back of her neck and pulled her in until their lips nearly touched.

And just like that, she was wet and trembling. What came next would feel so good. It did every time—his hands on her, his mouth on her, his cock inside her. She wanted to shove him back and demand he strip so she could have her way with him, but she also wanted to see where he would take this. To let him take the lead and take control of her body, something she'd never wanted and vowed she'd never give to a man.

But she trusted him completely. It was the scariest and most exhilarating realization.

"Pulse," she said, brushing their lips in the barest kiss.

"All I could think about was getting back to you," he whispered. "I cared more about that than the fucking vote."

Her knees weakened, and she grabbed his cut for support. This man would be her undoing.

"You gonna let me have you?"

God, the fact that he asked. He had her at his mercy, a quivering mess of need he could take advantage of, but he'd never. He asked because he knew her and what mattered.

"You gonna let me inside this beautiful body? In the one place where everything makes sense. The one place I know I belong, and I never want to fucking leave because it's as close to fucking heaven as I'll ever get."

"Pulse, please."

She could feel his smile against her lips. "Yes?"

"Yes. So much, yes. All the yes."

Their lips met in a slow, deep, soul-changing kiss she lost control of straightaway. Pulse held her where he wanted her and helped himself to her mouth as though it was custom-designed for him. And she supposed it was No man had ever kissed her so thoroughly, and she couldn't imagine letting another try in the future.

He swept his tongue into her mouth, gliding it along hers. She chased him when it retreated, only to be rewarded with another taste of him. He kissed her until she clenched his sides so hard she risked puncturing his cut with her nails. He curled his hand in her hair, which gave him complete control of where she went. One light tug had her chin tilting up. He took full advantage of her exposed neck, attacking the soft skin with nips and brutal kisses.

"You taste like champagne," he whispered when he reached her ear.

"Uh… oh God…"

He sucked her earlobe.

"The girls…"

"That was nice of them."

"Uh-huh."

What was he talking about?

He sucked the side of her neck beneath her jawline with enough sting to leave a mark.

Talia moaned and squirmed. Her panties were soaked, and she ached with an emptiness that couldn't be ignored much longer. Pulse must have sensed her desperation. He kicked her legs apart with one booted foot and stepped forward, pressing his thigh between hers. Talia needed no instruction as to what to do next. She ground her pussy against his denim-covered leg, brazen in her quest for relief.

Pulse worked his hands under her T-shirt. As soon as he found skin, she sighed in relief.

"You like my hands on you?" he asked as he stroked up and down her back with those warm, roughened fingers.

"I love when you touch me."

"Yeah?" He pushed her wireless bra up, releasing her breasts. "That's good because I can't seem to keep them off you." He brushed his thumbs back and forth over her nipples. She arched into him with a soft moan.

"You can touch me whenever you want."

"Yeah?" He increased the pressure, drawing another moan from her. "What about in public, where everyone will know you're mine? Can I touch you then? Show all the fuckers out there who you belong to?" He pinched her nipples.

She should have been horrified that a man wanted to claim her. Instead, she was trying to hold off on coming from his words alone.

"Show everyone who *I* belong to," he said in a low rumble.

Their gazes locked, and she didn't dare breathe. What was

he asking?

"What do you say?" he asked, still playing with her nipples, which made it nearly impossible to think. "You want to be my ol' lady?"

Her heart skipped a damn beat. "And you'll be my ol' man?"

"Only way it works," he said with the first grin she'd seen from him all day.

"Yeah, Pulse. I want that. I really want that."

Together, they worked her shirt and bra over her head. It took five times as long as it should because they couldn't separate their mouths long enough to complete the task.

Whatever, they weren't in a rush. They had all afternoon to celebrate.

Once she was bare from the waist up, Talia went to work on Pulse's clothes. She slid her hands into his cut, easing it off his shoulders. He caught it as it slipped down his arms, then tossed it over a kitchen chair. His T-shirt was next. Pulse grabbed a handful of fabric behind his back and tugged it over his head in a way women drooled over.

Various tattoos covered his body, detailing his life story before he met her. A lifelike motorcycle with flames shooting from the rear wheel adorned his entire right ribcage. A medical symbol she recognized as representing his career as a nurse ran the length of his left side. He had a storm cloud near his collarbone with six numbers inked inside. A date. The day Camila died and when he walked away from his former life if she had to guess.

He backed her through the small apartment toward the bed. The whole time, she ran her hands along his torso, tracing tattoos and absorbing the solid strength beneath her fingertips. When her calves hit the bed, he reached for the button on her denim shorts. Every time his knuckles brushed her lower belly, she shivered in anticipation.

Once nothing remained of her clothing but a heap on the floor, Pulse started on his jeans. She followed as he shoved them down his hips, running her hands down to his cock where she took him in her fist.

Pulse hissed, and his pupils flared as his stomach muscles contracted. What a rush to elicit such a strong reaction with nothing but the touch of her hand. She stroked him from root to tip, mesmerized by the pleasure playing across his face. His eyes darkened, and his nostrils flared as he clenched his fists at his sides. How he visibly struggled to hold himself in check and let her do as she pleased was a thrill like no other.

Her mouth watered, so she started to lower to her knees.

"Another time." Pulse caught her under her arms. "I'll fucking lose it in two seconds, and I want to be in your pussy when I come."

As though stating it's agreement, her pussy clenched.

"Bare?" she whispered.

He raised an eyebrow. "Your call."

They'd talked about it at length. Both were clean and hadn't been with anyone else in that way. Talia had been on birth control for years to regulate her cycle. Did she want him to be the first man to fuck her without a condom? Did she want to feel his cum inside her, dripping out when they finished?

"Yes. I want it."

He groaned. "Lie on the bed."

The dark promise in his voice had her limbs shaking as she sat on the bed and then scooted up to the pillows. The sheet's soft cotton felt cool on her overheated skin. Pulse watched every move she made with hungry eyes. He'd taken over stroking his cock in an intoxicating show. All those muscles and tattoos moving as he slowly pleasured himself could make him millions if he ever had the urge to film himself.

"Spread your legs."

She did as he asked so quickly it was almost comical.

"Christ." He swallowed. "I can see how fucking wet you are. Your pussy is soaked for me."

"I want you," she whispered. "I always want you."

"Fuck, I'm a lucky bastard." He released himself, chuckling at her pout, then crawled onto the bed between her legs. Starting at her ankles, he worked his hands up her legs in a torturous combination of massage and light, tickling touches. Talia fought to keep from squirming. When he reached her inner thighs, he walked his fingertips across the sensitive skin, and her back bowed off the bed.

She bit her lower lip and watched as his gaze zeroed in on her sex. The air felt thick and charged with electricity. She could almost hear crackling and popping as it sizzled around them.

Pulse scooted up and smoothed his hands across her lower belly and down to her sex, where he used his thumbs to part her folds, all while staring as though transfixed.

"So pretty," he whispered.

Never had her body been so exposed. If any other man had ever wanted to stare at her pussy this way, she'd have burst out laughing and kicked their ass to the curb.

But not Pulse. With him, it felt symbolic. Her body was as open and exposed to him as her heart. His for the taking, and he treated both with reverence and, dare she hope, love?

As much as she wanted him inside her and wanted to come, she never wanted this moment to end. Something shifted between them this afternoon. They'd created a bond, a connection that felt permanent and unbreakable as though their souls had merged.

If anyone had told her they felt that way about their significant other, she'd have politely smiled and nodded while internally rolling her eyes and vomiting. Talia spent her adult years convinced the love people wrote poems about was nothing more than a flight of fancy.

But right then, she understood.

And she was safe in that understanding because Pulse would never reveal her secrets.

He pressed a slick thumb to her clit, shocking a bolt of pleasure through her core. She lifted her hips in a silent invitation.

Further foreplay wasn't necessary. All she wanted was to be joined with him in every way she could think of. He rose on his knees and fisted himself again. Talia bent her legs to give him better access. She kept her gaze locked with his as he ran the tip of his dick through her wetness.

"Pulse…"

He fitted himself against her pussy, then pushed in— slowly. So slowly, it felt like he'd never bottom out. Every inch that sank into her brought a heightened pleasure. Part of her wanted to grab his hips and yank him fully inside her, but a more significant part wanted to stay in suspended need for as long as possible. It was the most delicious place to be, experiencing ecstasy while knowing there was still more to come.

She reached for him, and he captured her hands, then pressed them to the mattress by her head. The move had him looming over her.

"Kiss me," she whispered, letting her desperation bleed through her voice. "I want to feel you everywhere."

He did as she asked. Their lips met as he bottomed out inside her. She moaned into his mouth, and he greedily swallowed the sound. Pulse pressed her into the mattress with his firm body as he fucked into her at an unhurried pace.

She got what she asked for. She could feel him along the entire length of her body as well as inside her. Even their feet were hooked around each other in an embrace. Their legs slid against each other as he slowly thrust in and out of her pussy. Every movement made his solid chest brush against her nipples, and his stomach muscles flex against her softer belly. He held her arms captive against the bed, and their mouths licked and sucked in a passionate dance.

No part of her was neglected. Even their hearts seemed to beat against each other in a synchronized rhythm.

Time no longer mattered as they kissed, fucked, and shared the same breath. Instead of ramping up toward a consuming orgasm, Talia floated on a cloud high in the sky for what felt like hours. When she finally came, wave after wave of pleasure crested over her while she stared into the eyes of the man she could finally admit to herself she loved.

Chapter Twenty-Four

As usual, Talia left work late, but to her surprise, she found Spec sitting astride his motorcycle in her office's parking lot three days later. As the only vehicle besides hers in the parking lot, it was impossible to call his presence a coincidence.

She slowed as she exited the building. Was he there to finish the job and take her out of the equation? While he hadn't spoken to Pulse or her in the days since the club's vote, she'd been told he'd agreed to Curly's demand of civility.

Was it a lie to get her to let down her guard?

Was this revenge for what he believed was Pulse's betrayal?

"What are you doing here?" she called across the twenty or so feet that separated them.

His eyes flared with a hint of pride.

That's right, asshole, I won't cower to you or anyone.

He lifted his hands in surrender. "Relax. I mean you no harm." Then he shifted to reveal Liv sitting behind him on the bike.

"Surprise!" she said with a sunny grin. "I'm here to take you to drinks with the ladies. You'll take me since I rode with this lug, but you know what I mean."

"Oh, that sounds nice." She could use a few drinks after the day she had. Three hearings and one failed mediation with a defiant abuser who's made it his life's mission to make his divorce as contentious as possible. Maybe she could get the club to put a little discreet pressure on him.

Wow, after only a few weeks of dating a biker, she'd crossed to the dark side.

"Of course, it's nice. We're a fantastic time." Liv climbed off the bike, then took her helmet off before laying a long, passionate kiss on Spec. Guess she was through icing him out.

"Where's Lug?" she asked of the prospect who'd been on guard duty earlier. Talia didn't step any closer to Spec. Liv could come to her. Maybe down the road, she'd be comfortable around the man, but the memory of his gun against her temple was too fresh to be relaxed with him in her personal space.

"Sent him home." Spec grinned. "I'll tail you ladies to the bar and hang while you get sloshed. I imagine Pulse is hearing about it right now and will be here to rip me a new one before we get the chance to ride out of the lot."

Frowning, she glanced at the quiet road leading from the office.

No Pulse yet.

"I thought you wanted nothing to do with us." She folded her arms across her chest as Liv sashayed her way. It was the only accurate word to describe the woman's confident, sophisticated gait.

"I don't."

"*Spec.*" Liv huffed.

He shrugged. "It's true. But Livy wants to go out, and she wants you there, which means I go too."

Rolling her eyes, Liv slipped her arm through Talia's. "He's a little cavemanish when it comes to my safety. Come on.

Let's go meet the others."

"Am I dressed okay?" Talia asked as she looked down at her black pencil skirt and cream silk camisole. She could lose the cardigan for a bit of a more casual look, but the outfit screamed attorney.

"Yes, of course. You always look fantastic." Liv waved her concern away as though the woman didn't resemble a damn supermodel in her leather miniskirt and hot pink crop top. Talia wanted to hate her, but Liv made it damn impossible.

"All right. Let's do it. That's me down there," she said, pointing to her car at the far end of the lot. She always parked under the streetlamp at the end so clients could take the spots closer to the building.

"I'll be right behind you," Spec called. "Don't try to lose me."

Talia rolled her eyes. "I'm not an idiot," she mumbled.

"C'mon." Liv, the peacemaker, glared what seemed like a warning look at her old man before tugging Talia down the sidewalk toward her car. "Brooke texted and said they got a table. We picked a place close to here. It's only about a five-minute drive," she said as they reached Talia's vehicle.

"Perf—"

A sharp staccato cut through the night air.

"What the hell?" Liv started to turn just as a pain-filled grunt left her man. "Spec!" she screamed. "Oh my God," she shrieked, instantly hysterical. "Talia, he's been shot!"

Talia watched in horror as Spec crumbled to the ground next to his motorcycle. The bike provided the only protection from a continued barrage of bullets.

"Get down," he screamed.

The command jolted her into action.

Liv lunged forward toward Spec, who continued to scream at them to get down. Bullets bounced off Talia's car with an eerie metallic plink.

"No, Liv," she shouted to the woman trying to dash across the parking lot toward her man. "They're still shooting. We need to get behind the car." Talia grabbed her friend and tried to pull her to safety.

Liv fought her. "I have to get to him."

"Liv, we're sitting ducks."

A bullet whizzed by so close she felt the rush against her ear.

"Talia. I need to get to him."

Fuck.

Her heart thundered in her ears. "Liv, I'm sorry," she said as she slammed into her friend, tackling her to the pavement.

Liv screamed, and Talia grunted as they hit the ground. Gravel ground into her bare knees with a painful sting. No doubt Liv took the brunt of it, but they were alive.

For the moment.

She grabbed a struggling Liv around the waist and dragged her behind the car to safety.

"Talia, please let me go. I have to get to him. Please, please, please. We can't leave him there." Her eyes were wide with panic, and her clothes were a mess of dirt and gravel. A long scrape from the asphalt covered her upper arm.

"We won't leave him, Liv, I promise," she said as she held Liv against the wheel well. "Spec knows what to do. Your man is former special forces. He needs you safe so he can focus on getting himself to safety."

"Okay, yeah." Liv shook her head. "I hate it, but I get it."

Talia sat back on her heels with a gasp. "Holy shit, Liv, I think you've been shot."

"What?" Liv blinked. Blood poured down her face from a gash that traveled from her forehead to her temple. Based on where it was, it seemed like it would have hit dead center in her forehead had Talia not knocked her to the ground. She lifted her hand to her head as her eyes glazed over.

"Don't touch it." Talia wriggled out of her cardigan. "Here, press this to the wound."

"Talia, I don't care." Liv tried to swat the sweater away. "I need to check on Spec."

"Liv, baby, you okay?" Spec's shout made Liv burst into tears.

"He's all right, Liv, see? And listen… the shooting stopped." Their eyes met. Liv looked like an extra from an action movie as she held the sweater to her bloody head. "She's safe," Talia shouted back. Telling Spec Liv had been grazed by a bullet would not be a smart move. Her injury wasn't life-threatening, so he could find out that tidbit later. "Is it over?"

"Not sure," Spec hollered back.

The night was as quiet now as it had been when she left the building, except for Liv's choked breathing.

"Okay," she said, grabbing Liv's shoulders. "I'm going to try to get to Spec. You need to promise me you'll stay here, okay?"

"No, Talia…"

"Honey, I have no idea how much blood loss is too much, but you're bleeding a fuck ton. You need to stay here so I don't have to drag you back if you pass out from blood loss. I won't be able to help Spec if I have to help you too." A low blow, maybe, but she'd say whatever she needed to keep Liv out of harm's way.

Liv's shoulders slumped. "Okay."

"Call Curly."

Liv nodded. "Be careful." They shared a quick hug, and then Talia crawled around the side of the car toward Spec. She made it about five feet before the first bullet hit the asphalt, so close that gravel spray pelted her cheek.

"Talia, what the fuck are you doing? Get back." Spec roared.

"I'm coming to help you, you asshole," she growled as she crawled toward him as fast as she could while her palms and knees screamed in agony.

"Get back behind the fucking car!"

A loud rumble had their gazes whipping toward the road where Pulse headed their way on his motorcycle.

"No," Talia whispered. She wanted to jump up, wave her arms, and shout at him to turn back, but she'd be shot dead for sure. Instead, she had no choice but to watch with her heart in her throat as the man she loved turned into the parking lot amid a spray of bullets. His shout rang out at the same time his bike tilted.

Talia screamed as the motorcycle hit the ground. Pulse scrambled away on all fours as bullets hailed around him like lethal raindrops. The screech of metal on concrete had her wincing as the bike slid across the parking lot, showering the air with a spray of sparks. Pulse made it behind a large pad-mounted transformer directly across from them. He sat with his back to the large metal box, panting and wild-eyed.

"Spec?" Liv called.

"I'm okay, baby. Don't fucking move from behind that car."

Talia couldn't tear her gaze from Pulse. "You hit?" he asked, panic in his voice.

She shook her head. "No. But Spec is. He was shot in the leg, and he's bleeding a lot." A bullet pinged against the bike, and she flinched. "And we're not exactly safe here."

Pulse ran his hand through his hair. "Can you walk, brother?"

"Of course, I can fucking walk."

Beneath him, a large pool of blood continued to spread. He'd paled to an ashy gray color that had Talia shaking her head at Pulse. No way could this macho idiot walk. He'd probably pass out the second he tried to stand.

"Here's what we're gonna do. I'm gonna stand and draw

their attention. Talia, you book it the fuck over here behind this transformer. Then I'll scramble over to Spec and try to drag him back here."

What?

"No. No way," she said, shaking her head. "You're not standing and drawing their fire. I'll help you drag him over there. He's freakin' heavy," she yelled. "It'll be easier with both of us."

She glanced toward the car, where Liv peered around the side and watched with wide, terrified eyes. Long, red blood trails ran down her face, but she still kept the cardigan pressed to her head.

"Fuck that," Pulse yelled across the lot. "No way in hell."

Talia ground her teeth and scowled at him. "Do not fight me on this, Pulse. Either I help you or stand up and draw their attention so you can crawl over here and get him."

She'd do it too. No way would she allow him to potentially sacrifice himself for her. Did he think she'd ever be able to look herself in the mirror if he took a bullet while she hid like a coward?

"Goddamn stubborn woman," he grumbled while Spec laughed.

"You got a serious set of balls on you, counselor. Either that or you're fucking crazy."

"Yeah, well, I'm trying to save your ass even though you pulled a gun on me the other day, so it's probably the crazy option."

Spec snorted.

She kept her attention locked on Pulse, who held up three fingers, then two, then one. He sprang out from behind the transformer like an Olympian runner, but instead of sprinting toward them, he scrambled on all fours. Bullets immediately hit the ground around him, but he made the five-second trip unscathed.

She wanted to kiss him and hold him until she was convinced they were both completely unharmed. A single Harley didn't provide much protection for three grown-ass adults during a bullet storm.

"Fuck, you're bleeding like a stuck pig," Pulse said, frowning at Spec.

"Thanks for noticing."

"Okay, Tal, hook your arm under his like this." Pulse demonstrated the hold. "Then we can crawl back behind the transformer. At least we'll have better coverage there. Spec, you use your good leg to help push along. Ready?"

Spec's eyes had dulled from pain and blood loss, but he shook his head. "Fuck this. Get your woman to safety. Forget me. I don't deserve your help."

The critical level of adrenaline coursing through her system wasn't enough to stop the pang in her heart.

"Fuck off," Pulse growled. "Besides, I'm doing this for Liv. I'm afraid she'll stab me to death with one of those spikes she calls shoes."

Spec's weak laugh had Pulse cursing. "Ready?" he asked, staring at Talia with determination.

Was she ready to drag a giant man across fifteen feet of target practice?

Hell no.

"I'm ready."

"All right, baby, let's go."

She heaved with all her strength while crawling and trying to ignore the rough concrete digging into her abraded knees and palms. Thankfully, Spec's uninjured leg was on her side. The added boost of his assistance allowed her to keep up with Pulse as they scrambled the fifteen feet that felt more like a mile.

Spec ground his teeth, muffling his scream. His leg had to be in agony. Neither she nor Pulse tried to be gentle. All they cared about was getting back to safety.

A bullet hit directly in front of her, spraying gravel and drawing a shriek from her.

"You got this, baby. You're such a fucking badass. Almost there."

If she hadn't loved the man before, she certainly did now. For him to use his energy to encourage and compliment her had her blinking back tears amidst her terror.

They reached the transformer after what felt like an hour but had only been a few seconds. Liv shouted, but Talia couldn't hear it over her harsh breathing and pounding pulse.

"One more burst of effort, Tal. Haul his heavy ass behind this box."

She inhaled a deep breath and let out a long wail as she used the last of her energy to help heave Spec behind the transformer. All she wanted to do was slump against the box and breathe, or better yet, kiss the hell out of Pulse, but her man went straight to work on Spec's injury and might need help.

Now that they were once again hidden, the gunfire stopped. "H-how can I help?" she asked between rapid breaths.

Pulse grabbed the back of her head and yanked her in for a quick, hard kiss. "Fuck, I love you so much, Talia."

She blinked.

He didn't mean that, right? It had to be the heat of the moment.

Now, her heart was racing for a different reason.

Chapter Twenty-Five

Was there a more incredible woman than Talia?

Pulse doubted it.

Who else would risk their life to save a man who'd held a gun to their head not one week before?

He shed his cut, then his T-shirt. "Ball this up and hold it on the wound. Don't be shy. Push fucking hard."

Talia reached for it with trembling hands. She was terrified and running on adrenaline, probably with some lingering caffeine in her system. She tended to forget to eat and consumed gallons of coffee when she worked late. But she took his shirt and pressed it to Spec's leg with firm, confident pressure as though she dodged bullets and tended gunshot wounds every day.

Christ, he really fucking loved this woman. The timing sucked, but he'd meant what he said. Later, he'd repeat it hundreds of times if he needed to, whatever it took to make sure she believed him.

He could sit there all night and drool over her competence and trust in him, but each passing second meant more danger to Spec's life.

Thank fuck he wore a belt that day. Most of the time he didn't bother but had that day for some reason.

Some cosmic intuition he didn't believe in.

Working as quickly as possible, he undid his belt and slid it out of the loops with one long tug. Talia watched him with a slightly dazed expression as he slipped the belt under Spec's thigh as high as he could manage.

"Okay, brother, this is gonna hurt like a fucking bitch, not gonna lie. But the way you're bleeding makes me worry they hit the artery, and there's no fucking way you're bleeding out on me tonight. He threaded the belt through the buckle and looked Spec in the eye. "That means you gotta suck it the fuck up. Don't be a whiney pussy."

Spec's laugh was a weak testament to how much blood he'd lost in a few short minutes—minutes that felt like ages.

"Do your worst," he croaked.

With a nod, Pulse yanked as hard as he could, cinching the belt around Spec's thigh. His brother let out a primal wail of pain, but it worked. The fountain of blood streaming from his femoral artery slowed to a trickle.

At Spec's agonized scream, Talia's expression turned to one of horror, but she bit her lower lip and kept pressure on the wound. Her trust that he knew what to do and how to do it was goddamn everything.

"Spec?" Liv shouted through the quiet night. "Are you okay? What's happening?" She sounded seconds away from full-on hysteria. Being separated from him while listening to his spine-chilling cry had to be torture.

"I-I can't shout," he rasped, panting. "Not enough breath."

"H-he's okay," Talia shouted for him. "He's okay, Liv. Pulse is taking care of him."

Spec sagged against the transformer box in a half-conscious slump. Sweat poured down his ashen face, and he couldn't speak above a whisper, but he was alive and not losing much blood anymore.

"W-what do we do now?" Talia asked. "We can't call the police."

No, they couldn't. The pretend DEA agent on the other side of that parking lot would spin this entire disaster his way and land everyone's ass in jail.

"We need to draw him out." Pulse froze. He turned his head, straining to catch the distant sound. "You hear that?"

Talia tilted her head. "What? No. What do you hear?"

"Cavalry's coming." Spec's dazed grin held the same glee it always did when the club kicked ass.

"What?" Talia blinked once then gasped. "Motorcycles. Oh my God, I hear them. I told Liv to call Curly."

"And he sent the cavalry. Don't ease up on the pressure, Tal." Pulse would have offered to take over, but he couldn't release the tension on the belt, or fresh blood would resume gushing out of Spec.

The rumble grew louder and louder until it reached a deafening roar. The whole goddamn club had come to save their asses.

Talia closed her eyes and mouthed, *Thank God.*

God had nothing to do with it. This was all Curly and his loyal family of outlaws.

Bikes poured into the parking lot. Curly shouted orders to be on guard and search for the shooter.

Pulse held a finger to his lips. As soon as it was safe, he'd announce their presence, but he wasn't going to risk popping up to have his head blown off. It felt like forever before Tracker shouted. "All clear. Betty found where he was shooting from, but he must have split. There's no sign of anyone here now."

Betty White was Tracker's dog, trained in search and rescue. However, she also came in handy at times like this. The intelligent pup could sniff out gun residue, and it sounded like that was precisely what she did.

"Pulse? Spec?" Curly shouted. "Shooter fled the scene."

"We're here," Pulse called back as he raised his hand above

the transformer.

Liv burst from behind the car with an impressive explosion of speed. The sound of pounding boots alerted him to the rest of the crew heading their way.

"Fuck, Livy!" Jinx shouted. He grabbed her before she could reach Spec. "What happened to you?"

Of course, Spec picked up on that. "Liv? What happened?" He grabbed Pulse's arm with a scary-weak grip. "Is she okay?"

Pulse looked at Talia, who nodded. "She just has a gash on her head, Spec. You know, head wounds bleed a lot. It must have freaked Jinx out, but she's all right."

A gash on her head. Jesus, had a bullet grazed her? Talia must have read the question in his eyes because she nodded. Spec didn't need to know that. It was bad enough that he was about to see his woman looking like someone tried to scalp her.

"She's good, brother," he added. "But we'll get her checked out at the hospital while you're there."

"I don't need a fucking hospital."

Talia laughed a hysterical, high-pitched sound. "Yeah, you do, macho man. No one has ever needed a hospital more than you do right now."

Liv escaped Jinx's concerned grasp and dropped to her knees by Spec's head. "Baby," she said with a choked sob.

"Jesus, fuck, Livy." Spec tried to sit up, but Liv put her hands on his shoulder when he groaned. No one could tame the beast quite like that woman. "I'm okay, Scott. I promise. I'm much more worried about you. You almost died."

He grunted. "Please, it's a damn scratch. Put a Band-Aid on me, and I'll be good to go."

No one had ever spoken a stupider statement.

She shook her head. "You crazy idiot," she said while kissing all over his face. "If you don't go to the hospital, I don't either."

What a ridiculous conversation. If Spec didn't get to a hospital and into surgery to repair his artery, he'd die. But if Liv could get him to go without a fight, everyone involved would be much better off.

He scowled at her but relented as they all knew he would.

Everything happened quickly after that. Jinx took over, holding pressure on Spec's bullet wound while Ty held the belt tight.

"Do not let up the pressure even for a second. Either of you," Pulse ordered.

"Got it, boss," Ty said with a nod.

"What if he's super obnoxious on the way? Can I let up a little? Take some of the fight out of him?" Jinx asked with a deep chuckle.

"Jinx!" Liv slapped the back of his head.

"Ow, woman! I was kidding."

Pulse shook his head. "Let's just get him in the fucking car."

"Wait."

As Pulse went to slide his hands under Spec's shoulders to help lift him, Spec held up a hand. "Brother, I was wrong." His voice had weakened to barely a whisper. "I'm so—"

Christ, he refused to hear Spec's version of a deathbed apology. No one was dying tonight.

"Save your energy, Spec."

"No, I—"

Pulse shook his head. He wanted an apology. A better man might not need it, but Pulse did. It was necessary to fix their broken bond, but not when Spec was worried he wouldn't make it. "Tell me once you're up on your feet, and we can stand eye to eye, brother."

If he hadn't known how much danger Spec was in, the fact that his brother didn't fight him let him know. Spec nodded.

His eyes drooped. They needed to get this show on the road.

"Let's move. He needs medical attention *now*."

Curly helped Pulse lift a half-limp Spec and load him in the back seat of Brooke's SUV while Jinx and Ty did their best to hold the pressure. Brooke had arrived with her car after Curly sent her a text saying the area was safe. Of course, the president anticipated needing vehicles besides motorcycles to get everyone out of there. He was the president for a reason.

Now that she didn't need to hold Spec's leg together, Talia scooted off to the side of the parking lot and sat on a curb with her head in her hands. He itched to go to her. To wrap her in his arms and check every inch of her to make sure she hadn't been hurt. Someone had been shooting at her, for Christ's sake. She could have died in an instant.

Not yet. Don't think about that shit yet. Keep your head in the fucking game.

As soon as he was confident Liv's injury wasn't more serious than she claimed, he'd be all over Talia. Liv stood near the SUV, staring into the back seat where Jinx attempted to keep Spec awake with atrocious jokes.

"Livy, let me take a look at that wound."

She turned her head until he had access to the gash. The bleeding had slowed to a trickle.

"How's the pain?" he asked as he probed the skin around the wound.

"Um… I'm not even sure. I'm feeling kinda weird."

"Shock," he said.

"My face itches."

God, he hated the flat tone of her voice, as though she didn't have enough energy to speak.

"That's just dried blood. They'll get you all cleaned up in the emergency room."

She nodded.

She was missing a patch of hair, which would piss her off

to no end later, but she was alive and wouldn't require more than a dozen or so stitches.

"Let's get you to the hospital," he said as he guided her to the front passenger seat of the SUV.

"I want to sit with Spec. Let me sit in the back." Her voice held an edge of panic no one could blame her for.

"Honey, he's got Jinx and Ty back there with him. There isn't even enough room for all of them, let alone you. Sit in the front next to Brooke. You can reach back and hold Spec's hand, okay?"

Tears streamed down her face, and she shook her head. "No, I-I wan—"

"Shh, hey, come here. It's okay, Livy." Brooke drew Liv into her arms. "I got her," she whispered to Pulse with a grateful nod.

Brooke loaded Liv into the car and then jogged around to the driver's seat. They peeled out of the parking lot a few seconds later and sped off to the hospital.

Curly strode over with his mouth set in a grim line. "You injured?"

"No." Pulse ran his hand through his hair. "I'm good."

"And Talia?"

He glanced over to where she sat on the curb with her bloody knees hugged close to her body. She stared toward where Tracker had found their assailant's hiding place as though she didn't trust the danger had passed for the night.

"She's scraped up, but nothing major. I'll drive her to the ER to be checked out, though."

Curly nodded, then slapped Pulse on the back. "Tomorrow we go hunting."

The club would no longer sit back and wait for the chips to fall. Pulse was on board with that. Too bad their special forces enforcer would be out of commission for the coming battle.

"Go take care of your ol' lady," Curly said.

"She's—"

Curly raised an eyebrow that asked, *wasn't she*?

"Will do, Prez. Thank you." He tried to convey how much Curly's support meant in those two words, but words would never be enough to capture what the Handlers meant to him.

"Always," Curly said, slapping him on the back. "Let's roll, boys," he said to the remaining men. Frost had loaded Jinx and Ty's bikes in the back of a truck. No way would he risk leaving them unattended overnight.

As the guys mounted up, Pulse made his way to Talia. Before he reached her, she leaped from the curb straight at him. He wrapped his arms around her in a gentle hold. "I'm so sorry, baby," he whispered as he rocked her back and forth. She'd given Liv her sweater and wore nothing but a tank top and a torn skirt.

"Is Spec going to survive?" she whispered.

"Yeah, Tal. He'll be in pain and probably the world's shittiest patient, but he'll recover. I want to talk about you, though," he said against her hair. "Let's get you to the hospital so they can check you over and patch you up."

She shook her head so hard she almost smashed his nose. "No. Please, no. I just want to go home. Or the apartment. Wherever is safest." She drew back to look at him. The dried tears on her cheeks felt like a punch to the chest. "I'm only scraped. I promise. I just don't want to be around anyone besides you right now. Can you just bandage them for me? Please."

Fuck, he hated the thread of panic in her tone, as though she worried he might deny the request. Didn't she know by now? He'd do anything she asked. This woman had him wrapped around every one of her fingers. "Yeah, baby, I can do that."

"Thank you."

"Let's get the hell outta here." He guided her to the

passenger side of her car. As much as he loved her clinging to his back on the bike, riding with skinned knees and palms would suck, so the car it was. Curly would take care of his motorcycle along with the others.

Neither spoke much on the ride to the Handlers' compound. Pulse kept his hand on Talia's thigh while she rested back against her seat with her eyes closed. The silence helped give him time to process, but unfortunately, his mind kept returning to one stark fact—he'd come extremely close to losing Talia tonight.

Why had he ever let her get involved with him? He could have cut it off the night she'd been run off the road. Instead, as a selfish fuck, he'd let himself get deeper and deeper until they were so entwined even a crowbar couldn't separate them. Still, he had to try. He had to take a stab at distancing himself.

The clubhouse was lit up like they were having a damn party when he pulled onto the property Most likely, his brothers were updating their women and drinking as they waited for news on Spec.

As much as he loved them and owed them for tonight, Pulse had no desire to be around them. He wanted Talia and Talia alone.

So much for his plan to distance himself. It would never happen, and he shouldn't bother lying to himself.

He drove over the grass and parked at the barn door.

"Pulse, I can walk," Talia said with a huff.

"Fuck that." He jogged around and opened the passenger door before his stubborn woman could try to slip out on her own.

She winced as she swung her legs his way.

"Saw that," he said with a smirk.

"Yeah, yeah," she muttered, rolling her eyes.

The flash of normal banter had his lips quirking even

though he couldn't muster a full grin.

Pulse kept his arm around her waist as they walked up the stairs. She leaned against him from either pain or fatigue. Her gait was slower than usual, and every so often, she winced. The injuries might be minor, but that didn't mean she wouldn't ache like hell for the next few days.

When they reached the apartment, he ushered her straight into the bathroom. "Hop up," he said, patting the countertop. He grabbed her waist and hoisted her onto the counter. When he turned toward the tiny closet to retrieve the first-aid kit, Talia grabbed his cut and stopped him.

She tugged him close and widened her legs. He slipped between them. The added height from her sitting on the counter put their lips nearly level with each other.

"Just give me a minute like this. I'm so tired," she whispered, resting her forehead against his. "I could fall asleep right here sitting up. I almost feel like I drank too much."

"It's the adrenaline crash." He coasted his hands up and down her back, and she nearly purred.

"Makes sense. Mm… that feels nice."

"Good." He'd rub her back for the rest of her life if it made her happy.

When she spoke again, he had to strain to hear. "I've never let anyone see me like this before."

He stilled his hands. "Injured?"

"No, I mean, weak like this… rattled from a bad experience, messy, and helpless. Normally, I'd hide away and lick my metaphorical wounds until I was back to one hundred percent. I don't like people to know I'm not always strong or at my best, so I isolate myself in those moments. It's too easy for someone to take advantage of those moments and judge or hurt you." She straightened and looked him in the eye. "But with you, I'm not afraid of that happening."

Christ, what a fucking honor. He had to be the luckiest bastard in the universe. Of everyone she knew, he was the lucky fucker who got all of her—the good, the bad, and the vulnerable.

He cupped her face and pressed a lingering kiss to her lips. "I will make sure you never regret giving me this gift." He kissed her again. "I meant it, you know."

Her forehead scrunched, and she frowned. "Meant what?"

"Earlier tonight when I told you I love you. My timing was shit, but I meant it. It wasn't just a heat-of-the-moment confession. I love you."

She sucked in a breath, and her pupils widened. "Pulse…"

"I love you, Talia."

Her eyes filled with tears, and her throat moved as she swallowed. "I love you, too," she whispered.

His heart nearly exploded out of his chest. He'd told Camila he loved her countless times as part of the ruse. And he'd heard it back just as many times. It'd been easy to say, becoming a habitual phrase he'd spoken every time they left each other's presence. Saying or hearing those words hadn't meant anything to him.

They did now.

He could feel something shift inside him at her words. Like a missing piece of an elaborate puzzle, he'd assumed he'd lost and would never find.

"Let's fix you so we can go to bed."

"Okay."

She watched intently as he cleaned her palms and knees. He wasn't surprised by how stoic she remained even when he knew it stung. The task took longer than expected due to bits of gravel he had to pick out of her wounded knees one by one. By the time he finished bandaging her, she'd slumped back against the mirror and fallen asleep.

Gentle as he could, he scooped her into his arms and

carried her out of the bathroom. Her eyes fluttered and opened about halfway to the bed. "Sorry," she whispered.

"Don't apologize. I'm thinking I might carry you around everywhere we go. Seems like something you'd be excited about."

Talia's chuckle was heavy with sleep. "You know me well."

He set her down next to the bed. Once he was sure she was steady on her feet, he stripped off her clothes and then followed with his own. They crawled into bed and reached for each other like two powerful magnets.

Neither had the energy for more than sleep, but he'd never felt anything better than holding her beneath the warmth of the blankets with their bare skin touching from toes to noses.

Chapter Twenty-Six

"Talia, would you mind slicing these strawberries for me?" Brooke asked as she thrust a large carton of whole strawberries at Talia's chest.

"Yeah, that sounds like something even I couldn't screw up."

Chuckling, Brooke retrieved a large cutting board from a low cabinet. "Not much of a cook?" she asked as she slid the board across the counter to Talia.

"Definitely not. I think I'm solely responsible for my Door Dasher's down payment on their new house." She set the strawberries on the cutting board and then accepted the handle of a sharp knife Brooke held out.

"Liv isn't either," Kelsie said with a smile. "But we still find plenty of jobs for her, so no worries. There's always some way to contribute."

"Just slice them up. Doesn't need to be perfect," Brooke said. "They're topping for the pancakes Harper is working on. These guys don't give two shits what the fruit looks like."

Laughing, Talia grabbed a berry. "Yeah, I can't imagine Jinx being picky about the cut of his strawberries."

"Exactly," Brooke said with a smirk.

Brunch at the clubhouse was an event like no other. No store-bought pastries and cereal for these people. They made everything from scratch and had enough food to fuel an army. Nerves had hit hard when Pulse told her the club was planning on having brunch, and it was an all-hands-on-deck kind of situation when it came to preparing the meal. She wasn't lying when she said she didn't cook. She could barely boil water.

But, like most things with this club, brunch preparation was a chill, judgment-free affair.

The best part was how no one harped on what had happened last night. After ensuring she was okay, everyone went about their tasks like a typical day. Either they were used to flying bullets or understood she needed to focus on something else for her sanity.

Probably a bit of both.

Her knees stung like a bitch and looked like raw meat, but her palms were in much better shape. Aside from some shallow scrapes that had scabbed over already, they didn't look bad and weren't holding her back from getting things done.

Like cutting strawberries.

They chatted as they worked, getting the meal whipped up quicker than Talia expected. Liv's absence left a hole in their group, but she'd called hours ago to say Spec made it through surgery and had received a blood transfusion. She'd refused to leave his side despite him 'growling at me like an angry ogre' to go home and rest.

"So," Harper said as she pushed herself onto the island next to where Talia was adding champagne to a large pitcher of peach juice. "Liv's going to kill me for asking this when she isn't here to get the deets, but I can't wait any longer. What exactly is going on with you and Pulse?"

"Oh, yes, I've been dying for details," Jo said as she strode into the kitchen. She'd been finishing some work at the shelter, though Brenna theorized Jo wanted to avoid kitchen duty. The ladies claimed she often had something important pop up during meal prep.

Talia's face heated as all the ladies stopped what they were doing to stare at her.

"Oh, man, it must be hot," Jo said with a chuckle. "Your face is redder than those strawberries you're butchering."

If she could have crawled into an empty champagne bottle, she would have.

"Jo, leave her alone. Not everyone likes to blab their personal business," Kelsie said as she opened the oven. Immediately, the scent of apples and cinnamon filled the kitchen.

"Too bad," Jo said with a smirk. "I want details."

Harper rolled her eyes but was grinning and hadn't moved from the counter. "Come on," she pleaded, giving Talia her best puppy-dog look. "We all know you're together. We just want to know if it's a serious thing or more casual."

"Yeah," Jo added. "We'd like to keep you, so if it's casual, we'll do our best to convince you to make it more."

As embarrassed as she was being put on the spot, Talia couldn't help but chuckle. "You guys are crazy."

"Guilty as charged, counselor." Jo grabbed a slice of bacon from an enormous platter and bit into it with a satisfying crunch. "Ow!" she said, mouth full, as Brooke slapped her hand away.

"What the hell?"

"It's not time to eat."

Their little scene only diverted attention from Talia for about twenty seconds. Everyone's eyes were back on her way too quickly. "Uh... well, it's serious."

Harper squealed and clapped her hands. "That makes me so happy. How serious?"

Ugh, really? Were they going to make her give details? "He told me he loved me last night and asked me to be his ol' lady," she mumbled.

For one second, the kitchen fell utterly silent but for the sound of the percolator brewing coffee. Then it erupted in a loud chorus of cheers and shrieks followed by a swarm of ol' ladies piling on her in a group hug.

"Yay!" Harper squealed. "I'm so happy." She was the closest, so she squeezed Talia while the others joined in.

The door opened, and Jinx stuck his head in. "Everything okay? Dayum, what do we have here? A little girl-on-girl action?" He straightened and folded his arms as he leaned against the doorjamb. "Don't let me interrupt. Please proceed."

"Get out of here, you big oaf," Jo yelled as she hurled a biscuit at Jinx.

"Hey! Don't waste a perfectly good biscuit. I made that," Kelsie cried.

"It won't go to waste." Jinx swiped the biscuit out of the air and took a monster-size bite. "Mm… good job, Kels. Very buttery. Flakey too."

"Get out!" they all shouted, making Jinx jump like he'd been electrocuted.

"Jesus, y'all are scary mean," he muttered with half of a biscuit in his mouth before he fled.

"Did you say it back?" Brenna asked as the hug broke apart.

"I did." Talia's cheeks went hot, feeling like an inferno.

"Eeep! Liv really is going to be pissed she missed this," Harper said with a gleeful grin. "Not gonna lie, I'm kinda excited."

"Welcome to our wild family." Brooke gave her another hug. "You're perfect for each other," she whispered.

"Thank you." Her throat thickened.

I will not cry.

She'd embarrassed herself enough in front of these people

to last a lifetime. Bursting out in tears because they liked her would be too much mortification to bear. Once she collected herself, she helped carry the food to the tables in the main clubhouse area. Pulse wandered over as she set the pitchers of peach mimosas on the table.

"How are you holding up?" he asked, drawing her into his arms.

She inhaled. The scent of his bodywash had quickly become her favorite smell. It reminded her of the delightful shower they'd taken together just a few hours ago.

"I'm good," she said as she hugged him close. "Really good."

"The ladies didn't force you to cook?"

She laughed. "No. I was on strawberry slicing and drink making. And I think I nailed both tasks."

He grinned and kissed her.

"Aw, look at the love birds." Jinx made kissy faces at them across the room, earning him a double middle finger from Pulse.

Talia couldn't describe how great seeing Pulse comfortable and relaxed with his brothers felt. Gone was the tension that had lingered for a day or two after he'd confessed his past. Of course, Spec was noticeably absent, which could be the reason.

The door opened as though she'd conjured him with her mind, and Liv strode into the room, followed by Spec on a pair of crutches. Liv held the door for him as he hobbled through.

A few people gasped while others murmured to each other.

Jinx, of course, had no trouble speaking his mind. "Uh, dude, didn't you have surgery like five minutes ago? Shouldn't you be in a hospital bed?"

"Do not go there, Jinx," Liv snapped. She marched into the room ahead of Spec. How could she still look put together after spending a night hiding from a gunman and then waiting in the hospital?

Oh yeah, and being grazed by a bullet?

A row of neat stitches lined the side of her head, but the blood had been cleaned, and she didn't appear to be in much pain. She wore a simple, matching pastel pink sweatsuit, trendy and stylish as always.

On the other hand, Spec had unruly hair, a day's worth of beard growth, and skin so pale she wondered if they should have given him an extra pint of blood.

"Ah, I'm guessing he was his usual charming self to the hospital staff."

Liv's dark scowl had Jinx shrinking back.

"Yikes," he muttered. "She's frightening."

"I had the surgery last night. It was a success. There's no reason for me to be in the hospital anymore."

"Sure," Liv said, not trying to hide her sarcasm. "Why would you need to stay in a place with trained professionals monitoring you immediately after a life-saving operation?" She jammed her hands on her hips and glared at her man, but the woman couldn't hide the affection in her gaze.

Talia mashed her lips together. It was either that or let her laughter sneak out. These two were endless entertainment.

Spec snagged the front of Liv's top and yanked her to him, kissing her square on the mouth. "Love you, too, baby," he whispered.

Liv rolled her eyes but stopped arguing. It seemed she knew she was only wasting her breath. If Spec didn't want to be in the hospital, he wouldn't stay. Spec handed her his crutches when they separated and limped toward the table.

Talia's spine straightened as Spec neared. Beside her, Pulse tensed. He slipped his hand around her waist and drew her flush against his side. The protective move had regret crossing Spec's face, but it didn't last long, replaced by a pained wince.

After a few more slow, cumbersome steps, Spec made it to her and Pulse. No one spoke. Instead, they watched the show, all waiting to see what Spec would do.

Talia held her breath. This moment felt important—it was make-or-break for Pulse and his brother.

Would he thank Pulse for saving his life? Would it come with a 'but I still want nothing to do with you?'

Her insides wavered. Thank God for Pulse's strong arm around her. The tough façade she presented to the world would crumble if it weren't for his support.

She had to give Spec some credit. The man didn't back down in the face of an uncomfortable situation. He stood tall and looked Pulse square in the eye.

"I was so fucking wrong," he said.

Talia's jaw dropped, and Pulse's hand tightened on her hip.

"I know it might not mean much considering what I did, but I'm fucking sorry." He shifted his gaze to her. "You didn't know me before I met Liv, but I was an angry fucker spiraling and losing myself to that anger. Most days, I have it under control, but clearly, I still have work to do."

She gaped at him. Holy shit. This had to be the most sincere apology she'd ever received. Pulse stood warm and solid beside her. She'd kill to be in his head. Did he accept this? Could he feel Spec's genuine regret as she could?

Spec shifted so his weight was on his uninjured leg. Sweat dotted his forehead, and his breathing picked up. The man had to be in severe discomfort, yet he stood and faced the people he hurt without a complaint.

"You both saved my fucking life without one second of hesitation, even though I threatened you. I'll have to live with the shame of holding a gun on your woman for the rest of my life," he said, focusing on Pulse again. "Aside from incorrectly judging Liv when I met her, this is my biggest fuckup." He extended his hand to Pulse. "You're my brother forever, and I vow to protect your woman like I would Olivia and any of the ol' ladies." He looked at her again. "Swear on my life you'll never have anything to fear from me, brother."

His hand hung in mid-air. Pulse remained frozen beside her, and for one gut-wrenching moment, Talia feared he wouldn't take Spec's hand and mend the rift. Could the club survive such a permanent fracture?

But then he turned his head and gazed at her with questioning eyes. He was giving her the final say. Talia had been the one in the sights of Spec's gun, and if she couldn't move past that, Pulse would choose her over his brother.

Her heart swelled until it felt close to bursting. This moment would have sealed the deal if she hadn't already been in love with him.

It was time to put the conflict behind them.

She nodded once.

Pulse's arm disappeared from her waist as he stepped forward and grasped Spec's hand, then yanked him into a crushing hug. Talia winced along with Spec, but the man didn't make a peep of protest. He returned the hug, slapping Pulse on the back.

"Apology accepted," Pulse said as he released Spec, who was now sweating profusely. "Now sit your stubborn fucking ass down before you destroy the surgeon's hard work. I'm not saving your ass again if you start bleeding out all over the floor."

"Ya'll need to stop being a buncha mother hens," Spec grumbled. "I'm fine." But he collapsed into the chair, and the relief on his face showed instantly.

"Everyone, grab a seat," Curly announced. "Eat first, then we make a plan to take out this cartel fucker."

Pulse pulled her chair out.

Her cheeks flamed as she accepted a kiss from him as well. These little gestures were so unfamiliar to her that they'd take time to adjust to. Part of her wanted to balk and remind him she was perfectly capable of getting in her own seat, but she fought the urge. Pulse didn't do things like that for her because he found her unable to manage basic tasks. He simply wanted to do something for her.

Because he loved her.

Only two people had claimed to love her in her lifetime. Her mother passed early, and her father taught her the independence she clung to by never doing a single thing for her.

But now she had Pulse.

"Thank you," she whispered before sitting. He slipped between her and Spec, kissing her on the cheek as he sat. Face warm, she glanced around to see if the others were staring, but no one paid them any attention. Physical affection was standard practice around here, so instead of making herself feel awkward, she scooted her chair closer to Pulse's. If she were going to do this, she'd jump in with both feet as she did with everything in life.

Chatter kicked up immediately, and within minutes, plates were full, and laughter shook the walls. It was almost enough to make Talia forget what came next.

But then Pulse's phone rang.

It cut through the noise like a sharp blade, drawing all eyes. He placed his free hand on her thigh as he pulled the phone from his pocket.

"It's my old contact."

"Fuck yes," Spec said. "Maybe he's got something useful."

Pulse swallowed, then pressed answer as he lifted the phone to his ear.

The longest twenty seconds of her life passed as she sat there staring at the side of Pulse's head, straining to hear what the caller had to say.

"Thanks, man," Pulse said to conclude the call. He lowered the phone as his eyes narrowed, and a sinister grin curled his lips. Before her eyes, he transformed from a life-saving trauma nurse into a former undercover federal agent. This was a lethal man with skills that would make her lose sleep at night—a competent agent who could handle himself as well as Spec.

He spoke four words that had a chill running down her spine.

"We have a location."

Chapter Twenty-Seven

"This fucking blows. Swear to Christ, you guys better find someone for me to kill when I'm back on my feet."

Spec's disgusted voice reverberated through Pulse's earpiece. He'd stayed back but refused to be left out, so he listened on comms and joined in spirit.

"What? You want some kind of execution IOU?" Jinx asked with a laugh.

"That's exactly what I want, fucker, so you better be prepared to deliver."

Pulse rolled his eyes. Some days, he was amazed those two could function at all.

"You good, Pulse?" Spec asked.

He pressed his hand to the small communication device tucked in his ear. "All good. Just getting the lay of the land."

He sat in his truck in the parking lot of the Breezy Palm, a motel that could only be described as shitty. It was about an hour inland and south of Lithia, near Sweetwater, Florida. When he first pulled into the lot, Pulse barely believed the ten-room motel was operational. One door, room seven, stood wide open and hanging from the hinges. Room four had a cracked window and a remnant of crime scene tape dangling from the doorknob. A vacancy sign lit the dark parking lot with neon orange, or it would have had any letters beyond the 'C' glowed. The once-white building had a yellowish tinge he could see even in the dark. The paint was a peeling mess as well. Off to the right, past the last room, a rusted chain link fence surrounded a pool he could only imagine was a lovely shade of green. Tall palm trees surrounded the structure and provided the only pleasant sight.

Birdy had informed him their target booked room ten, next to the pool and farthest from the office, for the foreseeable future. At present, he was the only guest in this dump unless they counted the prostitute renting room two by the hour. She'd arrived with a greasy-haired john a few moments ago. Pulse would be keeping an ear out for trouble there as well. He had no problem doling out a few black eyes if the trick decided to get rough with her.

The second he'd pulled his vehicle into the motel's parking lot, instincts he'd buried five years ago came rushing back. He'd slipped into federal agent mode as though no time had passed. He registered every sound, smell, sight, and feeling. His observation skills might be rusty, but they hadn't fled and came surging back when he needed them most.

He'd been there for thirty minutes, scouting the area and preparing for the next step. One motel employee snoozed at the reservation desk. Their mouth dangled open as they slept in their desk chair, visible through a wide storefront window. They hadn't so much as twitched since Pulse arrived. Aside from that, the only other people he'd laid eyes on were the hooker and her client. No one had even driven past the motel. He'd spotted two exterior cameras, one outside the lobby entrance and one in the pool area. Neither appeared functional. The camera near the pool dangled from the side of the building by a fraying wire, and the other had a green moldy film over the lens.

The isolation and low risk of being recorded had to be the reason the cartel member picked this motel.

The ambiance sure wasn't a draw.

The rest of his club—minus Spec—sat in cars on the street, waiting for Pulse's instructions. Much to everyone's dismay, they'd left the bikes behind, being less identifiable without motorcycles and cuts.

"Okay, I'm confident I won't be seen. I'm going to engage the target."

Jinx snorted. "I'm going to engage," he mocked. "You sound like a damn fed."

"If the shoe fits," Tracker said.

"Funny," Pulse muttered. "Can you all shut your traps for a hot minute so you don't get me caught?"

"Quiet on comms," Curly ordered.

No one spoke.

He slid from the truck without making a sound, then shut the door quietly behind him. Pulse darted across the parking lot toward room ten, dressed in black from head to toe. None of the security lights in the lot or building worked, so he could easily remain unseen. He'd have blended with the shadows even if someone driving by took a long look at the crumbling motel.

Room ten's shades were drawn, but a light glowed along the bottom edge. The building's shitty insulation allowed Pulse to hear the rush of the shower through the closed door. "Target is in the shower," he whispered into his comms. "I'm going in."

"Stay safe," Curly replied. The others remained quiet as ordered.

Pulse pulled a lock pick kit from his pocket—thank you, Lock—and had the rusted lock open within seconds. A familiar surge of anticipation he hadn't experienced in ages flooded his system. Even years later, he could admit nothing matched the thrill of taking down a perp. This one would be extra satisfying since this shithead posed a threat to his woman.

He won't threaten anyone after tonight.

With excitement racing through his veins, he slipped into the room and shut the door behind him. The dull snick of the door wouldn't be heard above the shower, even with the bathroom door wide open. Steam wafted into the room, illuminated by the glow of the harsh bathroom lights. After securing the chain lock—the last thing he needed was an unexpected visitor—he turned to assess the room.

The inside of the hotel room was as nasty as the outside. A faded mauve comforter with at least two cigarette burns covered the single full-size bed. Two flat pillows were propped together against the headboard as though someone had been using them as a backrest. The walls were painted tan and stained yellow from cigarette smoke, which the entire room reeked of. Not recent smoke, but stale, years-old tar and nicotine.

The decades-old television played a telenovela on low. Next to the door, beneath the window, sat a small table and two wooden chairs. Empty Chinese food containers littered the table and overflowed a trash can beside the bed.

Pulse grabbed one of the chairs by the table and spun it to face the bathroom. Then he drew his gun and plopped down to wait, pointing the weapon toward the bathroom.

Not three minutes later, the water cut off, and the metallic scrape of the shower curtain along the rod announced his target was exiting the shower. Pulse readied his trigger finger but remained relaxed in the chair. At the wet slap of footsteps on the tile, he grinned.

Showtime.

His target came into view, striding into the room bare-assed and rubbing a towel over his dark hair.

"Jesus, fuck," he shouted as he spotted Pulse. He immediately dropped the towel down to his waist to cover his swinging dick.

Recognition bloomed inside Pulse, immediately turning to nausea. Birdy had told him Tomás Del Rios was resurrecting the cartel and posing as a DEA agent, but part of Pulse hadn't believed him. The Tomás he'd known had been a gangly, geeky teen who'd loved reading and playing *Dungeons and Dragons*. His father didn't involve him in cartel business, believing Tomás too soft for that life.

Looked like he'd been wrong.

"Tomás," he whispered. "For fuck's sake."

"Max. Gotta admit I wasn't expecting you to find me here."

"You didn't make it easy. You chose the shittiest motel in existence and paid cash."

Tomás shrugged. "It served its purpose."

Tomás. Fuck, he never would have thought. "Why?" Pulse asked because he couldn't think of anything else. When the cartel came down, the kid could have walked away and lived a safe and satisfying life.

The younger man snorted. "Come on, Max. The feds might not be rocket scientists, but they don't hire idiots. You know why. It's simple. You destroyed my fucking family."

"Your family ran the most violent and deadly drug cartel we've ever seen," he said, gun trained on Tomás. "You hated what they did."

"You spent years with my goddamn family." His voice broke as he spoke. "Fucking years. My family welcomed you. Accepted you. My father loved you like a son!" By the time he finished, he was red-faced and screaming.

"It was my job, Tomás. Countless lives have been saved since the takedown of the cartel. Your father murdered anyone who looked at you sideways. Thousands of fatal overdoses were directly linked to the Del Rios Cartel's supply. My job was to save lives, and I did it well."

"Too bad one of those lives you saved wasn't Camila,

huh?"

Shot fired.

Direct hit.

It felt like acid being poured into a fresh wound.

"Camila wasn't supposed to be there that day, Tomás. I did everything in my power to keep her away. I tried every damn day to get her to move away from your family. I showed her pictures that gave her nightmares and begged her to move somewhere safer. The risk of arrest was always high, and the risk of a war with rival cartels even higher. But Camila loved the lavish lifestyle your father provided. She loved the mansion and fancy cars. She loved the diamonds and envious stares everywhere she went. No, she didn't directly work for the cartel, but she benefited as much as anyone from the suffering of others. Even still, I did everything in my power to keep her alive and will regret her death for the rest of my life."

"Your regret doesn't mean shit to me, asshole. My father and brother are behind bars for the rest of their lives, and my sister is dead. The government seized every fucking dollar. I was left with nothing."

That wasn't entirely true. Tomás had a trust fund he'd been scheduled to receive when he turned eighteen, only three months after the cartel's takedown. The US and Mexican governments, working together, decided to leave that money for seventeen-year-old Tomás as a sort of twisted consolation prize for the loss of his family. Financially, he was set for life.

They should have considered his emotional security as well.

"So, this is all one big plot of vengeance against me? Seems like a lot of effort when you could have just hired someone to shoot me in the head."

Tomás snorted. "There's that arrogance you feds all have, thinking you're the center of the goddamn universe. You're just the first domino to fall, Max. I'm taking down the agency one evil operator at a time."

A conflicting mix of sadness and satisfaction warred within Pulse, giving him a familiar heaviness in his chest he'd battled with for months after leaving the DEA. Tomás had to be stopped. There wasn't any way to let him go free. The man couldn't be bargained with or bought off. Hatred had invaded his cells and ruled his life. Not only was he a direct threat to everyone Pulse loved, but he would topple an entire government agency if allowed to leave today.

Still, part of Pulse took no joy in ending the young man's life. He'd become collateral damage in a war he should have been shielded from. Another life destroyed by violent cartel life.

"So what's your plan here, Max?" Tomás asked with a smirk. He still had the towel covering his junk and stood dripping all over the thin carpet. "Shoot a DEA agent in cold blood? One who is down here specifically investigating your club? You think my superiors don't know where I am? The second I go off the grid, the entire agency will be so far up your club's ass they'll be peeking out your mouth."

"Give me a little credit." Pulse stood. "Like you said, the DEA doesn't hire idiots. No, Tomás, that's not how it will happen, although you are right about some of it." He took a step closer. The way Tomás frowned as though unable to fathom a way out of this for Pulse had him grinning. The man wasn't as clever as he thought.

"I am going to kill you."

"You'll never fucking get away with it."

"I promise you, I will. You think you covered your tracks so well. You think you scrubbed your history so clean no one could ever find a link between you and the Del Rios Cartel. I mean, hell, you passed the government's most invasive background check. But you'd be wrong. Or maybe my guy is just that good. You see, right now, as we speak, your immediate supervisor, his supervisor, and so forth until we reach the tippy top of the DEA, are receiving an email with very detailed background information on their hot-shot young agent."

Blood leached from Tomás' tanned face, leaving him with a sickly pale hue. Fuck, it felt good to have the upper hand, finally. To know Talia would be safe and his club could continue to thrive.

Pulse waved his gun with a flourish. "Things like who your father is, who your brother is, what you've been doing with the money the government generously let you keep when the cartel was dismantled. I think they'd give me a damn medal for shooting you, frankly, but they'll never know it was me."

Tomás' mouth flopped open and closed like the large fish Pulse had caught a few months ago out in the Gulf.

"You see, as we're talking, my club is waiting for my signal. As soon as I've… done my thing…" He smirked and wiggled the gun. "They'll be here to assist with cleanup and to transport your body to New Mexico."

The flash of fear in Tomás' eyes hit Pulse's blood like a caffeine surge.

"That's right," he said with a chuckle. "My sources are so good they even found out you purchased your father's old property in New Mexico. Your body will be there, surrounded by more proof of how you've resurrected the cartel these past few years. A nice present for the DEA, all wrapped up with a pretty bow."

He bowed as though having completed the grand finale of an epic performance.

Tomás stood frozen with the towel hiding his dick. The shrill shriek of an enraged telenovela character played in the background.

In an instant, a tsunami of rage transformed Tomás face into a furious snarl, and he lunged at Pulse. It happened so fast that only his decade of training made him react quickly. Muscle memory kicked in. He raised the gun and fired two rounds straight into Tomás' chest before the man could touch him.

The towel slipped from Tomás' fingers and floated to the floor, landing after his heavy body collapsed. Wide, hateful eyes stared up at him as blood erupted from the two wounds in his chest. Without clothing to absorb the liquid, blood spurted onto the floor, creating a large puddle in seconds.

Pulse stared down at Tomás as life left the younger man.

All he felt was peace—more peace than he'd experienced since before he'd walked into the Del Rios' world.

He pulled out his phone and shot a quick text to Curly. Ten seconds later, there was a light rasp on the door. Pulse turned from the naked dead body and went to open the door. Jinx pushed into the room, followed by Curly, Tracker, and Ty.

"Oh, for fuck's sake," Jinx muttered as he spotted the body.

"What? What the fuck is happening? This is fucking bullshit. I need to be there." Spec's tone matched his irritated words.

"Why the fuck couldn't you have asked him to put on some goddamned clothes? Now we gotta stare at his dick the whole time we're moving him."

"That's your biggest concern?" Tracker asked with a snort.

"What? The only dick I like looking at is mine, which, I might add, is much more impressive than this dude's."

"You're mind never grew past a damn thirteen-year-old," Ty muttered as he walked over to Tomás' crumpled body.

Jinx folded his arms and glared at Ty. "It sure as fuck did, VP. Trust me, the things I think of now did not cross my mind at thirteen." He waggled his eyebrows, earning a laugh from Tracker.

"Hey…" Curly strode over to Pulse. "You good, brother?"

He allowed himself a second to consider the question. "Yeah. I am, Prez."

Curly slapped him on the shoulder. "Why don't you head out? Your woman must be climbing the walls by now."

They'd be lucky if that's all Talia was doing.

"You guys got this?"

Curly nodded. "Not our first rodeo."

"Fair enough. Thanks, Prez."

He strode out of the shitty motel into the cool, clear night, only to stop when he saw the gorgeous woman leaning against his truck. One glimpse of her had him grinning like a damn fool. "Just couldn't be left out of the action, could you?"

Talia shrugged without an ounce of regret. "You don't seem surprised to see me," she said as she pushed off the car and strode his way.

Pulse stayed put so he could enjoy the show as she walked to him. She looked damn sexy in her black leggings and long-sleeve top, ready for a night of crime.

As soon as she was close enough to touch, he reached around her waist and yanked her to him. "Hi, baby," he said before kissing her.

"Is it done?"

He nodded. "It's done."

She blew out a breath and leaned into his embrace. "So we can leave here, be together, and just be normal?"

He chuckled. "I'm not sure anything is ever normal with the Handlers."

"Good point." She tipped her chin up, offering her lips for a kiss. "I'll take your club's brand of crazy any day."

"You better. You're stuck with us now."

"As long as I'm stuck with you."

"Forever." He kissed her until they were both panting, and

her eyes had glazed. "Now let's get the hell out of here, counselor. I've had a lot of trouble with the law lately, and I'm gonna need you to get me off."

Talia burst out laughing. "Oh my God, that is the worst attorney pun I've ever heard. You're lucky I love you, or that might be enough to have me running from you."

He slid his arm around her shoulders and guided her across the lot to his truck. "Trust me, I know how goddamn lucky I am."

Talia's soft grin warmed his insides. "Love you."

"Love you, too, baby."

He helped her into the giant truck, and then they sped off, finally leaving this part of Pulse's life where it belonged—in the past. Only this time, he had his brothers at his back, his woman at his side, and no secrets to jeopardize that perfection.

Epilogue

The roaring bonfire protected Talia from the chilly—not cold, it never got cold—Christmas Eve air. Well, the fire warmed her front since her back couldn't be more comfortable and toastier nestled against Pulse's muscular chest on the blanket set out for them.

Brenna, designer extraordinaire, had outdone herself. She'd banned everyone from the clubhouse for the entire day to set up what she'd been planning for weeks, and, man, had it been worth her efforts. Somehow, she'd transformed the space behind the clubhouse into a magical winter wonderland.

Thick blankets sat around the massive fire, one for each couple, with pillows and a tray of spiked hot cocoa and treats. Every detail was holiday-themed from the pillows to the mugs with reds, greens, and gold woven throughout. Brenna had found an enormous Christmas tree and must have paid a pretty penny to have it delivered and decorated in twinkling lights. The effect was warm and comforting, and when she got to enjoy it with the man she loved more than anyone, it was magical.

In the few months since Talia had tumbled into the Handlers' world, the club had become the family she'd never had. There wasn't anywhere she'd want to be than right where she was. Well, maybe one place, but the night was young with plenty of time for her and Pulse to tear up the sheets later. For now, she was beyond content right where she was.

"You good?" Pulse's warm voice rumbled against her ear.

"Good?" she asked, tilting her head to view her man. "No, Pulse, I'm perfect."

"You are," he whispered, tightening his hold.

That wasn't what she meant, nor was it close to the truth, but she had to admit there was something incredible about having a man who thought so. And Pulse really seemed to. Talia didn't consider herself an easy person to be in a relationship with. As an attorney, she could argue for days and never lose steam. Her independent streak bordered on pathological, and she tended to do the exact opposite when ordered around.

None of her flaws phased Pulse. Months into their relationship, he found them amusing, which boggled her mind but made for a sublime connection.

"You ready for your Christmas present?"

She straightened and whipped around as excitement zinged through her. "Now?"

Pulse nodded, then signaled to Brooke, who stood near the clubhouse's back door. Talia had been so caught up in enjoying the moment she hadn't noticed her friend leave the blanket where she'd sat cocooned with Curly.

It was then she noticed Brooke was holding something.

Wait. Is it moving?

Her breath caught, and she squeezed Pulse's thigh. "Oh my God. Is that what I think it is?"

Pulse grinned.

"Oh my God," she said again. Her throat thickened, and tears caused her to blink rapidly. Brooke started her way and with each step she took, Talia became more certain her hunch was correct.

Pulse got her a dog.

About fifteen feet out, Brooke crouched and set the wriggling puppy on the ground. It immediately began to attack her shoes.

"It's a girl," Pulse said. "She was left on Curly and Brooke's doorstep last week in the middle of the night. The vet thinks she's about ten weeks old."

"Oh, the poor baby." She pressed a hand to her chest and patted the blanket with the other. "C'mere, sweet girl," she said. The puppy's ears twitched at the high-pitched tone. She looked right at Talia and then scampered over, all gangly legs and oversized puppy feet. "Does she have a name?"

"Funny enough, the box she was in had a note that said her name was Judy. I thought that was kinda perfect since you're a lawyer."

"What does Judy have to do with being a lawyer?"

"Judge Judy, of course," Pulse said with a wide grin.

Talia burst out laughing just as Judy reached her. She had no fear, clambering right into Talia's lap and going to work on the drawstring of her joggers. Her soft fur was a dream to pet, and her big puppy eyes would melt even the iciest heart.

She was instantly smitten.

But she had never taken care of anyone or anything besides herself.

Could she do it? Did she have what it took to nurture and care for such a tiny, helpless creature?

"I know you're worried you won't be able to do this," Pulse whispered. "But that's crazy. You are the most warm, giving, and loving woman I've ever met. Being independent and strong as fuck doesn't take away from any of that. Besides, we'll be raising this little lady together."

They would, wouldn't they? Pulse had moved into her house the week before, and she couldn't have been happier.

At least, that's what she thought until that moment.

She blinked, but instead of dispelling the tears, it pushed one out and down her cheek. How did she get so lucky to have met this man when she did?

"Thank you," she whispered. It felt like an insignificant way to express the vast well of gratitude in her, but Pulse seemed to understand. Words couldn't capture the love she had for him.

"You're welcome." He kissed her as the puppy tried to dig a hole between her crisscrossed legs.

They stared down at Judy, who seemed to have worn herself out already. She flopped down and rested her adorable snout on Talia's knee. Two seconds later, a soft puppy snore filled the air.

"I'm so happy," she whispered as she settled back against the man she loved. "You've made me happier than I've ever been."

"Tell me if that ever changes," he whispered back. "Because your happiness is the most important thing to me."

That statement let her know they'd never need to have that conversation. She'd be happy with him for the rest of her days.

THIS WAS ONE of the most relaxing and satisfying nights Pulse ever had. He could have sat by the fire forever with Talia in his arms and died a happy man. But the night would come to a close soon, and everyone would head to their respective houses, where, for Pulse, things would only get better.

He'd strip Talia down, and they'd slide between the sheets to spend the next few hours pleasuring each other.

Unless, of course, their new fur child decided she couldn't sleep in her new house.

"Oh, Curly's coming over," Talia said. She tensed a bit.

"What's up, Prez?" Pulse asked as Curly reached them.

"Mind if I sit and chat for a minute?"

"Of course." Talia didn't move away from him, but she straightened between his legs so she wasn't resting on his chest. "Everything okay?"

Curly scratched Judy behind her fuzzy ears. "Damn, she's a cute one, isn't she?"

Talia beamed, already the proud doggy mama. "She is."

"Any time you want to drop her here or at our house to hang out with the rest of the pack, you're more than welcome. I know it can be hard to leave them alone when you have to work all day."

Talia's breath caught. "Thank you. We'll probably take you up on that."

"Thanks, Prez. That'll take a lot of worry off our shoulders since we both work crazy hours sometimes."

Nodding, Curly let the pup go back to sleep. "There's one other thing I wanted to talk to you two about." He turned his attention to Talia, whose eyes widened.

Pulse knew what was coming. After everything went down with Tomás last month, she'd told him about her father's connection to Curly and how it had come out at the same time as Pulse's secret. But hers ended up on the back burner and hadn't been discussed since. It weighed on her, so Pulse appreciated his president addressing it.

"My father," Talia whispered.

"Your father," Curly confirmed with a nod. "You were young when I was arrested."

"In my late teens. My father and I were never close. You weren't the only one he screwed over. I followed your case because I just knew he wouldn't do right by you. I never believed you were guilty. I even went to the cops to tell them my father was crooked. They pretty much patted my head and gave me a lollipop before sending me on my way."

Her sad grin tugged at Pulse's heart. This was the final string tethering Talia to her past. As soon as Curly cut it, she'd be free of the misplaced guilt that had plagued her for many years.

"You were a kid, and you tried to do more for me than most everyone I knew then. I can never tell you how much that means to me."

"I worried if I told you who I was, you wouldn't hire me to represent the club, and I wanted you to be represented by someone who truly had your back. I wanted to make up for my father's betrayal. I'm sorry I withheld the information."

Pulse pulled her back against his chest and splayed his hand across her stomach. He had to bite his tongue to keep from assuring her no one worried about her loyalty. He wasn't the one to fix this. Curly had to ease that worry.

"I knew who you were before I ever agreed to hire you. You might not want to hear this, but you look like your old man."

Talia winced. "I've been told that a time or two."

"When I started digging, I saw you got a few of his clients' convictions overturned."

"He took a lot of bribes and did a shit job of defending so many of his clients because of them."

"Your career has been the opposite. I also found an article in an obscure law journal where you commented on my trial and what a sham it was. How your father never tried to form a competent defense."

She gasped. "You saw that?"

"I did. So, Talia, you never have to worry that I'll question your loyalty. You're good people. You're family."

Talia blinked rapidly. "Thank you," she whispered.

Curly patted Judy on the head a final time before standing. "Merry Christmas," he said.

"Merry Christmas, Prez," Pulse said because Talia seemed

too choked up.

"I can't believe that," she whispered as she faced him after Curly returned to his ol' lady.

"Believe it, baby." He hugged her close and kissed the side of her neck.

"I needed that from him."

He knew she did. One more thing to be grateful to his club's president for. "I'm glad you finally got that closure."

She turned her head and met his gaze. "There's something I need from you too."

He raised an eyebrow. "Really? And what could that be?"

"Why don't you take me home, and I'll show you?" she asked as her eyes deepened with lust.

"Yes, ma'am," he said with a wink.

He wasn't sure he deserved the gift the universe gave him when Talia walked into that interrogation room, but he was smart enough to recognize her for what she was—his entire damn world.

Thank you for reading PULSE. If you enjoyed this book, please leave a review on Amazon or Goodreads.

Other books by Lilly Atlas

No Prisoners MC
Hook: A No Prisoners Novella
Striker
Jester
Acer
Lucky
Snake

Trident Ink
Escapades

Hell's Handlers MC
Zach
Maverick
Jigsaw
Copper
Rocket
Little Jack
Joy
Screw
Viper
Thunder

Hell's Handlers Florida Chapter

Curly
Spec
Tracker
Frost
Jinx
Lock
Ty

Mayhem Makers Series
Solo Rider
Series Page

Blue Collar Bensons
First Comes Loathe
Shock and Aww

Audiobooks
Audio

Join Lilly's mailing list for a **FREE** No Prisoners short story.
www.lillyatlas.com
Facebook
Instagram
TikTok

Pulse

Join my Facebook group, **Lilly's Ladies** for book previews, early cover reveals, contests and more!

About the Author

Lilly Atlas is an award-winning contemporary romance author. She's a proud Navy wife and mother of three spunky girls. Every time Lilly downloads a new eBook she expects her Kindle App to tell her it's exhausted and overworked, and to beg for some rest. Thankfully that hasn't happened yet so she can often be found absorbed in a good book.